WINGS OF FIRE

WINGS OF FIRE

THE DRAGONET PROPHECY

by
TUI T. SUTHERLAND

SCHOLASTIC INC.

No part of this publication may be reproduced, stored in a retrieval system, or transmitted in any form or by any means, electronic, mechanical, photocopying, recording, or otherwise, without written permission of the publisher. For information regarding permission, write to Scholastic Inc., Attention: Permissions Department, 557 Broadway, New York, NY 10012.

This book was originally published in hardcover by Scholastic Press in 2012.

ISBN 978-93-5275-085-6

Text copyright © 2012 by Tui T. Sutherland
Map and Border design © 2012 by Mike Schley
Dragon illustrations © 2012 by Joy Ang

First printing, May 2013
Book design by Phil Falco

This reprint edition : January 2023

Printed in India

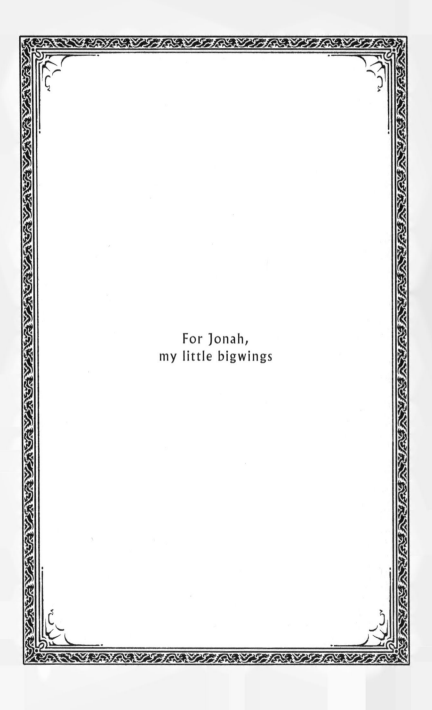

For Jonah,
my little bigwings

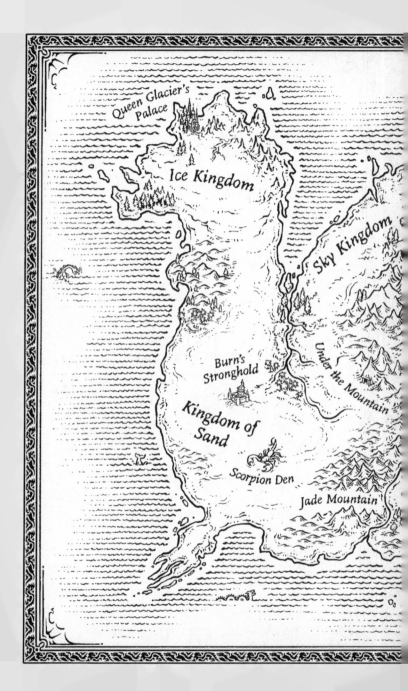

Queen Scarlet's
Palace

Diamond Spray River

Diamond Spray
Delta

Kingdom of
the Sea

Mud Kingdom

Scavenger
Den

Scavenger Den

Rainforest Kingdom

W   E

Ice Kingdom

Kingdom

A NIGHTWING GUIDE TO THE
DRAGONS

Sand

Scorpion Den

Jade Mountain

Queen Scarlet's
Palace

Dia

m of

OF PYRRHIA

Scavenger
Den

Scavenger De

Rainforest Kingdom

SANDWINGS

Description: pale gold or white scales the color of desert sand; poisonous barbed tail; forked black tongues

Abilities: can survive a long time without water, poison enemies with the tips of their tails like scorpions, bury themselves for camouflage in the desert sand, breathe fire

Queen: Since the death of Queen Oasis, the tribe is split between three rivals for the throne: sisters Burn, Blister, and Blaze.

Alliances: Burn fights alongside SkyWings and MudWings; Blister is allied with the SeaWings; and Blaze has the support of most SandWings as well as an alliance with the IceWings.

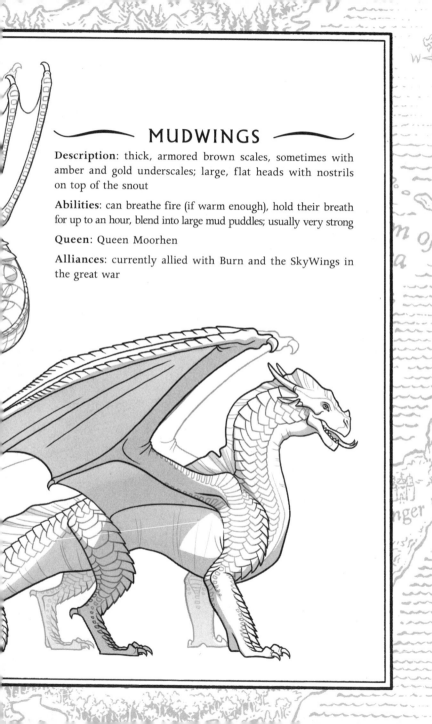

MUDWINGS

Description: thick, armored brown scales, sometimes with amber and gold underscales; large, flat heads with nostrils on top of the snout

Abilities: can breathe fire (if warm enough), hold their breath for up to an hour, blend into large mud puddles; usually very strong

Queen: Queen Moorhen

Alliances: currently allied with Burn and the SkyWings in the great war

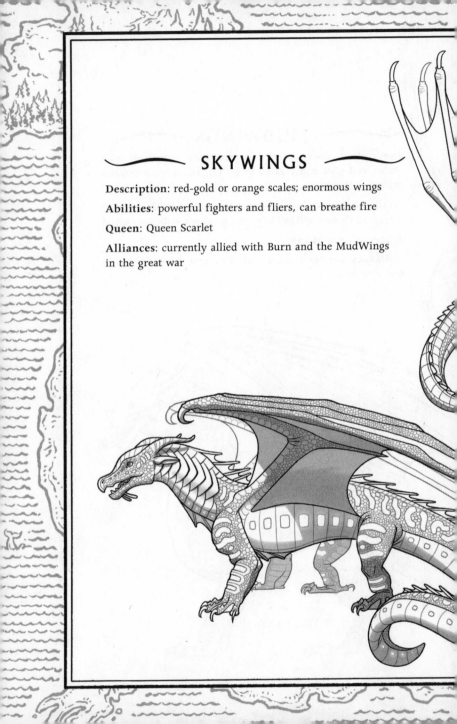

SKYWINGS

Description: red-gold or orange scales; enormous wings

Abilities: powerful fighters and fliers, can breathe fire

Queen: Queen Scarlet

Alliances: currently allied with Burn and the MudWings in the great war

SEAWINGS

Description: blue or green or aquamarine scales; webs between their claws; gills on their necks; glow-in-the-dark stripes on their tails/snouts/underbellies

Abilities: can breathe underwater, see in the dark, create huge waves with one splash of their powerful tails; excellent swimmers

Queen: Queen Coral

Alliances: currently allied with Blister in the great war

ICEWINGS

Description: silvery scales like the moon or pale blue like ice; ridged claws to grip the ice; forked blue tongues; tails narrow to a whip-thin end

Abilities: can withstand subzero temperatures and bright light, exhale a deadly freezing breath

Queen: Queen Glacier
Alliances: currently allied with Blaze and most of the SandWings in the great war

RAINWINGS

Description: scales constantly shift colors, usually bright like birds of paradise; prehensile tails

Abilities: can camouflage their scales to blend into their surroundings, use their prehensile tails for climbing; no known natural weapons

Queen: Queen Dazzling

Alliances: not involved in the great war

NIGHTWINGS

Description: purplish-black scales and scattered silver scales on the underside of their wings, like a night sky full of stars; forked black tongues

Abilities: can breathe fire, disappear into dark shadows, read minds, foretell the future

Queen: a closely guarded secret

Alliances: too mysterious and powerful to be part of the war

THE DRAGONET PROPHECY

When the war has lasted twenty years . . .
the dragonets will come.
When the land is soaked in blood and tears . . .
the dragonets will come.

Find the SeaWing egg of deepest blue.
Wings of night shall come to you.
The largest egg in mountain high
will give to you the wings of sky.
For wings of earth, search through the mud
for an egg the color of dragon blood.
And hidden alone from the rival queens,
the SandWing egg awaits unseen.

Of three queens who blister and blaze and burn,
two shall die and one shall learn
if she bows to a fate that is stronger and higher,
she'll have the power of wings of fire.

Five eggs to hatch on brightest night,
five dragons born to end the fight.
Darkness will rise to bring the light.
The dragonets are coming. . . .

PROLOGUE

A dragon was trying to hide in the storm.

Lightning flickered across the dark clouds. Hvitur clutched his fragile cargo closer. If he could make it over the mountains, he'd be safe. He'd escaped the sky dragons' palace unseen. And the secret cave was so close. . . .

But his theft had not been as stealthy as he thought, and eyes as black as obsidian were already tracking him from below.

The enormous dragon on the mountain ledge had pale gold scales that radiated heat like a desert horizon. Her black eyes narrowed, watching the gleam of silver wings far up in the clouds.

She flicked her tail, and behind her two more dragons rose to the sky and dove into the heart of the storm. A piercing shriek echoed off the mountains as their talons seized the moon-pale ice dragon.

"Bind his mouth," the waiting dragon ordered as her soldiers dropped Hvitur on the slick, wet ledge in front of her. He was already inhaling, ready to attack. "Quickly!"

One of the soldiers grabbed a chain from the pile of smoldering coals. He threw it around the ice dragon's snout, clamping his jaws together with a sizzling smell of burning scales. Hvitur let out a muffled scream.

"Too late." The sand dragon's forked tongue slithered in and out of her mouth. "You won't be using your freezing-death breath on us, ice dragon."

"He was carrying this, Queen Burn," said one of the soldiers, handing her a dragon egg.

Burn squinted at the egg through the downpour. "This is not an IceWing egg," she hissed. "You stole this from the SkyWing palace."

The IceWing stared back at her. Hissing steam circled his snout where the hot chains met cold silver scales.

"You thought you got away unnoticed, didn't you?" Burn said. "My SkyWing ally is not a fool. Queen Scarlet knows everything that happens in her kingdom. Her lookouts reported an IceWing thief sneaking away, and I decided finding you might add some violence to my boring visit."

Burn held the large egg up to the light of the fire and turned it slowly. Red and gold shimmered below the pale, smooth surface.

"Yes. This is a SkyWing egg about to hatch," Burn mused. "Why would my sister send you to steal a SkyWing dragonet? Blaze hates any dragon younger and prettier than she is." She thought for a moment as rain drummed on the ledge around them. "Unless . . . the brightest night is tomorrow. . . ."

Her tail flicked up like a scorpion's, the poisonous barb inches from Hvitur's eyes. "You're not in Blaze's army, are you? You're one of those insipid underground *peace*mongers."

"The Talons of Peace?" said one of the soldiers. "You mean they're real?"

Burn snorted. "A few worms crying over a little blood. Unwrap his chains. He won't be able to freeze us until his scales cool down." The enormous sand dragon leaned closer as her soldier pulled the chain away. "Tell me, ice dragon, do you really believe in that pompous old NightWing's prophecy?"

"Haven't enough dragons died for your war?" snarled Hvitur, wincing at the pain in his jaws. "All of Pyrrhia has suffered for the last twelve years. The prophecy says —"

"I don't care. No prophecy decides what happens to me," Burn interrupted. "I'm not letting a bunch of words or baby dragons choose when I die or what I bow to. We can have peace when my sisters are dead and *I* am queen of the SandWings." Her venomous tail dipped closer to the silver dragon.

Rain pattered on Hvitur's scales. He glared up at her. "The dragonets are coming, whether you like it or not, and they'll choose who the next SandWing queen should be."

"Really?" Burn stepped back and turned the egg slowly between her talons. Her forked tongue slipped in and out of her smile. "So, IceWing. Is this egg a part of your pathetic prophecy?"

Hvitur went still.

Burn tapped lightly on the eggshell with one long talon. "Hello?" she called. "Is there a dragonet of destiny in there? Ready to come out and end this big bad war?"

"Leave it alone," Hvitur choked out.

"Tell me," Burn said, "what becomes of your precious prophecy . . . if one of the five dragonets is never hatched at all?"

"You wouldn't," he said. "No one would harm a dragon egg." His blue eyes were fixed desperately on her talons.

"No 'wings of sky' to help save the world," Burn said. "What a sad, sad story." She began tossing the egg from one front claw to the other. "I guess that means you should be very, very careful with this *terribly* important little — oops!"

With an exaggerated lunge, Burn pretended the wet egg was slipping through her talons . . . and then she let it fall over the side of the cliff into the rocky darkness below.

"No!" Hvitur shrieked. He threw off the two soldiers and flung himself toward the edge. Burn slammed her massive claws down on his neck.

"So much for destiny," she smirked. "So much for your tragic little movement."

"You're a monster," the IceWing gasped, writhing under her talons. His voice cracked with despair. "We'll never give up. The dragonets — the dragonets will come and stop this war."

Burn leaned down to hiss into his ear. "Even if they do — it'll be far too late for you." Her claws ripped through the silver dragon's wings, shredding them as Hvitur shrieked in agony. With a swift movement, she stabbed her poisonous tail through his skull and flung the long, silver body over the edge of the cliff.

The ice dragon's screams cut off long before the echoes of his corpse slamming into the rocks below.

The SandWing turned her black eyes to her soldiers. "Perfect," she said. "That should be the last we hear about that stupid prophecy." She held out her talons so the rain could wash away the glistening dragon blood. "Let's go find something else to kill."

The three dragons spread their wings and lifted off into the dark clouds.

Some time later, far below, a large dragon the color of rust crawled over the rocks to the broken body of the ice dragon. She nudged his tail aside and lifted a shard of eggshell from underneath it, then slipped back into the labyrinth of caves under the cliffs.

Stone walls brushed against her wings. She breathed out a plume of flame to light her way along the dark passage, deep into the mountain.

"I stand with the Talons of Peace," hissed a voice in the shadows. "Kestrel? Is that you?"

"We await the wings of fire," answered the red

dragon. A blue-green SeaWing emerged from a side cave, and she tossed the eggshell at his feet. "Not that it'll do us much good now," she snarled. "Hvitur is dead."

The SeaWing stared at the eggshell. "But — the SkyWing egg —"

"Broken," she said. "Gone. It's over, Webs."

"It can't be," he said. "Tomorrow is the brightest night. The three moons will all be full for the first time in a century. The dragonets of the prophecy *have* to hatch tomorrow."

"Well, one of them is already dead," Kestrel said. Rage flickered in her eyes. "I knew I should have stolen the SkyWing egg myself. I know the Sky Kingdom. They wouldn't have caught me a second time."

Webs grimaced, scratching one claw over the gills along his neck. "Asha is dead, too."

"Asha?" A spurt of flame shot from Kestrel's nose. "How?"

"Caught in a battle between Blaze's and Blister's forces on the way here. She still made it with the red MudWing egg, but she died of her wounds soon after."

"So it's just you, me, and Dune to raise the little worms," Kestrel growled. "For a prophecy that can never be fulfilled. Let's break the cursed eggs now and be done with it. We'll be long gone before the Talons of Peace return for the dragonets."

"No!" Webs hissed. "Keeping the dragonets alive for

the next eight years is more important than anything. If you don't want to be part of that —"

"All right, enough," Kestrel snapped. "I'm the strongest dragon in the Talons of Peace. You need me. It doesn't matter how I feel about nasty little dragonets." She eyed the eggshell on the floor, rubbing her scarred palms together. "Although I thought at least one of them would be a SkyWing."

"I'll find us a fifth dragonet." Webs pushed past her, scales scraping against rock.

"There's no way back into the Sky Kingdom, brainless," she said. "They'll be guarding the hatchery closely now."

"Then I'll get an egg somewhere else," he said grimly. "The RainWings don't even count their eggs — I could take one from the rain forest without anyone noticing."

"Of all the horrible ideas," Kestrel said with a shudder. "RainWings are wretched creatures. Nothing like SkyWings."

"We have to do something," Webs said. He hissed as his tail sent the eggshell skittering across the floor. "In eight years, the Talons of Peace will come looking for five dragonets. The prophecy says five, and we're going to make it come true . . . whatever it takes."

Ice Kingdom

Sky Kingdom

Under the Mountain

Burn's
Stronghold

Kingdom of
Sand

Scorpion Den

Jade Mountain

PART ONE

UNDER THE MOUNTAIN

———— CHAPTER 1 ————

Clay didn't think he was the right dragon for a Big Heroic Destiny.

Oh, he wanted to be. He wanted to be the great MudWing savior of the dragon world, glorious and brave. He wanted to do all the wonderful things expected of him. He wanted to look at the world, figure out what was broken, and fix it.

But he wasn't a natural-hatched hero. He had no legendary qualities at all. He liked sleeping more than studying, and he kept losing chickens in the caves during hunting practice because he was paying attention to his friends instead of watching for feathers.

He was all right at fighting. But "all right" wasn't going to stop the war and save the dragon tribes. He needed to be extraordinary. He was the biggest dragonet, so he was supposed to be the scary, tough one. The minders wanted him to be *terrifyingly dangerous.*

Clay felt about as dangerous as cauliflower.

"Fight!" his attacker howled, flinging him across the cavern. Clay crashed into the rock wall and scrambled up again, trying to spread his mud-colored wings for balance. Red talons raked at his face and he ducked away. "Come on," the red dragon snarled. "Stop holding back. Find the killer inside you and let it out."

"I'm trying!" Clay said. "Maybe if we could stop and talk about it —"

She lunged for him again. "Feint to the left! Roll right! Use your fire!" Clay tried to duck under her wing to attack her from below, but of course he rolled the wrong way. One of her talons smashed him to the ground, and he yelped with pain.

"WHICH LEFT WAS THAT, USELESS?" Kestrel bellowed in his ear. "Are all MudWings this stupid? OR ARE YOU JUST DEAF?"

Well, if you keep that up, I will be soon, Clay thought. The SkyWing lifted her claws and he wriggled free.

"I don't know about other MudWings," he protested, licking his sore talons. "Obviously. But perhaps we could try fighting without all the *shouting* and see —" He stopped, hearing the familiar hiss that came before one of Kestrel's fire attacks.

He threw his wings over his head, tucked his long neck in, and rolled into the maze of stalagmites that studded one corner of the cave. Flames blasted the rocks around him, singeing the tip of his tail.

"Coward!" the older dragon bellowed. She smashed one of the rock columns into a shower of sharp black pebbles. Clay covered his eyes and almost immediately felt her stamp down hard on his tail.

"OW!" he yelled. "You said stomping tails was cheating!" He seized the closest stalagmite between his claws and scrabbled up on top of it. From his perch near the roof, he glared down at his guardian.

"I'm your teacher," Kestrel snarled. "Nothing *I* do is cheating. Get down here and fight like a SkyWing."

But I'm NOT a SkyWing, Clay thought rebelliously. *I'm a MudWing! I don't like setting things on fire or flapping around in circles biting at dragon necks.* His teeth still ached from Kestrel's jewel-hard scales.

"Can't I fight one of the others?" he asked. "I'm much better at that." The other dragonets were his own size (nearly), and they didn't cheat (well, most of the time). He actually *liked* fighting with them.

"Oh, yes? Which opponent would you prefer, the stunted SandWing or the lazy RainWing?" Kestrel said. "Because I'm sure you'll get to choose out on the battlefield." Her tail glowed like embers as she lashed it back and forth.

"Glory's not lazy," Clay said loyally. "She's just not built for fighting, that's all. Webs says there's not much to fight about in the rain forest because the RainWings have all the food they want. He says that's why they've stayed out of the war so far, because none of the rival queens want RainWings in their armies anyway. He says —"

"STOP YAMMERING AND GET DOWN HERE!" Kestrel roared. She reared up on her back legs and flared her wings so she suddenly looked three times bigger.

With a yelp of alarm, Clay tried to leap to the next stalagmite, but his wings unfurled too slowly and he smacked into the side of it instead. Sparks flew as his claws scraped down the jagged rock. He let out another yowl of pain as Kestrel snaked her head between the columns, seized his tail in her teeth, and yanked him out into the open.

Her talons closed around his neck as she hissed in his ear. "Where's the violent little monster I saw when you hatched? *That's* the dragon we need for the prophecy."

"*Gawp,*" Clay squawked, clawing at her grip. He could feel the strange burn scars on her palms scraping against his scales.

This was how battle training with Kestrel always ended — with him unconscious and then sore or limping for days afterward. *Fight back*, he thought. *Get mad! Do something!* But although he was the biggest of the dragonets, they were still a year away from being full grown, and Kestrel towered over him.

He tried to summon some helpful violent rage, but all he could think was, *It'll be over soon, and then I can go have dinner.*

So, not the most heroic train of thought.

Suddenly Kestrel let out a roar and dropped him. Fire blasted over Clay's head as he hit the floor with a thud.

The red dragon whirled around. Behind her, panting defiantly, was the SeaWing dragonet, Tsunami. A red-gold scale was caught between her sharp white teeth. She spat it out and glared at their teacher.

"Stop picking on Clay," Tsunami growled. "Or I'll bite you again." Her deep blue scales shimmered like cobalt glass in the torchlight. The gills in her long neck were pulsing like they always did when she was angry.

Kestrel sat back and flicked her tail around to examine the bite mark. She bared her teeth at Tsunami. "Aren't you sweet. Protecting a dragon who tried to kill you while you were still an egg."

"But luckily you big dragons were there to *save* our *lives*," Tsunami said, "and we sure appreciate it, because now we get to hear about it *all the time*." She marched around to stand between Clay and Kestrel.

Clay winced. He hated hearing this story. He didn't understand it. He'd never want to hurt the other dragonets.

So why had he attacked their eggs during hatching? Did he really have a killer monster inside him somewhere?

The other minders, Webs and Dune, said he'd been ferocious when he hatched. They'd had to throw him in the river to protect the other eggs from him. Kestrel wanted him to find that monster and use it when he fought.

But he was afraid if he ever did, he would hate himself, and so would everyone else. Thinking about what he'd nearly done to his friends made him feel like all the fire had been sucked out of him.

He didn't particularly *want* to be a violent angry monster, even if Kestrel thought that would be an improvement.

But maybe that was the only way to make the prophecy come true. Maybe that monster was his destiny.

"All right," Kestrel said dismissively. "We're finished here anyway. I'll mark another failure in your scroll, MudWing." She snorted a small flame into the air and swept out of the cave.

Clay flopped down on the floor as soon as her red tail had vanished from sight. It felt like every one of his scales was stinging from the burns. "She's going to be so mean to you during your training tomorrow," he said to Tsunami.

"Oh, no," the SeaWing dragonet gasped. "I've never seen Kestrel be mean before! That'll be so unexpected and out of character!"

"Ow," Clay groaned. "Don't make me laugh. I think my ribs are broken."

"Your ribs are not broken," Tsunami said, poking him in the side with her nose. "Dragon bones are almost as hard as diamonds. You're fine. Get up and jump in the river."

"No!" Clay buried his head under his wing. "Too cold!"

"Jump in the river" was Tsunami's solution for everything. Bored? Aching bones? Dry scales? Brain overstuffed with the history of the war? "Jump in the river!" she'd shout whenever any of the other dragonets complained. She certainly did not care that she was the only one who could breathe underwater or that most other dragon tribes hated getting wet.

Clay didn't mind being wet, but he couldn't stand being cold, and the underground river that flowed through their cave home was always freezing.

"Get in," Tsunami ordered. She seized his tail between her front talons and started dragging him toward the river. "You'll feel better."

"I will not!" Clay shouted, clawing at the smooth stone floor. "I'll feel colder! Stop it! Go away! Argh!" His protests went up in a cloud of bubbles as Tsunami dumped him in the icy water.

When he resurfaced, she was floating beside him, ducking her head and splashing water over her scales like a beautiful overgrown fish. Clay felt like a gawky brown blob next to her.

He sploshed into the shallows and lay down on a submerged rock ledge, with his head resting on the bank of the river. He wouldn't admit it, but the burns and aches did feel better in the water. The current helped wash away the smoky rock dust caught between his dry scales.

Still too cold, though. Clay scratched at the rock below him. Why couldn't there be just a *little* mud down here?

"Kestrel will be sorry one day, when I'm queen of the SeaWings," Tsunami said, swimming up and down the narrow channel.

"I thought only a queen's daughters or sisters could challenge her for her throne," Clay said. Tsunami swam so *fast*. He wished he had webs between his talons, too, or gills, or a tail like hers, so powerful she could nearly empty the river with one big splash.

"Well, maybe the SeaWing queen *is* my mother and I'm a lost princess," she said. "Like in the story."

Everything the dragonets knew about the outside world came from scrolls picked up by the Talons of Peace. Their favorite was *The Missing Princess*, a legend about a runaway SeaWing dragonet whose royal family tore up the whole ocean looking for her. At the end she found her way home, and her parents welcomed her with open wings and feasting and joy.

Clay always skipped the adventures in the middle of the story. He just liked that last part — the happy mother and father. And the feasting. The feasting sounded pretty great, too.

"I wonder what my parents are like," he said.

"I wonder if any of our parents are still alive," Tsunami said.

Clay didn't like to think about that. He knew dragons were dying in the war every day — Kestrel and Webs brought back news of bloody battles, scorched land, and burning piles of dragon bodies. But he had to believe his parents were still safe. "Do you think they ever miss us?"

"Definitely." Tsunami flicked a spray of water at him with her tail. "I bet mine were frantic when Webs stole my egg. Just like in the story."

"And mine tore apart the marshes," Clay said. They'd all imagined scenes of their parents' desperate searches ever since they were young dragonets. Clay liked the idea that someone out there was looking for him . . . that someone missed him and wanted him back.

Tsunami flipped onto her back, gazing up at the stone roof with her translucent green eyes. "Well, the Talons of Peace knew what they were doing," she said bitterly. "No one would ever find us down here."

They listened to the river gurgle and the torches crackle for a moment.

"We won't be underground forever," Clay said, trying to make her feel better. "I mean, if the Talons of Peace want us to stop this war, they *have* to let us out sometime." He scratched behind his ear thoughtfully. "Starflight says it's only two more years." He only had to hold on that long. "And then we can go home and eat as many cows as we want."

"Well, first we save the world," Tsunami said. "And *then* we go home."

"Right," said Clay. *How* they were going to save the world was a little fuzzy, but everyone seemed to think they'd figure it out when the time came.

Clay pulled himself out of the river, his waterlogged wings heavy and drooping. He spread them in front of one of the torches, arching his neck and trying to get warm. Feeble waves of heat wafted against his scales.

"Unless . . ." Tsunami said.

Clay lowered his head to look at her. "Unless what?"

"Unless we leave sooner," she said. She flipped over and pulled herself out of the water in one graceful motion.

"Leave?" Clay echoed, startled. "How? On our own?"

"Why not?" she said. "If we can find a way out — why should we have to wait another two years? I'm ready to save the world now, aren't you?"

Clay wasn't sure he'd ever be ready to save the world. He figured the Talons of Peace would tell them what they had to do. Only the three guardian dragons — Kestrel, Webs, and Dune — knew where the dragonets were hidden, but there was a whole network of Talons out there getting ready for the prophecy.

"We can't stop the war by ourselves," he said. "We wouldn't know where to start."

Tsunami flapped her wings at him in exasperation, showering him with cold droplets. "We can too stop the war on our own," she said. "That's the whole *point* of the prophecy."

"Maybe in two years," Clay said. *Maybe by then I'll have found my dangerous side. Maybe then I'll be the ferocious fighter Kestrel wants me to be.*

"Maybe sooner," she said stubbornly. "Just think about it, all right?"

He shifted his feet. "All right. I'll think about it." At least that way he could stop arguing with her.

Tsunami cocked her head. "I hear dinner!" The faint sound of dismayed mooing echoed up the tunnel behind them. She poked Clay cheerfully. "Race you to the hall!" She whirled and pounded away without waiting for a response.

The torches in the battle room seemed dimmer, and cold water was seeping under Clay's scales. He folded his wings and swept his tail through the debris of the smashed rock column.

Tsunami was crazy. The five dragonets weren't ready to stop the war. They wouldn't even know how to survive on their own. Maybe Tsunami was brave and tough like a hero should be, but Sunny and Glory and Starflight . . . Clay thought of all the things that might hurt them and wished he could give them his own scales and claws and teeth for extra protection.

Besides, there was no way to escape the caves. The Talons of Peace had made sure of that.

Still, part of him couldn't help wondering what it would be like to go home now instead of waiting another two years. Back to the marshes, to the swamps, to a whole tribe of MudWings who looked like him and thought like him . . . back to his parents, whoever they were . . .

What if they could do it?

What if the dragonets could escape, and survive, and save the world . . . their own way?

CHAPTER 2

Clay swept the bones of dinner into the river with his tail. The stripped white shapes bounced away in the current.

Fires flickered around the edges of the great central cave. Echoing space yawned overhead, dripping with stalactites, like huge teeth. The cave dome was big enough for six full-grown dragons to fit across with their wings extended. The underground river flowed along one wall, muttering and gurgling as if it were plotting its own escape.

Clay glanced at the two small sleeping caves that opened onto the hall — currently empty — and wondered where the other dragonets had gone while he was cleaning up.

"AHA!" yelled a voice behind him. Clay threw his wings over his head.

"What'd I do?" he yelped. "I'm sorry! It was an accident! Or if it's the extra cow, Dune said I could have it because Webs would be out late but I'm sorry and I can skip dinner tomorrow!"

A small snout poked his back between his wings. "Calm down, silly," Sunny said. "I wasn't aha-ing at you."

"Oh." Clay smoothed his crest and twisted around to

look at her, the smallest and last-hatched of the dragonets. A pale lizard tail was disappearing into her mouth. She grinned at him.

"That was my fierce hunting cry," she said. "Did you like it? Wasn't it scary?"

"Well, it was certainly surprising," he said. "Lizards again? What's wrong with cows?"

"Blech. Too heavy," she said. "You look all serious."

"Just thinking." He was glad Kestrel and Dune couldn't read minds like NightWing dragons. He hadn't been able to stop thinking about the idea of escape all through dinner.

Clay lifted one of his wings, and Sunny nestled in close to him. He could feel the warmth from her golden scales radiating along his side. Sunny was too small and the wrong color — tawny gold instead of sand pale like most SandWings — but she gave off heat like the rest of her tribe.

"Dune says we should go study for an hour before bed," she said. "The others are in the study cave already."

Dune, the maimed dragon who taught them survival skills, was a SandWing, and so was Sunny . . . more or less. There was something not quite right about the littlest dragonet. Not only were her scales too golden, but her eyes were gray-green instead of glittering black. Worst of all, her tail curled into an ordinary point like the tails of most dragon tribes, instead of ending with the poisonous barb that was a SandWing's most dangerous weapon.

As Kestrel often said, Sunny was completely harmless . . .

and what good was a harmless dragon? But her egg fit the instructions in the prophecy, so she was their "wings of sand," whether the Talons of Peace liked it or not.

Of course, there were no "wings of rain" in the prophecy at all. The dragonets had all heard — many times over — about how Glory was a last-minute substitute for the broken SkyWing egg. Kestrel and Dune called her a mistake and growled at her a lot.

Nobody knew whether the prophecy could still happen with a RainWing instead of a SkyWing. But from what Clay knew of SkyWings, he was very glad they had Glory instead of another grumpy, fire-breathing Kestrel under the mountain.

Besides, if anyone was likely to mess up the prophecy, it was him, not Glory or Sunny.

"Come on," Sunny said, flicking him with her tail. He followed her across the central cave.

Twisting stone tunnels led off in four directions: one to the battle area, one to the guardians' cave, one to the study room, and one to the outside world. The last was blocked with a boulder too big for any of the dragonets to move.

Clay stopped and pushed against the rock with his shoulder as they went by. He often tried to open it when the big dragons weren't around. Someday it would move when he did that. Maybe not a lot, but even a tiny shift would let him know he was finally getting close to full grown. He *felt* big. He was constantly bumping into things and accidentally knocking stuff over with his tail or his wings.

Not today, he thought ruefully when the boulder didn't budge. *Maybe tomorrow.*

He followed Sunny down the tunnel to the study room. His enormous feet and thick claws thumped and scraped along the stone floor. Even though he'd lived under the mountain his whole life, it still hurt to walk on bare rock. He was constantly stubbing his talons, and they always ached by the end of the day.

Tsunami was strutting around the study cave barking orders. Sunny and Clay sat down by the entrance, folding their wings back. A breath of air drifted down from the hole in the roof, far overhead — the only window to the outside in any of the caves. At night, without the distant hint of sunlight, the room felt colder and more hollow. Clay stretched up and sniffed at the darkness that had fallen on the other side of the hole. He thought it smelled like stars.

A map of Pyrrhia hung on the wall between the torches. Tsunami and Starflight loved staring at the map, trying to figure out where their hidden cave was. Starflight was pretty sure they were somewhere under the Claws of the Clouds Mountains. SkyWings preferred to live high among the peaks, so anything could happen in the deep caves below without being noticed.

"All this history is so confusing," Sunny murmured to Clay, swishing her tail back and forth. "Why don't the three sides just sit down and talk out an end to the war?"

"That would be great," Clay said. "Then we could stop studying it."

Sunny giggled.

"Stop that," Tsunami said bossily, stamping her feet at them. "No whispering! Pay attention. I'm assigning parts."

"This is not proper studying," Starflight pointed out. His black NightWing scales made him nearly invisible in the dark shadows between the torches. He swept a few scrolls between his talons and began to neatly sort them into stacked triangles. "Perhaps I should read to everyone instead."

"Dear moons, anything but that," Glory said from the ledge above him. "Maybe later, when we're *trying* to fall asleep." Her long, delicate snout, glowing emerald green with displeasure, rested on her front claws. Ripples of iridescent blue shimmered across her scales, and tonight her tail was a swirl of vibrant purples.

If it weren't for Glory, Clay thought, none of them would know how many colors there were in the world. He wondered what it must be like in the rain forest, where there was a whole tribe of dragons that beautiful.

"Shush," Tsunami scolded. "Now, obviously I'd be the best queen, but let's make Sunny the queen, since she is a real SandWing." She bustled over and pushed Sunny into the center of the cave.

"Well, sort of," Glory muttered under her breath.

"Hsst." Starflight flicked her with his tail. None of the dragonets ever talked about why Sunny didn't look like a regular SandWing. Clay's guess was that her egg had been taken from the sand too early. Maybe SandWing eggs needed the sun and desert sand to keep them warm until hatching, or else they'd come out half baked and funny looking — although personally he thought Sunny looked just fine.

Tsunami tapped her talons on the cave floor, studying her friends. "Clay, you want to play the scavenger?"

"That's hardly fair," Starflight pointed out. "He's twice Sunny's size. A real scavenger would be smaller than her, according to this scroll over here. It says that scavengers have no scales, no wings, and no tail, and they walk on two legs, which sounds very unstable to me. I bet they fall over all the time. They like treasure nearly as much as drag- ons do. The scrolls say scavengers attack lone dragons and steal —"

"OH MY GOSH, WE KNOW," Glory snapped. "We were all here for the fascinating lectures about them. Don't make me come down there and bite you, Starflight."

"I'd like to meet a real scavenger!" Clay said. "I'd rip off its head! And eat it!" He pounded his front talons on the stone below him. "I bet it would taste better than the mouth- fuls of feathers Kestrel keeps bringing us."

"Poor, hungry Clay," Sunny teased.

"When we're free, we'll go find a scavenger nest and eat all of them," Tsunami promised, nudging Clay with one wing.

Sunny blinked at her. "When we're free?"

Oops. Tsunami and Clay exchanged glances. Sunny was sweet and trusting and absolutely terrible at keeping secrets.

"I mean, after we fulfill the prophecy, of course," Tsunami said. "Clay, be the scavenger. Here, this can be your claw." She swung her long tail in an arc and smashed a stalagmite loose. Shards of rock flew across the cave, and the other dragonets ducked.

Clay hefted the sharp rock spear in his claws and grinned wickedly at Sunny.

"Don't *actually* hurt me," she said nervously.

"Of course he won't," Tsunami said. "We're just acting it out. And the rest of us will be the princesses. I'll be Burn, Glory can be Blister, and Starflight will be Blaze."

"I had to be a princess last time, too," Starflight observed. "I'm not sure I like this game." He stretched his wings and the scattered silver scales underneath glittered like stars in the night sky.

"It's not a game, it's *history*," Tsunami said. "And if we had any other friends, we could play it differently. But there are three sand dragon princesses, so you have to be one, so stop complaining."

Starflight shrugged and settled back into the shadows, the way he always did when he couldn't win a fight.

"All right, go ahead," Tsunami said, hopping onto the ledge next to Glory.

"Um," Sunny said. She eyed Clay warily. "Right. Here I go, la la la, Queen Oasis of the SandWings. I'm *so* very important and, uh — royal — and stuff."

Tsunami sighed. Glory and Starflight hid their smiles.

"I've been queen for ages and ages," Sunny went on. She strutted across the cave floor. "No one dares challenge me for my throne! I am the strongest SandWing queen who ever lived!"

"Don't forget the treasure," Tsunami hissed, pointing at a pile of loose rocks.

"Oh, right," Sunny said. "It's probably because of all my treasure! I have so much treasure because I'm such an important queen!" She swept the rocks toward her and gathered them between her talons.

"Did someone say *treasure*?" Clay bellowed, leaping out from behind a large rock formation. Sunny yelped with fright.

"No!" Tsunami called. "You're not scared! You're Queen Oasis, the big, bad queen of the sand dragons."

"R-right," Sunny said. "Rargh! What is this tiny scavenger doing in the Kingdom of Sand? I am not afraid of tiny scavengers! I shall go out there and eat him in one bite!"

Glory started giggling so hard she had to lie down and cover her face with her wings. Even Tsunami was making faces like she was trying not to laugh.

Clay swung his stalagmite in a circle. "Squeak squeak squeak!" he shouted. "And other annoying scavenger noises! I'm here to steal treasure away from a magnificent dragon!"

"Not from me, you won't," Sunny said, bristling. She stamped forward, spread her wings, and raised her tail threateningly. Without the poisonous barb other SandWings had, Sunny's tail was not very menacing. But nobody pointed that out.

"Yaaaaaaah!" Clay shouted, lunging forward with his rock claw. Sunny darted out of the way, and they circled each other, feinting and jabbing. This was Clay's favorite part. When Sunny forgot about trying to act queenly and focused on the battle, she was fun to fight. Her small size made it easy for her to dodge and slip under his defenses.

But in the end Queen Oasis had to lose — that was how the story went. Clay drove Sunny back against the wall of the cave and thrust the fake claw between her neck and her wing, pretending it went right through her heart.

"Aaaaaaaargh," Sunny howled. "Impossible! A queen defeated by a lowly scavenger! The kingdom will fall apart! Oh, my treasure . . . my lovely treasure . . ." She collapsed to the ground and let her wings flop lifelessly on either side of her.

"Ha ha ha!" Clay said. "And squeak squeak! The treasure is mine!" He scooped up all the rocks and paraded away, lashing his tail proudly.

"Our turn," Tsunami said, jumping off the ledge. She hurried over to Sunny, clasped her talons together, and let out a cry of anguish. "Oh, no! Our mother is dead, and the treasure is gone. But worst of all, none of us killed her — so who should be queen now?"

"I was about to challenge her," Glory cried. She flapped her wings dramatically. "I would have fought her to the death for the throne. *I* should be queen!"

"No, *I* should be queen!" Tsunami insisted. "I am the eldest and biggest and would have challenged her first!"

They both turned to look at Starflight, hidden in the shadows. The black dragon looked as if he was trying to become even more invisible.

"Come on, Starflight," Tsunami said. "Don't be a lazy —" She caught herself just before saying "RainWing." The teachers said things like that all the time: "If you don't study, you're no better than a RainWing"; "What's the matter, someone replace your brains with a RainWing's?"; "Still sleeping? Anyone would think you were a RainWing!" (That last one was mostly for Clay.)

But the dragonets all knew Glory hated it, no matter how much she pretended she didn't care. It also seemed really unfair. Glory was the only RainWing any of them had ever met, and she studied and trained harder than anyone else.

"Er . . . dragon," Tsunami finished awkwardly, with a quick glance at Glory. "Starflight, get out here."

The NightWing shuffled forward and looked down at Sunny, who had her eyes scrunched shut. "Oh dear, oh dear," he said. "Well, now I should be queen. As the youngest princess, I could have the longest reign. That would be good for the SandWings. Also . . ." He paused and gave a long-suffering sigh. "Also, I am by far the prettiest."

Sunny giggled, and Tsunami poked her to keep still. Clay swept his treasure rocks into a pile and sat on them.

"I should kill you both right now," Glory snarled.

"You and what army?" Tsunami taunted her.

Glory stretched her neck up and bared her teeth. "That's a great idea. I'll go *get* an army — an army of SeaWings — and then you'll be sorry."

"You're not the only one who can make alliances," Tsunami said. "I'll get the SkyWings on my side. *And* the MudWings! Then we'll see who wins this war!"

There was a pause. They both looked at Starflight again.

"Uh, yeah," he said. "You do that, and I'll ally myself with the IceWing army. Also, by the way, most of the SandWings want me to be their queen."

"They do?" Sunny said, opening her eyes. "Who says?"

"Stop talking," Tsunami said, poking her with one talon. "You're dead."

"There are lots of recent scrolls about it," Starflight explained pompously. "Blaze is very popular with her own tribe."

"So why can't she be queen?" Sunny asked. "If that's who they want?"

"Because Burn is bigger and scarier and could crush her like a bug if they actually fought claw to claw," Glory chimed in. "And Blister — that's me — is smarter than both of them put together. She knew she couldn't kill Burn in a regular duel. It was her idea to involve all the other tribes and turn their SandWing throne battle into a world war. She's probably waiting for the other two to kill each other."

"Which one do *we* want to be queen?" Sunny asked. "We get to pick, right? When we fulfill the prophecy?"

"None of them," Starflight said gloomily. "Blaze is about as smart as a concussed sheep, Blister is most likely plotting to become queen of all the tribes somehow, and if Burn wins, she'll probably keep the war going just for fun. They're all pretty nasty. I guess we'll see what the Talons of Peace decide."

"The Talons of Peace don't *get* to decide," Tsunami said, bristling. "They only *think* they're in charge of us."

"We can still hear them out," Starflight argued. "They want what's best for us and Pyrrhia."

"Easy for you to say," Glory snapped. The ruff around her neck flared orange. "You weren't stolen from your home. The NightWings were pretty eager to hand over your egg, weren't they?" Starflight flinched as if she'd burned him.

"Boring!" Clay shouted from his pile of rocks. "Stop fighting with each other! Come fight me for this treasure instead!"

"No one knows what the scavenger did with the sand dragon treasure," Starflight said in his "top of the class" voice, turning away from Glory. "Among other things, he stole the Lazulite Dragon, the gold SandWing scepter, and the Eye of Onyx, which had been in the SandWing treasury for hundreds of years."

Clay stamped his feet. Starflight's lectures always made his scales itch. "I just want to fight somebody!" he said. Somebody who wasn't trying to beat him into a violent rage, preferably.

As if the thought had summoned her, Kestrel suddenly loomed in the entrance of the cave.

"WHAT is going on in here?" Kestrel's booming voice made all five dragonets jump to attention. Sunny slipped as she tried to scramble to her feet, and Starflight jumped forward to catch her.

The enormous red SkyWing slithered into the cave, glaring down at them. "This doesn't look like studying," she hissed.

"We're s-s-s-sorry," Sunny stammered.

"No, we're not." Tsunami shot the SandWing a glare. "We *were* studying. We were acting out the death of the queen that started the whole war."

"You mean play-acting," Kestrel growled. "You are too old for games."

"When were we ever *young* enough for games?" Glory muttered.

"It wasn't a game," Tsunami said. "It was a different way of learning the history. What's wrong with that?"

"And now you're talking back," Kestrel said. She looked smug, as she always did when Tsunami got in trouble. "That means no sleeping in the river tonight." Tsunami scowled. Kestrel tapped the pile of scrolls by the entrance with one claw. "The rest of you, learn from the SeaWing's mistakes and study the correct way."

"That's not fair." Clay spoke up as Kestrel turned to go, even though it made his heart pound. "We were all doing the same thing. We should all be punished." Glory shook her head at him, but beside him, Sunny nodded.

Kestrel stared down at Clay. "I know who the ringleader was. Cut off the head, and the problem goes away."

"You're going to cut off Tsunami's head?" Sunny squeaked.

Glory sighed. "It's a metaphor, featherbrain."

"Now go to bed," Kestrel said. She turned and swept out of the cave, knocking over Starflight's neat stacks of scrolls as she went.

Clay nudged Tsunami's dark blue shoulder with his snout. "Sorry. We tried."

"I know, thanks," Tsunami said, brushing her wing against his. "Hey, Sunny, would you mind taking those scrolls back to our sleeping cave?"

The small gold dragon brightened. "Sure, I can do that!" She hurried to the entrance, gathered the scattered scrolls in her front talons, and whisked out of the cave.

"I can't stand this much longer," Tsunami said as soon as Sunny was gone. "We have to get out of here, and soon."

Clay glanced at Glory and Starflight, who didn't look surprised. "You talked to them about it?"

"Of course," Tsunami said. "I needed their help figuring out an escape plan." Clay couldn't help but notice that she hadn't asked *him* for any escape plan ideas. Even the dragons who liked him thought he was pretty useless.

"I'm not sure we're ready," Starflight said, wrinkling his forehead. "There's so much we haven't learned yet. . . ."

"That's what the teachers want us to think!" Tsunami's blue scales shifted as she shook herself from head to tail. "But we'll never know until we get out of these horrible caves and see the world for ourselves."

"What about the prophecy?" Clay asked. "Shouldn't we wait two more years?"

"I don't see why," Glory said. "I'm with Tsunami. Destiny is destiny, right? So whatever we do must be the right thing. We don't need a bunch of ancient dragons telling us how to save the world. *They're* not in the prophecy."

"When do we tell Sunny?" Starflight asked, glancing at the cave's dark opening.

"Not until the last minute," Tsunami said fiercely. "You know she can't keep a secret. Starflight, *promise* you won't say anything to her."

"I won't, I won't," he said. "She's not going to like it, though. She thinks everything is great here."

"Of course she does," Tsunami said. "She doesn't care that we get treated like cracked eggs even though we're supposed to be the key to peace or whatever."

"She cares," Starflight said defensively. "She just doesn't whine about it."

"Yowch," said Glory.

Tsunami whirled to glare at Starflight, her gills pulsing. "Say that to my face."

"I *am* saying it to your face," he said. "Or was I saying it to your rear end? It's easy to get the two confused." He ducked behind Clay before Tsunami could even bare her teeth at him.

"Hey, stop. Quit snarling at each other like mini Kestrels," Clay said, standing up to keep his bulk between Tsunami and Starflight. "Nobody's happy here. Sunny deals with it differently, that's all. But remember what we decided — we five stick together or else everything gets worse, right?"

Starflight hunched his wings forward, muttering.

"Clay's right," Glory said. "The last thing we want is to be like Kestrel or Webs or Dune."

Tsunami hissed for a moment, then shook herself. "All right, I know. I'm trying. But this place is slowly killing me," she said. Clay shivered at the fierce look on her face. He would not want to be the dragon standing in her way.

"As soon as we have a plan, we go," Tsunami said, looking them each in the eye. "Let's see them force our destiny on us when they can't find us anymore."

CHAPTER 3

Suddenly there was a thundering crash from the central cave. Clay heard the entrance boulder slam back into place, and then the rumble of heavy footsteps. From the extra squish-flap sound of them, he knew that it must be Webs.

"Something's happening," Tsunami said. She hurried to the door, her ears twitching and the spiny ridge along her back standing straight up. "We have to go listen."

Starflight spread his wings slowly. "I'm sure we'll find out what the fuss is in the morning."

"I don't want to wait that long." Tsunami spun around to jab his underbelly with her tail, and he tipped backward with a grunt. "Don't be a smoke-breather! Let's go!" She whirled out of the cave.

Clay winced as his sore muscles sprang into action. He followed Glory to the central cave. Glory's scales were already changing to match the mottled gray-and-black rocks. In a moment she'd be nearly impossible to see.

Starflight slipped past to join her, and the two of them hurried away toward the tunnel that led to the big dragons' cave. They vanished almost immediately into the shadows.

Hidden by their coloring, they'd get as close as they could to eavesdrop.

But Clay and Tsunami had an even better shot of hearing everything, if they hurried. Tsunami was already charging across the cave to the river.

"What about Sunny?" Clay called quietly. He could hear the little SandWing rummaging around in her sleeping cave, putting scrolls away.

"We'll come up with something to tell her later," Tsunami hissed back.

Clay felt sorry that Sunny was the only one who didn't know about their spying games, but they'd learned their lesson about trusting her with secrets years ago. Sunny hadn't *meant* to tell Dune about the pile of rocks the dragonets were collecting. Their plan was to build a tower to the sky hole, back when they were too small to fly. They'd only wanted to stick their heads out and look around. But one day Sunny forgot to be careful around Dune, and the next day all the collected rocks were gone from their hiding place. That was the end of that plan — and of Sunny getting to know anything.

Tsunami disappeared into the river with a nearly soundless splash. The pale green flecks under her dark blue scales shimmered as she swam upriver. Clay dove in after her, wishing he could see in the dark like she could. At least she'd remembered to activate the glow-in-the-dark stripe along her tail.

MudWings couldn't breathe underwater like SeaWings,

but they could hold their breath for more than an hour. So whenever the dragonets wanted to spy on their guardians, Clay and Tsunami could use the river to get closer than the others.

He caught up to the SeaWing as she was wriggling through the underwater gap in the cave walls. It made Clay nervous every time, squeezing through such a small space. He wished he hadn't eaten that extra cow at dinner.

His claws scrabbled on the rocks, catching in the crevices. There was a brief, terrifying moment as his midsection got stuck. Would he drown down here? Would the prophecy be ruined because of an extra cow?

Then, with a whoosh of bubbles, he popped through and shot after Tsunami.

Her tail stripe went dark as they swam quietly into the guardians' cave. The three older dragons hardly paid any attention to the river, except for Webs, who sometimes slept in the shallows. It would never occur to them that two pairs of dragonet ears might be poking out of the water, listening.

Clay drifted to a stop near the entrance while Tsunami swam to the far side of the room. That way at least one of them could hear, no matter where the minders were talking.

Tonight, however, Clay was pretty sure everyone could hear everything, including Glory and Starflight in the passageway outside. From the way Kestrel was shouting, it was possible even the SkyWings up in the mountain peaks could hear her.

"Coming *here*? With no warning? After six years, suddenly he's interested?" A jet of fire shot out of her snout and blasted the nearest rock column.

"Maybe he wants to make sure they're ready to stop the war," Webs suggested.

Dune snorted. "These dragonets? Then he's going to be very disappointed." He eased himself onto a flat boulder, stretching his foreleg stump and mangled wing toward the fire. The big SandWing dragon never discussed his scars or how he lost his foot, but the dragonets could guess from the anger in his voice whenever he talked about the war.

The fact that he couldn't fly was probably why he was chosen for underground dragonet-minding duty. He clearly wasn't picked for his warm, nurturing personality.

"We've done our best," Webs said. "The prophecy chose these dragonets, not us."

"Does he even know what happened?" Kestrel demanded. "Does he know about the broken egg and the RainWing? Or the defective SandWing?"

Clay winced. Poor Sunny. He floated closer, keeping his bulky brown length below the surface of the dark water. Through the ripples he could see the blurred shapes of the large dragons gathered around the fire.

Webs flapped his wings. "I'm not sure what he knows or why he cares. The message just said 'Morrowseer is coming.' I'm supposed to meet him and bring him here tomorrow."

Morrowseer. That sounded familiar. Clay racked his brain. A dragon from history class? One of the tribe rulers? No, it couldn't be; all the tribes were ruled by queens.

"I'm not worried about Sunny," Dune said. "We followed the prophecy's instructions. It's not our fault she's the way she is. But the RainWing — he's not going to like that."

A deep growl rumbled in Kestrel's throat. "I don't like it either. I never have."

"Glory's not that bad," Webs argued. "She's smarter than she wants us to know."

"You overestimate her because you brought her here," Dune said. "She's lazy and worthless like the rest of her tribe."

"And she's not a SkyWing," Kestrel snapped. "We're supposed to have a SkyWing."

Clay wished Glory didn't have to hear all this. The guardians never hid how they felt about her, and she never acted like she cared. But he wished he could tell her she was just as important and smart as any SkyWing.

"Well, I never thought Morrowseer would come look at them!" Webs said. "After he dropped off Starflight's egg, I assumed we'd never see him again. The NightWings have nothing to do with the war."

So he's a NightWing. Which means superpowered and mysterious and full of himself. That was all Clay could remember about NightWings. He found himself actually wishing he could get a lecture from Starflight. The epic wonderfulness of NightWings was the black dragonet's favorite topic.

"Did the Talons say what he wants?" Kestrel asked.

"Well, it's his prophecy," Webs said. "I guess he wants to make sure it'll actually come true."

Morrowseer. Clay felt a jolt run through him, like the stinging shock he sometimes got when Dune whacked him with his barbed tail for not paying attention.

Morrowseer was the NightWing who had spoken the dragonet prophecy ten years ago. They had learned about him in history, but it was one of many facts Clay could never remember. Who had delivered the prophecy never seemed as important as who was *in* the prophecy.

But maybe Morrowseer was more important than Clay had realized. After all, he was coming to see them. Perhaps he would take them out into the world. Perhaps they didn't need to escape after all.

Perhaps everything was about to change.

CHAPTER 4

Clay had never really believed the legends about NightWings. Secretive dragons who could read minds? A hidden kingdom that no one could find? A mystery queen, the power to see the future, the way they appeared from darkness to deliver prophecies that shaped the world . . . it all sounded like fairy tales, about as likely as a world ruled by scavengers instead of dragons.

Besides, Clay knew Starflight, and Starflight was many things — annoying, long-winded, smart, too serious — but he had no magical powers and he was never, ever scary.

But the next evening, when a dragon black as a bottomless pit loomed out of the shadows of the entrance tunnel, Clay felt all the rumors about NightWings come crashing into his head like a collapsing rock wall.

Morrowseer was even bigger than Kestrel, and five times more terrifying. He spread his jagged, batlike wings and peered down at the dragonets lined up in front of him. He had silver scales like stars on the underside of his wings, like Starflight did, but on him they seemed to glitter from a great distance and cast a cold glow.

He looked like he could easily rip off each of their heads in one bite. He also looked like he already hated the five dragonets. Which wasn't what Clay had expected at all. Were they such a disappointment already?

Maybe Morrowseer was reading their minds and knew how confused they were about the prophecy. Or maybe he was seeing the future and his visions were all of failure, failure, failure.

Clay could feel Sunny trembling at his side. He felt the same way, petrified in place, as if his scales were being slowly peeled off, one by one, while the giant NightWing inspected them.

On his other side, Starflight was more still than Clay had ever seen him. Starflight always froze when he was frightened. It was as if he hoped that by not moving, he'd disappear from view and the danger would pass right by.

Clay couldn't see Glory, but he knew when Morrowseer saw her. The huge black dragon stared down at the RainWing dragonet for a small eternity. His snout twitched with ripples of disgust. A forked black tongue slipped over his teeth.

Clay wished his own wings were as vast as the cavern itself so he could hide his friends from Morrowseer. He wished his talons were as huge as the stalagmites and as sharp as the rock shards. He wished he were big enough to be brave and brave enough to be big. He'd never wanted anything so much as he wanted to protect his friends from this tall, hissing, scornful, immensely dangerous dragon.

He really, really hoped that Morrowseer wasn't reading his mind right then. *Think about cows think about cows think about delicious fat cows. . . .*

Morrowseer pivoted his head slowly to glare down at Kestrel. He lifted one long claw and pointed at Glory.

"What. Is. THAT?" he said, his voice loaded with enough venom to kill twenty dragons in midflight.

Starflight took a step back, and Clay saw Glory. She was sitting on her haunches with her long tail curled over her talons. Trails of violet and gold chased each other through her scales. Only the shades of flame around her feathery ears hinted that she was upset. She stared calmly back at Morrowseer.

"There was an accident," Kestrel said. "We lost the SkyWing egg, so we had to get another one somewhere —"

"From the *RainWings*?" Morrowseer interrupted scathingly.

"It was his idea," Kestrel snarled, whipping her tail toward Webs. "*He* brought her egg here!"

"At least we have five dragonets," said Webs. "That's what matters."

Morrowseer peered down his long black snout at Glory. His eyes shifted to Sunny, who let out a tiny squeak and sank a little lower toward the ground. "More like four and a half," he grunted. "Are you supposed to be the SandWing? Don't you eat? What's wrong with you?"

There was a long, horrible pause while Sunny tried to squeak out an answer.

"She does," Tsunami blurted. "She eats fine. As much as anyone."

"It's not her fault she's small," Starflight chimed in, to Clay's surprise.

"She's a good fighter," Clay said. "And so is Glory."

"Stop talking now," Morrowseer said, and silence dropped over them. His sharp, menacing gaze landed on Clay.

THINK ABOUT COWS THINK ABOUT COWS THINK ABOUT COWS. . . .

The tall NightWing turned to the three guardians. "Something has gone very wrong here."

"Yes!" Tsunami burst in again. "It has, and I can tell you what. We're treated like prisoners! We've never been outside these caves, not once. All we know about this world we're supposed to save is what we've learned in scrolls. We're supposed to be the most important dragonets in the world, but those three treat us like blind salamanders!"

Clay couldn't believe it. Wasn't she scared of Morrowseer, too?

"Tsunami, hold your tongue," Dune snapped.

"I will not," she cried. "Please get us out of here," she said to Morrowseer. "Take us away with you."

Please DON'T, Clay thought. *I mean, think about cows, think about cows. . . .* Now that he'd seen the NightWing, he'd rather stay trapped here.

"Ungrateful lizard!" Kestrel growled.

Without warning, Morrowseer lunged at Tsunami. His teeth flashed like bright white lightning, darting toward her neck. *It really is like the night sky falling on you*, Clay thought, and then discovered he was moving, too. He flung himself at the NightWing's huge, ridged back before he could stop to think about what he was doing.

His claws sank into the small gaps between the shifting black scales, scrabbling for a hold. His tail thrashed as he tried to balance. Below him he saw Tsunami rolling away and spinning to fight back. Her blue talons slashed at Morrowseer's nose and underbelly.

Clay tried frantically to remember his battle training. He flattened himself along the big dragon's back, snaked his neck forward, and bit down as hard as he could.

OW. His jaw exploded with pain, and he reared back. In the black-on-black scales, it was impossible to find a weak spot.

Morrowseer jumped away from Tsunami and shook his whole body violently. Clay lost his grip and went flying through the air. He landed with a jarring thud, sliding halfway into the river.

As he staggered to his feet, he saw Tsunami and Morrowseer facing each other in battle positions. Morrowseer made a grinding noise deep in his throat. He stepped back and swung his tail around into view.

Clinging to Morrowseer's tail, her teeth firmly planted in the vulnerable spot near the end, was Sunny. Clay wished *he'd* remembered about that spot, which every dragon had, no matter which tribe they were from.

"Ha," Morrowseer rumbled. "That's a surprise." He pried Sunny loose with his front talons, as if she were just a tiny bloodsucking insect.

"That one will do," Morrowseer said, pointing at Tsunami. None of the big dragons had moved at all as he attacked their charges.

Neither had Glory.

Neither had Starflight.

Clay staggered up beside his NightWing friend, who was doing an excellent imitation of a stalagmite. Starflight lowered his head and avoided Clay's eyes.

"And that one will do." Morrowseer nodded at Clay. Kestrel snorted.

The NightWing approved of *him*? Clay was confused. It wasn't as if Clay's attack had done any good. Even when Clay was defending his friend, apparently he couldn't get angry enough to drag out his inner monster. Couldn't Morrowseer hear everyone thinking about how Clay was going to let them all down?

"This one . . ." Morrowseer studied Sunny, from her harmless tail to her weirdly golden scales and moss-green eyes. "We'll have to see."

"We followed the prophecy," Dune insisted. "She wasn't in a clutch of eggs — I found her egg alone, buried out in the desert. Just like the prophecy said."

The guardians never talked about where they got the dragonets' eggs. Sunny stared at Dune hopefully, but he fell silent under Morrowseer's dark eyes.

"As for you," Morrowseer said to Starflight, "I assume you used your NightWing powers to figure out that I wasn't going to harm the SeaWing. Perhaps you even had a vision of my visit today. No doubt you already know that I'm going to take you into the next cavern for a private conversation."

Clay shuddered. A "private conversation" with Morrowseer sounded about as much fun as having his ears roasted. He did not envy Starflight as the two NightWings slithered toward the study room. Morrowseer paused in the archway and looked back at the guardians.

"We'll talk about *her* later." He didn't look at Glory, but everyone else did. She flicked her ears and lifted her chin a little higher as Morrowseer's footsteps faded away down the tunnel.

What does that mean? Clay worried. What was there to talk about?

"Stupid SeaWing," Kestrel shot across the cave and struck Tsunami's snout. "Complaining to the first strange dragon you see! Trying to make us look bad! Whining about your life, after all we've given up for you!"

"If you hate this, too, why don't you let us go?" Tsunami shot back.

"This is for your safety," Webs interjected. His voice was gentler than Kestrel's, but Clay could tell he was angry from the way his long blue-green tail lashed on the floor. "That's what all of this is for. The Talons of Peace need you to survive long enough to fulfill the prophecy. You have no idea how many dragons would love to get their claws on you five."

"Or what they'd do to you if they did," Dune growled.

"Our job is to keep you alive," Kestrel said. "Or else I'd have strangled you myself a long time ago."

"Great," Tsunami said. "Well, it's been a terrific life. Thanks very much."

Kestrel made the hissing, fire-is-coming noise. Clay grabbed Tsunami's tail and tugged her back toward the river.

"We are grateful," Sunny said, jumping in front of Kestrel. She stood up on her back legs, not even half the red dragon's size. Her golden ears twitched. "We would much rather be alive than not alive! We're glad you keep us that way, really we are."

"Come on," Webs said. He prodded Kestrel and Dune toward their cave. "We need to talk."

"*Now* he has something to say," Kestrel grumbled as the three of them clambered over the broken stalagmites.

Tsunami threw herself into the river and sank to the bottom in a stream of furious bubbles, where she curled up with her talons over her head.

It got very quiet in the cave. Sunny and Clay exchanged glances, then looked over at Glory.

The RainWing was sitting in the same spot, with her tail still neatly curled around her feet. She yawned. Clay wished he could ever be that calm. It was as if nothing bothered her at all.

"Are you all right?" Clay asked. He came around and sat in front of her, studying her face. Sunny sidled up beside Glory, brushing her violet wings with her own smaller golden ones.

"Of course," Glory said. "I mean, we knew that was going to happen. It's not like the minders have been talking about how awesome I am this whole time."

"But you are," Clay said. Glory tilted her head at him. "Awesome," he insisted. "They just don't see —"

"They see a RainWing," she said with a shrug. "I don't care. It's their own fault for bringing me here."

"Why didn't you fight Morrowseer when we did?" Sunny asked. "Then maybe he'd know how brave and fierce you are, too."

"Why bother?" Glory said. "It was obviously a test, and I'd already failed." A splotch of sky-blue scales on her back pulsed, and then the color began to spread across her other scales, eating up the purple and gold.

"Well, we don't care what the prophecy says or what Morrowseer thinks," Clay said stoutly. "You're our fifth dragonet. We don't want anyone else."

Glory gave him a rueful look. "That's very sweet." She yawned again. "I'm going to take a nap."

"Now?" Sunny said, alarmed. "Is that a good idea?"

Glory fell asleep every day, usually after lunch, for a

couple of hours, but Clay had expected her to stay awake while Morrowseer was around. He knew he wouldn't want the big dark dragon to catch *him* sleeping. He glanced at the tunnel to the study room, wondering uneasily how far the NightWing's telepathy reached and whether he could read Clay's mind through rock.

"I'm tired," Glory snapped. "And they all think I'm lazy anyway. Nothing I do can change that."

Clay knew Glory wasn't lazy. She worked harder than everyone at battle training and learning the dragon war's history, even though none of the big dragons ever noticed. She just had to nap in the middle of the day, probably for some RainWing reason. Although it didn't seem to help: Glory was just as prickly and tired after napping as she was before.

"Wake me if anything exciting happens," Glory said. "But make sure it's actually exciting, not Sunny-exciting." She gave Sunny a friendly nudge with her snout, and the SandWing squeaked in protest.

"I don't think *everything* is exciting!" Sunny flapped her wings. "But you guys don't think *enough* things are exciting."

"Think of it this way," Glory said. "Time to leave the caves and fulfill the prophecy: exciting. You caught another weird-looking white crab in the river: not exciting. Got it?" She poked Sunny again, uncurled her tail, now fully blue, and slipped inside her sleeping cave.

Sunny blinked at Clay.

"I know," he said. "That last crab *was* really weird looking."

"It was, wasn't it?" she said.

"I wouldn't have minded if you'd woken *me* up to see it," Clay added kindly.

"Well, good," she said. "I know. That's why you got to eat half of it instead of anyone else." She headed for her favorite stalagmite and started to climb it, hooking her claws in the holes that dotted the bulbous shape.

Clay clambered up the rocks beside her. "Hey, Sunny," he said. "What would you think about running away?"

She paused and looked at him with shocked green eyes. "You mean leaving the caves? Without our guardians? Oh, no, we couldn't. We have to do what the prophecy says."

"Do we?" he asked. "I mean, we do," he said quickly as she nearly lost her grip on the stalagmite in surprise. "But what if the Talons don't understand the prophecy any better than we do? Maybe we need to get out and stop the war our own way."

Sunny settled on top of the stalagmite and coiled her tail around it, balancing on her back legs. She reached up toward the stalactites that were poking sharply down from the top of the cave. "I don't think that's a good idea, Clay. If we just follow the prophecy, everything will be all right." Her claws batted at the tip of the lowest stalactite, but she was still too small to reach it. She sat back down with a frustrated sigh.

Clay glanced at the soft blue glow coming from Glory's cave. *Follow the prophecy.* But he couldn't help thinking that a real prophecy would have included Glory.

What if the prophecy was wrong?

CHAPTER 5

It seemed like a long time later when Starflight finally slunk back into the main hall with Morrowseer close behind him. Clay couldn't tell whether Starflight had told Morrowseer the truth — that he didn't have visions or read minds. He was just ordinary, like the rest of the dragonets. But who would be brave enough to tell Morrowseer that?

The enormous NightWing slithered off to the guardians' cave without a word to Sunny or Clay. Starflight glanced at them, then turned and headed for his sleeping cave.

Clay hurried after him.

"What happened?" he asked. "What did he say to you?"

"I'm not supposed to talk about it," Starflight said stiffly. He sat down in the middle of their cave, his wings askew behind him, and started poking through the scrolls on the floor.

"It's over here," Clay said, nudging a fat scroll with silver letters that had rolled under his sleeping ledge. Starflight hooked it over with one talon, tucked it under a wing, and carried it up to his ledge. He curled up with his tail draped over his nose and started reading.

"Wow," Clay said. "So it was that bad?" *Tales of the NightWings* was Starflight's favorite scroll, and he always read it when he was upset or fighting with one of the other dragonets.

The tip of Starflight's tail twitched. "I have a lot to learn," he said.

"But you already know everything!" Clay said. "You have to be the smartest dragonet in all of Pyrrhia. Couldn't he tell that by reading your mind?"

Starflight didn't answer.

"I thought he liked you," Clay said. "Surely he said something about what a great and noble dragon you must be because you're a NightWing."

A long, tired breath whooshed out of Starflight's snout. "Yeah," he said. "That's exactly what he told me, actually."

"Oh," Clay said. "Well, that's good, isn't it? Did he say when you'll get your powers?"

Starflight fidgeted with the scroll, shredding a corner of it between his claws. Clay had never seen him upset enough to damage a scroll without noticing. He wished he could say something helpful, but he couldn't think of a single useful thing to say about NightWings.

"At least you're not a RainWing," he tried. "Did Morrowseer say anything about Glory?"

Starflight frowned at him over the edge of the rock. "Not much. He said, 'Don't worry about the RainWing. I'll take care of it.'"

Clay felt a cold chill climb up through the stone floor and spread through his scales. "What does that mean? What's he going to do?"

"How should I know?" Starflight poked his nose back into the scroll. "Maybe she'll get to go home. She's probably the luckiest of all of us."

The pulse of fear pounding in Clay's head disagreed. He couldn't see the guardians just releasing Glory, not after all the years of secrecy.

"We have to go spy on them," he said, jumping to his feet. "We have to know what they're planning." He stopped halfway out of the cave and stamped one foot in frustration. "Oh, no, we can't. Morrowseer will know we're there."

"Right," Starflight said. "He'll hear you thinking all your big, loud, worried thoughts."

"You don't know that my thoughts are loud and worried," Clay said. "Maybe they're quiet and very serene."

Starflight snorted with amusement, the first happy sound he'd made since Morrowseer showed up. Even through his worry, Clay was pleased.

"What are you doing?" Sunny's anxious voice echoed across the main hall. "What's that for?" The heavy tread of dragon footsteps reached their ears, along with an ominous clanking. "Stop! Wait! You don't have to do that!"

There was an enormous splash.

Clay raced into the big cave with Starflight close behind him. He skidded to a halt, horrified. Kestrel and Dune were standing on the bank of the river, holding a length of iron chain between their talons. Behind them, Morrowseer was holding Sunny back with his tail as the tiny golden dragon tried to climb over him.

Webs emerged from the river, dragging a writhing, hissing ball of blue scales. Kestrel and Dune threw the chain around Tsunami's neck and wrapped it around one of her legs. The three guardians hauled her over to one of the rock columns that stretched from the floor to the ceiling high above. Dune flung the chain around the column twice, binding Tsunami with barely three steps to move in any direction.

Kestrel took the two ends of chain and blasted them with a bolt of flame. The metal melted into a bubbling mass, welded together.

Tsunami was trapped.

"Maybe some time away from the river will teach you to be grateful for what you have," Kestrel growled.

It all happened so fast, Clay didn't have time to figure out what was happening, let alone stop it, before it was too late. He let out a yell of dismay and charged across the cavern.

"Let her go!" He grabbed the chain and let go at once, hissing with pain at the searing heat.

"You'll regret this," Tsunami snarled. She clawed at the chain around her back leg, but pulling on it tightened the loop around her neck. With a hiss, she stopped struggling. "When we're free — when my family hears about this — when the rest of the world finds out how you treated the dragonets of destiny —"

"All your big dreams of your wonderful family," Kestrel mocked her. "They don't care about you. When it's time to fulfill the prophecy, you'll be alive, and the Talons of Peace will have you, and that's all that matters."

"Why are you doing this?" Sunny cried. "Tsunami's the good one! She's wonderful! If anyone can save the world, it's her."

"Actually, tiny SandWing," Morrowseer rumbled, "the dragonet you should believe in is Starflight over there." He nodded at Starflight, still rooted in place by the sleeping cave. Starflight ducked his head. "NightWings are natural leaders. You do what he says, and you'll be all right."

Clay glanced over at Starflight and saw Glory standing in the archway of her own sleeping cave. Morrowseer narrowed his eyes at her.

"I'll be back tomorrow," he said to the guardians. "To make sure that everything has been . . . dealt with."

"We understand," Kestrel said. Together she and Dune rolled the boulder aside. Morrowseer squeezed through the gap and disappeared into the blackness without a backward glance.

"This is for your own good," Webs said, stopping in front of Tsunami. She raked her talons at him, and he stepped back. "We only want to keep you safe. Maybe this isn't the perfect way, but —"

"But dragonets don't know what's best for them," Dune said as the boulder thudded back into place. "You need us, whether you like it or not."

"You were all awful today," Kestrel said. "No dinner for any of you. Go to bed, and I don't want to hear a squawk out of anyone until morning."

"Really? What else are you going to do to me?" Tsunami challenged her. "What if I feel like singing all night?" She started howling in her off-key voice. *"Oh, the dragonets are coming! They're coming to save the day! They're coming to fight, for they know what's right, the dragonets, hooray!"*

"Your fault," Dune snarled at Webs. "I told you not to teach them that horrible bar song."

"OH, THE DRAGONETS ARE COMING!" Tsunami bellowed even louder.

"We have more chains!" Kestrel yelled in her ear. "We could throw one around your snout if you would like me to *force* you to be quiet."

Tsunami paused, glaring at her mutinously, then took another breath in and opened her mouth.

"Or we could chain up one of your friends," Kestrel offered. "Perhaps Clay would like to spend the night hanging from a stalactite, so you have some company out here."

Clay shifted uneasily on his feet, wondering if there was anywhere he could hide out of Kestrel's reach before she could grab him.

Tsunami snapped her jaws shut and lay down with her head turned away from all the dragons. Her gills fluttered furiously, but she kept quiet.

"Much better," Kestrel said. She stomped off to her tunnel, her red scales flaring brightly in the fire's reflection. Webs followed her with his wet tail leaving a darker trail behind them.

Sunny pounced on Dune's tail before he could go after them. "Please don't leave her like this," she said. "I know you're not that mean."

Dune shook her off. "We're doing what we have to." He went after the others.

As soon as they were gone, Clay tried tugging on Tsunami's chains again. They were hopelessly strong.

"Clay, stop," Tsunami whispered. "You know what you have to do. Go, quickly!"

Clay shivered, dreading the cold water, but she was right. For the first time, spying on the guardians was really important.

He ran over to the river and dove in. Through the water, he could hear the muffled echo of Sunny's nervous squeak as he swam against the current to the rock wall. Without Tsunami's glow-in-the-dark scales to guide him, it took longer than usual to find the gap that led through to the other cave. But finally he felt open space under his claws, and he ducked and squeezed through.

His heart was hammering in his chest as he popped through into the cave. Slowly he paddled to the surface and poked his ears out into the air.

This wasn't the loud confrontation they'd heard the

previous night. This time, the three big dragons were huddled around the fire, whispering. None of them glanced at the river as Clay floated closer.

"When tomorrow?" Webs asked.

Kestrel leaned toward the fire, baking her scales an even brighter red. "He'll be back by midday. It has to be done by then." Her tail was coiled in a tight knot beside her. "He doesn't want to see her again."

Clay clenched his talons under the water. They had to be talking about Glory.

"Well, I'm not doing it," Webs said.

Dune shot him a withering look. "No one thought you would."

"Even though this is all your fault," said Kestrel.

"I still think we need five of them," Webs snapped. "What's he going to do about that?"

"He'll find us a SkyWing," Kestrel said. "Properly this time. No colorful substitutions."

They all went quiet for a moment, staring into the fire.

"So, how and when," Dune said in his no-nonsense military voice. "Drowning would be simplest." He glared at Webs.

"I joined the Talons of Peace to *stop* killing dragons," Webs said. "I won't argue with Morrowseer, but I'm not doing it myself."

"It has to be me," Kestrel said in a choked, tense voice. "She's just a RainWing, but she still might get away from you." She nodded at Dune's missing foot and the long scar that ran through his mangled wing.

"But can you go through with it?" Webs asked. "Isn't it too much like — I mean, we all know what happened —"

"That was totally different," Kestrel snapped. "Glory is just a RainWing. I don't care about her. I don't even like her." She blasted a ball of flames at the fire so it blazed up.

"If you're sure . . ." Webs started.

"I'll do it tonight while she's sleeping," Kestrel said. "I can get in there and break her neck before the others know what I'm doing, especially with the bossy one safely chained up. Tsunami's the only one who could stop me."

Shudders of horror were running through Clay so violently that he was afraid one of the big dragons would notice the waves on the water. He began paddling softly backward, but froze when he heard his name.

"Not Clay?" Dune asked. "He might try, at least."

"He'll definitely try," Webs said. "Dumb as a rock, but he's devoted to the other four."

"It's not natural, that much loyalty in a dragon," Dune said. "Especially to dragons outside your own tribe."

"I can handle him," Kestrel said. "Even if he finally gets mad like we want him to, there's nothing he can do to stop me."

Clay had heard enough. He sank down below the surface and swam toward the gap in the wall.

What do we do? What can we do? What can I do?

There's no time.

How do I save her?

— CHAPTER 6 —

"It's not true," Sunny said. "They wouldn't."

"They definitely would," said Tsunami. "They'll do anything if they think it's right for the prophecy." The dragonets all looked at Glory, whose scales had gone pale green. Even her usual aloof expression was gone. She paced around Tsunami's rock column, lashing her tail.

"But we won't let them," Clay blurted. He was still panting and dripping icy water on the stone floor. "Right, Tsunami? We'll stop them."

"You don't have to get involved," said Glory. "This is my problem, not yours."

"How will you stop them?" Tsunami asked Clay, ignoring her. "Even all of you together are no match for Kestrel, especially with Dune helping her. And I can't do anything." She bared her teeth and snapped at her chains, pulling the one around her neck dangerously tight.

"So we escape," Clay said. "Just like you wanted. We get you out of there and we escape, tonight. Right now."

"Escape?" Sunny squeaked.

"Seriously," Glory said. Apple-red stripes flickered

across her ruff like lightning. "You don't have to do anything. I'm the one that doesn't fit in. I'll — I'll fight her or — or figure something out. . . ."

"Of *course* we have to do something," Clay said fiercely.

"If escape were that easy, we'd have done it already," Starflight pointed out. He stepped around Glory, stood up on his back legs, and tapped on the boulder that blocked the entrance. "This is the only way out. And they have it rigged on a mechanism that only the big dragons can move."

"They do?" Clay said.

Starflight nodded. "You know how Dune never leaves, because he can't fly? He has a stone that fits in this slot." He tapped a grooved niche in the stone wall. "He turns it in here to unlock something so they can roll the boulder from inside the cave. But when Kestrel or Webs come from outside, there must be a lever or switch they use to open it from out there."

"Oh." Clay felt like an idiot for trying so hard to roll the big rock all these years. He'd never even noticed that Dune unlocked something before moving the boulder. He'd never thought twice about the oddly shaped stone that was always around the sand dragon's neck.

"So can we steal Dune's rock?" Sunny suggested.

"Terrible idea," Glory said immediately.

"They'd catch us for sure," Starflight said to Sunny, more kindly. "Especially tonight, when they're already on high alert because of Morrowseer."

"Well, then what about the sky —" Sunny asked.

"Is there any way to move the boulder without the rock?" Tsunami interrupted her.

Starflight shook his head. "Only from the outside. It's impossible from in here. Believe me, I've thought about it."

"Maybe the sky —" Sunny said.

"And we couldn't force it?" Clay asked Starflight. "Even if we all leaned on it really hard?"

Starflight shook his head as Glory said, "This is all really sweet, guys, but you shouldn't get in trouble for me. Morrowseer likes the rest of you. Just let me handle myself."

"Stop that," Tsunami snapped at her. "Acting like a martyr won't help right now."

Glory bristled. "I'm not *acting like a martyr*. I'm trying to make sure nobody gets killed for no reason."

"Besides you," Tsunami argued. "It's fine if it's you getting killed for no reason?"

"It just doesn't matter," Glory said. "I'm not even in the prophecy, so who cares what happens to me?"

"I swear I'm going to kill you myself," Tsunami growled.

"Glory, she's trying to say that *we* care," Clay interjected. "In her usual gentle way."

"Guys, what about the sky hole?" Sunny said in a rush, jumping into the brief pause in the conversation. "In the study room? Couldn't we fly up to it and squeeze out?"

"Oh, Sunny, don't be ridiculous," Tsunami said.

"It's way too small," Starflight explained. "We'd never fit, especially Clay."

"But maybe I might," Sunny said. "I could climb out and then go around and open the boulder from the outside, like Starflight said. Right? And I could let you all out?"

Clay brushed her wing and twined his tail around hers. Sunny hadn't even thought of escaping before today, and yet she was volunteering for the most dangerous part of it without any hesitation.

"It won't work," Starflight said. "I'm sorry, Sunny. I've flown up to the hole when no one was around."

"Me too," said Tsunami.

"Me too," said Glory.

Clay felt slow. He'd sat below the sky hole often enough, watching the stars or clouds or rain overhead, but he'd never flown up to it or tried to climb out. Apparently the other dragonets had thought about escape a lot more than he had.

"The hole is smaller than you think," Starflight said to Sunny. "I can barely fit my head through it. It's not a way out."

"The minders wouldn't have left it there if it was," Glory said. She stopped next to Tsunami, waves of dark green pulsing from her ears to her tail. "They're too careful. There's no way to escape."

"There *must* be," Clay said desperately. He could feel time slipping away. Kestrel might come down to kill Glory at any moment. She wouldn't care if they all saw her do it.

He could tell that Tsunami was thinking hard. She kept looking at him like she wanted to say something, then stopped herself.

"What if we tried talking to them?" Sunny offered hesitantly. "Maybe we could convince them to let her go instead?"

Glory snorted. Nobody else answered. Sunny sighed, pressing her wings back against her sides.

"You have an idea," Clay said to Tsunami. "I can tell. You've been working on an escape plan forever."

She wound her talons through the chains, hissing. "It's too dangerous," she said. "It was supposed to be me."

He caught her sideways glance and followed her eyes to the river.

The river.

They'd only ever gone upstream, into the guardians' cave. Downstream, the river flowed from the main cavern along the tunnel into the battle cave and then . . . Clay had no idea where it went. The roof of the battle cave sank lower and lower until the river disappeared. Clay had never explored underwater in the battle cave; he'd never wondered about where the river went.

But of course Tsunami had.

"Do you know where the river goes?" he asked.

"No — I mean, I've seen the gap in the wall, but it's even smaller than the one to the guardians' cave," she said. "I've never been through in case I couldn't get back. But the river has to go somewhere."

"Can we get out that way?" he asked.

"Not all of us," she said. "Only me."

"And me," he said.

She shook her head. "Clay, you can't. We have no idea what's on the other side. You can only hold your breath for an hour — you could get trapped with no air and drown. And you can't see in the dark like me. You'd be swimming blind into who knows what. It has to be a SeaWing who goes. It has to be me."

"And even if you did get out," Starflight said, "how would you find us again? How would you get back to this cave from the outside?"

"The sky hole," Clay said, pouncing on an idea of his own at last. "You guys start a fire in the study room, and I'll follow the smoke back to you. Then I'll know the entrance is nearby, and once I find it, I can let you all out."

Glory's eyes glinted. "I can think of a few scrolls I'd like to burn."

Clay grinned at the shocked expression on Starflight's face. "Yeah, me too," he said. "Throw *The Sluglike Qualities of MudWings* on there and think of me."

"Stop joking about this," Tsunami cried. "Clay, you can't go, and that's final. You'll almost certainly die."

"But Glory *will* die if I don't," he said. "Right? There's no other way."

Tsunami growled and thrashed her whole body, straining against the chains. The heavy links pressed into the scales of her neck, and she stopped with a cough.

"Wait, you won't be able to see the smoke until daylight," Sunny said worriedly. "Won't Kestrel come for Glory before then?"

Clay's hopes dropped like a boulder in his stomach. He hadn't thought of that. He might not make it back in time — it might all be for nothing.

Then Glory smiled, and her scales shifted into a warm, rosy pink. "I know what to do," she said. "Starflight's method."

"Act like a lump and hope no one notices you?" Tsunami said sarcastically.

"Hey!" Starflight protested.

"Exactly," Glory said. She crouched down to the floor. Slowly, as if the stone were eating her alive, grays and browns and blacks crept over her scales. All her beautiful colors faded away. The shadows and crags behind her appeared perfectly reproduced, as if the dragonets were seeing right through her.

She closed her eyes and vanished.

"Wow," Sunny said faintly. "I mean, I knew you could, but . . . I'd never . . ."

"The guardians don't know I can do this." They all jumped as Glory's voice came from the top of a stalagmite. "I guess it's a good thing we never studied RainWings after all. I'll find a corner and hide. You don't even have to risk the river, Clay. I could just stay like this."

"For how long?" Starflight said. "Until you starve or one of them catches you accidentally?"

"Tsunami was right earlier," Clay said. "We do need to get out of here, as soon as we can."

Sunny gave Tsunami an unhappy look. "Why didn't anybody tell me?" she asked, but no one answered her.

"All right," said Glory with a sigh. Her green eyes appeared again, halfway across the cave. She was looking straight at Clay. "Do what you want, as long as you're not doing it only for me. I'll stay out of the way until Clay comes back to get us."

Clay felt like the rosy pink color was rising up through his scales now. Glory trusted him. She believed he could do this.

He could save her. He could save all of them.

He just had to survive the river first.

— CHAPTER 7 —

"I hate this," Tsunami called softly. "I hate this a lot." She beat her wings against the chains that trapped her.

"I don't love it either," said Glory's voice.

"Shhhh," Starflight scolded from the riverbank. Clay stood in the shallows, shivering as the icy water washed over his talons. He wished he could take fire with him underwater. He wished he knew what he was getting into. He really, really wished he didn't have to go alone.

But he had to do this. He glanced at the corner of the cave where Glory had disappeared.

"Are we sure this is the only way?" Sunny asked, splashing the river with her tail. "I bet I could think of some more ideas, with a little more time."

"We don't have any more time," Clay said.

"Follow the current," Starflight said to Clay. "Don't leave the river. If it goes out into the world anywhere, the current should take you there."

If, Clay thought.

"Stop and rest anytime you find a place to breathe,"

Starflight went on. "If you can't find a place where the river surfaces, don't panic or you'll run out of air faster."

Clay felt like he was panicking already. When he thought about swimming into inky blackness with no idea if he'd ever breathe again, his whole body tightened with fear.

He felt the brush of wing tips next to his and turned. The river eddied around the blurry outline of Glory beside him.

"Go hide," he whispered.

"Thank you, Clay," she said quietly. "I'll never admit I said this, but . . . I want you to know I would never have made it through the last six years without the four of you."

"Same here," Clay said. Growing up under the mountain without Glory, Sunny, Tsunami, and Starflight would have been too miserable to bear.

"Me too," Starflight said.

Sunny nodded. She twined her tail in Glory's and touched one of Clay's talons.

"Good luck," said Glory. She stepped out of the river and melted back into the shadows.

"Be really, really careful, Clay," Tsunami said. Her chains were taut around her legs and neck as she leaned toward them. "Come back if you have to. Don't keep going if it's too dangerous."

"Don't you dare die," Sunny added, flinging her forearms around his neck and beating his wings with hers.

"You all stay safe, too," Clay said. He took a deep breath, then another. "I'll be rolling away that boulder before you know it." He couldn't delay any longer. He nodded to his friends and dove into the river.

Swimming helped warm him a little, but his scales still felt crusted with ice by the time he'd made it down the tunnel to the battle cave. He swam to the far wall, where the rock sloped down into the water. He floated for a moment, feeling the current tugging him. Then he inhaled and dove down.

By the flickering light of the torches above, he could see the patch of wall that was darker than the rest. Tsunami was right; this hole was smaller than the gap to the guardians' cave. Well, it was flatter, but wider, too, more like a snarling dragon mouth, complete with sharp outcroppings like teeth. He couldn't see anything but darkness on the other side.

Clay reached one forearm into the hole and felt nothing but emptiness. Dark water rushed past him.

He arrowed to the surface and took the longest, deepest breath of his life, hoping it wouldn't be his last. The water closed over his head in an awful, final kind of way. He tried not to think about that.

With a few swift kicks, he swam back to the hole and grabbed the rocks on either side to brace himself. He folded his wings tightly to his body and snaked his head through the hole. His shoulders followed, then his wings, scraping painfully against the stone teeth. His front talons found a lip of rock ahead of him and he seized it, pulling himself forward.

He felt his shoulders slip into open space just as his haunches got stuck. His back claws scrabbled for a grip. He tried to flatten himself to the rock, squishing himself sideways. He wriggled as hard as he could, remembering Starflight's instructions. *Don't panic. Don't panic. Don't —*

He popped loose so suddenly that he spun forward, head over tail, and had to flail around with his wings to straighten himself out. As he did, he felt stone brushing his wing tips on either side. Cautiously he reached out into the darkness.

Rock pressed closely around him. The river was narrow here and the current was strong. It carried him forward even when he wasn't trying to swim. Everything was pitch dark.

He tried paddling up to find the surface of the river, but his head barked painfully against a rock ceiling. There was no air here, only a tight channel filled by the river. He wasn't even sure there was space to turn around if he wanted to go back.

But I don't want to go back. I can't go back.

Clay forced himself to swim, kicking his back legs, and waving his wings as much as he could in the cramped space. Water gurgled in his ears, as if it were laughing at his efforts. His heartbeat seemed louder than he'd ever noticed before.

He didn't know how long he swam through the dark, twisting channel, but after a while his chest began to hurt. He had never actually tried holding his breath for an entire hour before. The dragonets only knew he could because that's what it said about MudWings in a couple of scrolls.

What if it took practice? What if only full-grown MudWings could do it? What if his lungs were still too small?

What if he drowned down here, alone, and his friends never knew what happened to him, and Kestrel killed Glory, and he really was the most useless dragonet in Pyrrhia?

I will not panic.

Clay climbed toward the surface for the hundredth time, setting his jaw stubbornly. Still only solid rock above him. But — it seemed like the rock was slanting upward. Was it? He reached his wings up to brush against the stone and swam faster.

The channel was definitely getting wider. He couldn't feel the walls on either side of him anymore. Suddenly the rock above him disappeared as well. The strength of the current dropped away. It felt as if he'd swum out into a wide-open pool.

Clay beat his wings, rising up and up through the dark water, his tail lashing to drive him forward. He was deeper than he'd realized, far below the surface.

But — were those stars above him? He nearly sucked in a mouthful of water in excitement. Could he have made it outside already? Something was shining overhead. He could see small spots of light, like the night sky through the hole.

His head burst out of the water. Clay yelped with glee as he breathed in and out, in and out, grateful for air like he never had been before.

But his voice echoed back to him, bouncing off cave walls. This air didn't smell like the sky, and he couldn't hear anything beyond the stillness of rock and the fading echoes of his own cry.

He floated on the surface of the pool. The current was still moving sluggishly somewhere below his talons. All was darkness around him except for those points of light overhead.

Glowworms.

He was still under the mountain, in a cave full of thousands of glowworms.

The eerie little insects pulsed with a greenish light. Glowing tendrils hung from several of them, like a shimmering star curtain far above him and around him in the pool's reflection. By their dim light, he could faintly see the distant arch of cave walls.

He wasn't outside, but at least he was breathing. He followed Starflight's advice, resting for as long as he dared. It was so cold in the water that he couldn't feel the tip of his tail or the outer ridge of his wings. He tried breathing a spurt of fire up into the air, but his chest was too frozen to produce more than a flicker of flame. It was almost more than he could bear to make himself duck under the water again.

But finally he took another deep breath and dove.

For a terrible moment he was afraid he'd lost the current. He had no idea where he'd come in. He had no idea if the river even left this cave. What if this wide, silent pool was the end? Could he make it back to his friends, fighting that strong current the whole way?

Then he realized that when he floated, there was something carrying him along. It was weaker, but the current was still there. He spread his wings wide and stretched his tail down, letting himself drift like a leaf until he was sure which direction it went.

On the far side of the cave, in the dim light of the glowworms, he found a passageway where the river left the pool. The ceiling was still far above him. He could swim and breathe for a while longer.

Clay beat his wings to push himself forward through the water. It was peaceful and creepy at the same time, with all those star-worms glowing overhead like a million burning eyes. But it was much preferable to solid rock, complete darkness, and no air.

After a while, the current started to pick up again. Clay's wings brushed against rocks jutting out of the river, and the glowworms were fewer and farther between. The darkness seemed to press down like Kestrel crushing him during battle training.

And then he heard the roaring.

Clay's ears pricked up. Was it dragons? His first thought was that he was hearing Kestrel, roaring in fury as she discovered she had lost Glory and Clay. But he was too far away to hear anything like that.

Then he started to worry. What *would* Kestrel do when she found Clay and Glory missing? Would she punish the others — especially Tsunami, all chained up and unable to fight back?

He was so distracted worrying about his friends that it took him a while to notice that the roaring was getting louder. Suddenly he bashed into a boulder sticking out of the river. Reeling with pain, Clay spun in the water, flailing for a hold on something.

He crashed into another rock, bounced off, and slammed into yet another. The river was going so fast now that he couldn't stop himself. He was being dragged toward the roaring at top speed.

With a jarring shock, he hit a spur of stone and dug in with all his talons. The rushing water whipped past him, seizing his tail and his wings with icy, desperate fingers. Clay fought his way out of the river until finally he stood, gasping, on bare rock.

He swept his tail around, trying to feel how big a rock he was standing on. It was big — it stretched farther than he could reach. He edged forward until he was sure he was standing on the bank of the river. A slope beside him rose away from the water.

He could feel a small trickle of a stream bubbling down the slope, joining the river near his talons. Clay dropped his head, trying to think. Now that he was out of the water, the cold was penetratingly deep. It coiled and twisted around his bones.

He coughed, hoping to summon a flame, but it was no use. Some dragons carried fire within them always — a SkyWing or a NightWing could blast flames anytime. SeaWings and IceWings could never breathe fire. But others, like MudWings, needed the right conditions — warmth most of all.

Remembering all his fire-breathing failures, Clay could hear Kestrel's scornful voice hissing about what a disappointment he was. *Not this time*, he thought. *I will figure this out.*

He could guess what the roaring was, although he had never seen a waterfall. And he certainly didn't want to experience one for the first time in total darkness. Even if he could fly over it, without his sight he'd be sure to run into something and crash.

But he couldn't leave the river — could he?

Clay set one claw in the trickling stream and was surprised to find it was a little warmer than the river. Where did it come from? Up . . . surely up meant closer to the surface and the outside world.

He inhaled, hoping to catch the scent of the outside. But the only faint smell was of rotten eggs.

He set his jaw. The stream had to lead somewhere. Somewhere not over a waterfall. Clay spread his wings to feel the cave walls and crept up the stream, slipping now and then on the slick stone.

Soon he felt a ledge ahead of him. He climbed over it and splashed into a deeper pool. The rotten-egg smell was much stronger up here. He tried to wade forward, and the water crept up his legs. Suddenly he felt a stinging pain slice through the softer scales of his underbelly. With a hiss, he scrambled back up on the ledge.

His wings caught on something sticky overhead, and he felt the same sharp pain shivering through his tendons. He pulled his wings in close to his body, quickly, but the stickiness came with it and suckered onto his scales like enormous, globby leeches. It felt like the poison in Dune's tail stabbing him in a thousand places, dissolving his skin from the inside out.

Clay let out an agonized yell and tried to stumble back down the slope to the river. But he'd lost the feel of the stream under his claws. He was stumbling blind over bare rocks. Frantic to escape the pain, he lunged toward the sound of the waterfall.

His head collided with something hard that knocked him to the cave floor.

As he lost consciousness, his last thought was, *I failed them.*

CHAPTER 8

Freezing water splashed over Clay's head. He woke up with a gasp as the rest of his body was plunged into the river. Strong talons gripped his shoulders, shoving him under the water.

He thrashed, terrified, and the current nearly dragged him away. The other dragon yanked his head into the air and shouted, "Quit struggling! I'm saving you!"

Clay went limp and let himself be shoved under again. He felt the sticky poison washing from his scales, although the pain lingered. As his panic died down, memory clicked on. He lunged back to the surface.

"Tsunami!" he yelped. He tried to wrap his wings around her, flapping and splashing in the dark.

Her claws dug into the spines along his back. "Seriously, Clay, stop moving!" She whacked his tail back into the water with her own. "I don't know what this white stuff is, but it smells awful, and I think it's trying to dissolve your scales. You stay in the water until it's all gone."

She moved his claws to the rock and helped him hang on against the fierce current while she poured more water over his head. He strained his eyes, trying to see her, or even a black shadow that might be her, but it was too dark. He clung to the feeling of her cold, wet scales against his. She was really here.

"How did you get free?" he asked through chattering teeth. They had to shout to be heard over the roaring waterfall.

"Fire," Tsunami said. "I realized, if Kestrel's flames could merge the chains together, maybe more fire would break them apart. She knew I couldn't do it, and as usual she figured we wouldn't help each other, because that's not 'dragon nature' or whatever. It took Sunny and Starflight together to get their fire hot enough, but they blasted one of the links until it melted. And then I followed you, as fast as I could."

Clay rested his head on the rock by her talons. It felt like the cracks between his scales were singing high-pitched arias of pain. "Well," he said, "as you can see, it's going great so far. I was just about to save the day."

"You would have," Tsunami said. "I'm sure you would've woken up soon and made it to the river on your own." She batted one of his wings lightly with hers.

Clay wasn't sure of that at all. But he wasn't about to add "whining" to the list of things wrong with him.

"Did you see the glowworms?" he asked instead. "Kind of cool, right?"

"Oh, I can beat that." A moment passed, and then Tsunami's stripes began to glow along her wings and tail. She even turned on the whorls of light along her snout.

Dimly, the cave took shape around them. Clay had never been so happy to see anything in his life.

"Thanks," he said. "It seems kind of unfair. You guys can see in the dark — it's the rest of us who actually *need* glowing scales."

Tsunami ducked her head in an odd, embarrassed way. "Well, they're not meant to help us see," she said.

Clay stretched his legs and tail under the water. The goop on his scales was gone, but the stinging was still there, battling the freezing numbness caused by the river. "Really?" he said, trying to take his mind off the pain. "Then why do you glow?"

"It's — well —" He'd never seen Tsunami stammer over anything. Now he was really curious.

"Tell," he said, splashing her.

"You know, you're doing that thing you do," she said, "where you talk about something ridiculous so you don't have to deal with something serious."

"Am not!" Clay protested. "*You're* the one who's ducking the question."

"All right, fine!" she said with a grimace. "Glowing in the dark — Webs says it's to attract other SeaWings. That's how we choose our partners, or whatever." She shoved his head under the water again, and he came up sputtering. "Now aren't you sorry you asked?"

He was, a little bit. The idea of Tsunami leaving them for another SeaWing with cool glowing scales made Clay feel extra-blobby and drab.

"So, we can't go up the rocks," he said. "What do we do about the waterfall?" He hoped she wouldn't ask whether his scales still hurt. He just had to tough it out until the pain went away.

She grinned. "We dive right over it!" she said. "How high could it be?"

"And how many sharp rocks could there be at the bottom?" he countered. "I'd like to see what we're jumping off first, please."

"All right, let's go check it out," she said, releasing him and leaping into the water. The current whooshed her away, and he had to let go of his rock to follow her quickly, before the light of her scales disappeared.

"Tsunami!" he called. There was no way she could hear him over the roaring waterfall. An underwater boulder slammed into his belly, and he inhaled a mouthful of river. Choking and coughing, he paddled after the blurry glow in the distance.

Suddenly the glow vanished, and he was plunged into darkness again. "TSUNAMI!" he roared.

A heartbeat later, Clay felt the air suddenly yawn wide in front of him. Some instinct kicked in, and he lashed out with his talons and tail. One of his claws caught a jagged spur of rock, and he flung his front talons around it just as the rest of him flew out into space.

He was dangling over the waterfall.

He dug his claws into the rock and hung on for dear life, scrunching his eyes shut even though the darkness was dark enough. His poison-riddled skin screamed with agony as it stretched below his scales. He couldn't bear to think of how far Tsunami might have fallen. He could picture her broken body, somewhere far below him. . . .

Something whacked his foot.

"Watch out, Clay!" Tsunami's voice teased. "It's really dangerous! You might stub a claw!"

Clay opened his eyes.

The waterfall crashed along beside him, cascading into a foamy pile of bubbles only a short distance below his dangling back claws. Tsunami was splashing and somersaulting in the pool, flipping waves at him with her tail.

"Hang on tight!" she cried. "Whatever you do, don't let go!"

"Ha ha ha," he said. He stirred the water below him with his tail, checking for rocks, then let himself drop. The waterfall gently battered his head as he resurfaced. "You knew how short it was," he said accusingly.

"Maybe," she said with a grin. "All right, yes. I'd just gotten to the edge when I heard you yell and went back for you."

"Lucky I'm not the type to suffer and die in silence," Clay said. But he couldn't help thinking . . . *What would have happened if I hadn't cried out? What if we had missed each other?*

"Come on, the river keeps going this way," Tsunami said. Her webbed feet swooped through the water, shooting her out in front of him. He followed her through the pool into another narrow channel, with rocky banks on either side.

"But —" He cocked his head. His ears twitched. "I think — that can't be all the roaring, then? Is there more up ahead?" There were weird echoes in these caves. He couldn't tell if he was hearing the roar of the small waterfall magnified, or if there was something else.

Tsunami suddenly spread her wings and spun to a halt, gazing up at the ceiling. "Did you see that?"

Clay squinted into the darkness. Her luminescent scales didn't cast light very far; he couldn't even see the stalactites that were probably up there. "No."

"It was a bat!" Tsunami excitedly slammed the river with her tail, submerging Clay in a tidal wave of water.

He came up gasping for air. "A bat? Why are we drowning me over a bat?" Once a bat had blundered in through the sky hole. It had flapped pathetically around the study cave until Sunny begged Dune to catch it and set it free. Clay was half convinced that Dune had eaten it instead, but at least he'd done it where Sunny couldn't see him.

"Because it must have come from somewhere," she said. "Bats go outside to hunt. So if bats can get in and out, I bet we can, too. We must be close."

"Bats are a lot smaller than we are," Clay pointed out, but Tsunami had already started swimming. He flexed his wings under the water, worried. The pain wasn't going away. It felt like tiny, sharp teeth biting him all over, under his scales.

"Look," Tsunami yelled from up ahead. "I see light!"

Clay beat his wings quickly, trying to catch up. It helped that the current was getting faster again.

But then — was the roaring getting louder, too?

He came around a bend in the river and saw a circle of silvery light in the distance. The dark outline of Tsunami's head was barreling toward it.

Clay couldn't believe his eyes. It was moonlight, just like he'd seen through the sky hole. There really was a way out, and they'd found it.

He was speeding along now, barely using his legs to paddle as the river whisked him toward the light.

Suddenly, a piercing shriek echoed through the cave, and Tsunami disappeared.

Please be another joke, please be another joke, Clay prayed, swimming as fast as he could. The moonlit entrance yawned wide in front of him, and then, abruptly, he shot out into open space.

The river plunged out of the cave and straight down a tall, sheer cliff.

Clay's wings flew open and he banked, catching the air before he fell.

He was flying!

CHAPTER 9

Clay had flown before — short hops around the caves, dodging the stalactites and flapping in circles — but that was nothing, nothing compared to this.

Everything was *so big*.

The sky was everywhere, it just . . . went on and on and on, like nothing could ever fill it up. It was night, but the light of the three moons was dazzling after a lifetime of caves and sputtering torches. Craggy mountain peaks bit into the sky all around him. In the distance he thought he saw a glimmer of sea.

And the stars!

Clay had thought he knew stars from gazing out of the sky hole. He'd never known how many there were, or how they looked like a silver net cast across the dark.

He felt like he could keep flying up and up forever, all the way to the moons. He wondered if any dragon had ever tried to do that.

This is what we've been missing. All this time . . .

Even the sharp lines of pain between his scales couldn't take away his excitement.

"Can you believe this?" he called, spinning in the air. "Tsunami! Isn't it amazing?"

There was no answer.

Clay lashed his tail to stop spinning and hovered, his eyes darting around the sky. He couldn't see Tsunami anywhere. She wouldn't have flown off without him . . . would she?

Maybe she'd seen the faraway sea. Maybe she saw her home and couldn't resist. Clay knew she wouldn't abandon her friends, but he also knew how desperately she wanted to return to the ocean.

He glanced down toward the horizon and spotted her, far below him, flapping in a frantic downward spiral.

Something was wrong.

It looked like only one of her wings was working.

Clay twisted into a dive and barreled toward her. He tucked his wings close to his body, fighting back the terror as he plummeted. Wind whistled past his face — wind! He'd imagined it all wrong. It was like a live thing: grabbing his tail to throw him off balance, whisking in his eyes to blind him, flaring under his wings to slow him down. It seemed to dig icicle-sharp claws into his skin, slicing under his scales.

The waterfall and the cliff shot past at lightning speed. Was he falling too fast? The ground hurtled toward him, shadows and moonlight mixed in shapes he'd never seen and couldn't understand. He had no idea how far away it was, or how soon he would reach it. He'd never dealt with distances like this before.

Would he be able to stop? Would it hurt when he did?

But he could see Tsunami below him, still struggling, so he knew that she hadn't hit the bottom yet, and that made him braver.

He fell, and fell, and fell, and she got closer and closer until . . .

Clay passed her and instantly flared his wings open. His body slammed upright like he'd run into a wall, and then a moment later he was whammed again, this time by a heavy SeaWing landing on him from above.

He tumbled, nearly losing Tsunami over his head, but they caught on to each other with their talons and held tight. With her claws wrapped fiercely around his neck, Clay battled to stay aloft, beating his wings in wide arcs. He wasn't strong enough to lift her, but at least he could slow her fall.

Tsunami let out a yelp, and then Clay felt something like claws snag his wings and tail. They lost their hold on each other as they fell through the trees, smashing branches and ripping off leaves before they thudded to earth.

It took Clay a moment before he could breathe again. Tsunami's tail was flopped across his snout. He pushed it aside and sat up, creaking with pain. Tsunami rolled over onto her back, letting her wings flop out to either side. Close up, Clay could see that he was right. One of her azure-blue wings was crooked, as if it had been wrenched out of her shoulder.

He touched it with one claw, and they both winced.

"What happened?" Clay asked.

"Getting out of the chains," Tsunami said. "I think I dislocated it."

"And you came after me anyway?" Clay said, appalled. "Why didn't you tell me you were hurt?"

She shrugged and winced again. "It didn't hurt so much in the river, but once I tried to fly . . ."

"DIRT!" Clay yelled suddenly. *"I'm standing on dirt!"* He stabbed his claws into the ground, and they sank right into the earth. A thrill ran through him from snout to tail.

Tsunami sat up to look at him. "Yay?" she said.

"It's amazing!" he cried. "Feel how soft it is!" He seized a handful of dirt and flung it at her.

"Hey, quit that!" she protested, defending herself with her good wing.

Clay flattened himself to the grass, feeling the warm earth crumble around his legs and clump against his scales. Scents of green and brown and buried sunshine overwhelmed him. It was nothing like the hard, cold, bare rock under the mountain. The ground here was welcoming and full of life. A worm burrowed past his nose, and he snapped it up.

"Well, now we're even," Tsunami said. "I saved you, you saved —"

"I hear the river!" Clay cried, jumping up and shaking himself. Tsunami ducked the shower of dirt that flew off him. "River plus dirt means mud!" He spun around and raced through the trees toward the sound of bubbling water.

Tsunami found him rolling blissfully in the muddy banks of the river. "I don't think most dragons get this excited about being so dirty," she said wryly.

"I bet my kind do," Clay said, ignoring her sarcasm. "I've never been this warm in my whole life." For the first time ever, his claws didn't ache, his scales didn't itch, his wings didn't feel too dry, and he wasn't worried about stubbing his talons every other step. He felt the mud squelch into the gaps between his scales and realized that the pain from the cave poison was fading, as if the mud was healing him. He sighed happily, squishing himself farther down into the damp riverbank.

"Wow," Tsunami said. She stuck her front talons in the river. "And we're not even at the MudWing swamps yet. I wonder if I'll be this excited when I get to the sea."

"You will," Clay said, suddenly feeling certain and brave and confident. "And when you can fly. Can we fix your wing?" He tilted his head, studying her injury.

The waterfall poured down a cliff that towered over them, with even higher mountains beyond. The three moons were low in the sky. Clay guessed it would be morning soon, and then they could look for the smoke signal that would lead to their friends. But Tsunami couldn't fly, she'd be stuck down here . . . easy pickings for any hostile dragons flying by.

Clay glanced up at the sky, remembering that they'd popped out into a world at war. It seemed so peaceful here. From the way the big dragons talked, he'd imagined the entire world as a giant battlefield. It was strange to be in a quiet clearing, with no sights or sounds of war or even other dragons anywhere nearby.

But he knew that the Talons of Peace — and, by extension, the dragonets — had enemies everywhere. The three SandWing queens distrusted the prophecy and would kill anyone who got in their way. And there was a whole list of dragons who might do terrible things to the dragonets of destiny, if they ever found them.

Tsunami twisted to look at her dislocated wing. "I'm sure I can fix it," she said. "I saw this in a scroll once. It just needs to be banged back into place. Maybe if I run myself into a tree." She glanced around at the forest, then suddenly charged at the nearest solid tree trunk.

Clay leaped out of the mud and pounced on her tail, yanking her back before she crashed.

"Ow!" Tsunami stormed. "Get off! I can fix it! This will work!" She snapped her teeth at him.

"Stop being a grumpy SkyWing. Smashing yourself into a tree is a terrible plan," Clay said. "Can I look at it?"

Tsunami settled down on the grass, grumbling, with her wings spread out. Clay circled her, then stood back and looked at the uneven line of her wings and shoulders.

"If you can stay still," he said, "I think I can shove it back into place."

"Is that a good idea?" Tsunami asked, flinching away from him.

"Better than running into a tree," he pointed out. "Dig your claws in and brace yourself."

Tsunami clutched the ground and closed her eyes. Clay felt gently along her shoulder with his front talons. It was easy to find the spot where a bone had slipped out of its socket. He touched it lightly until he was sure where it was and where it needed to be. Then he grabbed and shoved the bone into place in one quick, strong movement.

"OW!" Tsunami roared, rearing back. Her powerful tail whipped around and slammed Clay into a thicket of prickly bushes.

"I'm sorry! I'm sorry," Clay yelped, floundering free. "I really thought that would work." He stopped. Tsunami was turning in a circle, flexing and extending both wings. They looked perfectly matched again.

"It did work," she said. "It's a little sore, but I can move it now. Pretty fierce, Clay." She helped disentangle his tail from the branches. "Sorry I whacked you."

Clay opened his mouth to respond, but Tsunami suddenly

seized his snout and held it shut. She raised one talon, her ears twitching.

"What's that?" she whispered.

Clay tried to swivel his head around, but Tsunami's grip was too tight. He strained his ears to listen.

Something was crashing through the forest toward them.

CHAPTER 10

"Not big enough to be a dragon," Tsunami whispered. "I think."

Now Clay could hear a huffing, panting sound and the cracking of branches. It sounded more prey than predator. He pried Tsunami's claws off his snout and whispered, "Maybe we can eat it." They couldn't rescue the other dragonets until sunrise anyway, and he wanted to test his hunting skills outside the caves.

A short, pale creature stumbled into the moonlit clearing in front of them. The top of its furry head was barely as high as Clay's shoulder. It had two long, thin legs and two dangling arms that ended in floppy, clawless talons. One arm held something pointy, like a giant dragon's claw, and the other was wrapped around a bulky sack.

It spotted Tsunami and Clay, dropped everything it was holding, and shrieked a long high-pitched note, like the birds Clay had sometimes heard through the sky hole.

"It's a scavenger," Tsunami cried with delight. "Look, Clay! Our first time outside, and we're already seeing a real live scavenger."

"It's so little," Clay said. "And look, it's scavenging something right now." He reached out to poke the bulky sack. The creature screamed again, backing away and covering its head with its arms.

"I thought they'd be scarier," Tsunami said, disappointed. She lowered her snout to peer at it. "One of these killed Queen Oasis? Really?" She picked up the metal claw it had been carrying, which was about four times as long as a regular dragon claw. "I guess these are pretty sharp, but still . . . it must have been some kind of unlucky accident."

"Can we eat it?" Clay asked. His tongue flicked out and in.

"Starflight says they're endangered," Tsunami said. "But I say it's their fault we're all in this war, so eat as many as you like." She swung the claw in a circle and glared down at the scavenger.

The scavenger was gibbering strange noises at them, waving its arms at the sack and the claw. Some of its movements were almost dragonlike, as if it was trying to communicate with them.

"Maybe it wants us to have whatever's in here," Clay said, lifting the sack. He upended it, and a pile of jewels and trinkets tumbled out, bouncing and sparkling across the grass. Clay saw three large rubies and a scattering of white diamonds among the gold shapes.

"Treasure," Tsunami cried. She picked up a silver medallion with a spiral carved into it, studded with tiny sapphires.

"Glory would love that," Clay said.

"So would I!" Tsunami said. "I know you like bringing her pretty things to cheer her up, but I saw this first."

"All right," Clay said diplomatically. "Maybe something else, then. Can we keep all this treasure?"

"Certainly not," said a new voice. "Not unless you want to fight me for it, which I don't advise." An orange SkyWing dragon, slightly bigger than Clay, landed soundlessly in the clearing behind the scavenger. Wreaths of smoke coiled around her horns. As the scavenger shrieked again, she bent down and bit off its head.

"Blech," she said, spitting it out again immediately. The head bounced across the grass as the body slowly toppled over, blood pouring out of its neck.

"Now, that's just unfair," said the orange dragon. "First of all, thieves are always trying to steal my beautiful treasure. And *then* they aren't even delicious when I catch them." She poked the body. "All stringy and tasting like fish. Yuck."

Clay took a step back from the spreading pool of blood. He didn't feel hungry anymore.

"Who are you?" Tsunami asked. She was turning the medallion over between her claws as if she wondered whether it might be worth fighting for.

The orange dragon stared at her, her yellow eyes narrowing to slits. Clay noticed that a fine coat of golden chain mail, hung with rubies and amber drops, was fitted around the dragon's torso. A row of tiny rubies was embedded between the scales over each of her eyes, and more rubies edged the top of her wings. Whoever she was, she had a lot of treasure, which meant she must be important.

"You don't know who I am?" the strange dragon said. "How upsetting. I'm really very hurt. Either I need to get out more, or you're not a very good spy, are you, SeaWing?"

"I'm not a spy!" Tsunami said. "We don't even know where we are. We've been — held prisoner, kind of, and we just escaped."

The orange dragon tilted her head at Clay. "A SeaWing and a MudWing together," she said. "Let's see. I know you're not from my dungeons, unless I'm getting horribly forgetful . . . so who was holding you? Blaze? I don't think she has prison camps. Wouldn't fit with her everybody-love-me act."

Clay took another step back. He didn't like the sound of a dragon who had her own dungeons. "Tsunami," he said quietly, "just give her back her treasure, and let's go."

"A MudWing using his head," said the orange dragon. "You don't see that very often." She slid menacingly toward Tsunami, stepping right through the scavenger's blood and leaving red claw prints on the grass. Small flames flickered in her nostrils, and a steady stream of white smoke poured out and gathered more thickly around her horns.

"All right," Tsunami said, holding out the medallion. "We don't want any trouble."

"Oh, neither do I," said the orange dragon. "That's why it makes me *so sad* when trouble keeps coming to me." She reached out and grabbed Tsunami's talon with the medallion still in it, squeezing hard. Clay started forward, but the strange dragon shot a bolt of flame at him so he had to duck back. She glared at Tsunami. "*Nobody* touches my treasure."

"We didn't know!" Tsunami protested. "We don't even know who you are!"

"Oh," the dragon hissed, "didn't I say? My name is Scarlet. But I highly recommend you call me *Your Majesty* if you want to live."

Clay inhaled sharply. Even *he* recognized that name.

They were standing face-to-face with the queen of the SkyWings.

CHAPTER 11

She was smaller than he had expected — smaller than Kestrel — but Clay knew they shouldn't underestimate the SkyWing queen. She'd held on to her power for thirty years, despite fourteen brave, foolish, extremely dead-now challengers. She was one of the longest-lived and deadliest queens in Pyrrhia. Not to mention one of the worst possible dragons to get her claws on the dragonets of destiny, especially since she was allied with Burn, who hated the prophecy and had destroyed the SkyWing egg six years ago.

Clay tried to remember anything else they'd learned about Scarlet. All he could think was *scary*.

Queen Scarlet let go of Tsunami's talons and slipped the medallion over her own neck. She turned and ran one claw down Clay's snout.

"Now you, MudWing, make me curious. We're on the same side. So why didn't you recognize me?"

"Like I said —" Tsunami started. Queen Scarlet silenced her with a flick of her tail.

"I like to hear the MudWing speak," she said. "All rumbly and deep and nervous."

"We, uh," Clay stammered. "We've been underground awhile . . . kind of always . . ." Tsunami made a face at him behind the queen's back, which he guessed meant he shouldn't give too much away. But what was he supposed to say?

He glanced up at the mountains looming overhead and realized that they were outlined with a golden glow. The sun was coming up. They needed to go rescue their friends, and fast, before Kestrel took out her anger on the dragonets she *could* find.

"We're just passing through," he said to Queen Scarlet. The rows of rubies over the queen's eyes arched disbelievingly. "I mean — it was an honor to meet — a — it was very —" *Terrifying* was the only word he could think of. "We have to go," he blurted.

"Already?" said the queen. "But that's heartbreaking. I hate being abandoned mid-conversation. There's so much more I want to know about you." She brushed the tip of her claw along the bottom of Clay's chin. "I think the only place you should go is back to my palace in the sky. Doesn't that sound thrilling? Don't say no, it'll hurt my feelings. You're just what I've been looking for."

Clay had no idea what that meant, but he was too petrified to respond anyway. He stared up into her unfriendly amber eyes, thinking for the first time in his life that maybe Kestrel was right about everything. Most especially about staying under the mountain and avoiding all the bad dragons out in the world.

Behind Scarlet, Tsunami raised the scavenger's sharp claw. Her eyes met Clay's. He felt the same chilling fear she must be feeling. If they attacked the SkyWing queen, they'd instantly have a new, powerful enemy who hated them.

But they couldn't tell her the truth about themselves. She'd take them captive or sell them to her ally Burn or kill them just to mess with the prophecy. And they couldn't go with her either — they had to get back to their friends.

He nodded slightly. *Do it. We have no choice.*

Tsunami stabbed the claw through Queen Scarlet's tail at the vulnerable spot, driving it straight into the ground beneath.

The queen roared with fury and pain. She whipped her head around and blasted fire in all directions.

"Fly!" Tsunami yelled. She rolled under the flames and shoved Clay's tail. He spread his wings and bolted into the sky with Queen Scarlet's fire scorching his claws. Tsunami flapped beside him, her wingbeats wobbly but determined.

"It won't take her long to get free," Tsunami called. "Quick, we have to lose her in the peaks." She soared up the cliff, and Clay followed.

They flew past the top of the waterfall, where the river flowed out of a hole in the cliff. They flew up and up until they reached the top and whooshed out onto a rocky plateau studded with dark green trees and bushes. Even up here, the mountains loomed over them, impossibly high and unbearably big. The peaks zigzagged to the north and south like crooked dragon teeth, a jagged row that went on and on and on.

The bigness of everything kept overwhelming Clay. How would they ever find their friends again in all of this? And even if they did, what could five dragonets do to save a world this big?

Tsunami led the way, staying low and swooping around trees, diving into chasms where they found them. Her wing-beats were getting stronger as she flew. Sunlight spread across the mountains, dazzling Clay's eyes. He wasn't used to so much brightness — and this was only dawn. The ferocity of the midday sun was still ahead.

"Here!" Tsunami called, jerking her head toward a dent in the side of the mountain. They spiraled down to land on the ledge outside a small cave. From here they could look over the rocky plateau, with valleys and mountain peaks spread out around them. Clay peered down nervously. The roar of the waterfall was a faint rumble in the distance. There was no sign of Queen Scarlet.

"I can't believe you did that," he said to Tsunami.

"I had to, didn't I?" she asked, but without her usual conviction. She scratched at her gills, looking worried, then slipped into the shadows of the cave to check that it was empty.

Clay wanted to reassure her, but he was worried, too. He closed his eyes and turned his face toward the rising sun. The heat soaked down through his scales until even his bones felt warm at last.

"You should see yourself," Tsunami said from the cave. "You're practically glowing. I didn't know MudWings had so many colors in them."

Clay opened his eyes and glanced down. He'd always thought of himself as just brown — plain brown scales, ordinary brown claws, the color of flat mud from horns to tail. But now, in the full sunlight for the first time, he could see gold and amber glints between and beneath his scales. Even the browns seemed richer and deeper, like the mahogany trunk where Webs kept the most delicate scrolls.

"Huh," he said.

"You're so pretty," Tsunami joked, emerging into the light. Clay had to bite back a gasp. While the sun brought out his colors, it made her look bejeweled, like a dragon made of sapphires and emeralds or summer leaves and oceans.

He thought of Glory and how beautiful she already was in the gloomy caves. None of them would be able to look at her in full sunlight, or else they'd be too dazzled to ever speak to her again.

Glory. Clay squinted out at the mountainside. There were crags and holes and rocky outcroppings that might lead to tunnels everywhere. He had no idea what the outside of their home looked like. They could see a lot of the mountain from here, but no smoke signal yet.

The sun had nearly cleared the horizon now, climbing slowly up the sky and chasing away the three moons. Clay saw several red shapes flitting around the distant mountain peaks. At first he thought they were birds, until he spotted fire flickering around them like lightning, and realized they were dragons.

This was definitely SkyWing territory. Starflight was right about where their secret cave was. But Clay had no idea how they'd escape the mountains now that the SkyWing queen was probably hunting them in a towering rage.

Tsunami seized his shoulder. "Over there!" she cried, pointing.

A thin column of smoke was starting to rise from a hole partway down the slope. Clay flung himself into the air and swooped over the hole. It was enclosed and partly hidden by a thicket of branches, so he couldn't land next to it. But it was open to the sky and looked like the shape of the sky hole to him.

It had to be his friends.

Tsunami swept up beside him. They both hovered around the smoke, trying to peer down into the hole.

"Starflight and Sunny must be right there," Clay said. "Right below us!" The smoke smelled of old paper. He felt a twinge of pity for Starflight, burning some of his beloved scrolls.

"So we're close, but we have to find the entrance," Tsunami said. "The tunnel must come out somewhere nearby." She spiraled down to the rocky ground outside the bushes. She started pacing as if she were trying to count off the distance from the study room to the entrance tunnel.

Clay stayed up in the air, circling. He had the same funny feeling he'd had looking at Tsunami's crooked wing — that if he relaxed and just looked, he could see how things should fit together. He'd walked the caves under the mountain a million times. He knew them better than his own claws.

He could still hear the faint roar of the waterfall, so he could guess which way the underground river flowed. He pictured the tunnel from the study cave to the central hall and mapped it out on the craggy rocks below.

"Here," he called to Tsunami, swooping down to land. "The boulder blocking the exit should be right below here. So the tunnel to the outside would go that way —" He turned to look.

"The ravine," Tsunami said. A crevasse cut through the rocks a short distance away. When they peered down into it, they could see a stream running over pebbly gravel and sandy mud. "The entrance must be down there somewhere."

Clay hopped down to the bottom of the ravine, keeping his wings spread to slow his fall. Mud squelched between his talons as he landed. He felt a wave of anger wash over him. Here was mud and sunlight and warm fresh air, this close to their cave. Why hadn't the guardians ever brought the dragonets outside? Even small trips to this ravine would have made life so different.

He knew they'd say it was for safety. They'd say it was to protect the dragonets, in case the distant SkyWings spotted them.

But Clay guessed it was really because the guardians didn't trust him and his friends. They didn't trust them not to fly away. They didn't trust them to act smart and avoid drawing attention to themselves.

He dug sharp gashes in the mud with his claws. The dragonets never even had a *chance* to be trustworthy. Maybe Clay didn't deserve it, after attacking the others at hatching. Maybe the guardians thought that something inside him might snap at any moment. But there was no reason to have kept Sunny and Glory and Starflight and Tsunami in the dark all these years.

Tsunami thumped down beside him and nodded at a mossy pile of boulders up ahead.

"Let's check there first." They squished and splashed down the stream.

Clay spotted something in the mud in front of them. He flared his wings up to stop Tsunami from going any farther.

"Look!" he said. "Dragon tracks!"

Fresh dragon prints were stamped into the riverbank, with the deep line of a tail dragged between them. They disappeared suddenly as if the dragon had lifted off into the sky.

Clay gingerly fit one of his own feet into a print. It was dwarfed by the size of the other dragon's talons.

"If it came from our cave," Tsunami said, "and I'm sure it did — then it must be Kestrel."

"How do you know?" Clay asked.

Tsunami put her own foot down next to one of the prints. "No webs between the claws," she said, "so it's not a

SeaWing. They're too recent to be Morrowseer's from yesterday. And you can see all four feet here, so it's not Dune."

"Oh," Clay said, feeling foolish. "Of course."

"There are prints leaving, but not coming back," Tsunami said, her voice rising with excitement. "Maybe she went out looking for us this morning. If she's still away, this is our best chance to get the others out." She started running down the riverbank, following the line of prints to where it began. "Come on, Clay, hurry!"

Clay raced after her. The tracks led right to the tumble of boulders. When they climbed up onto the large rocks, they could see down into a dark tunnel in the side of the ravine. It was almost entirely hidden from view unless you looked from the right angle.

"This is it," Tsunami whispered.

"Why didn't she hide her tracks better?" Clay worried. "What if it's a trap?"

"It's not," Tsunami said confidently. "Kestrel doesn't know we're coming back for the others. She doesn't think like that. If she were one of us, she'd escape and leave everyone else behind without a second thought."

That sounded true to Clay. Kestrel never believed that dragons could keep their word or care about other dragons.

"She was in a hurry to find us, that's all," Tsunami pointed out. Clay glanced up at the sky anxiously. If Kestrel hadn't bothered to be cautious, she must be *really* angry with them.

Tsunami lowered herself into the tunnel, and Clay slid down beside her. He was warm enough now to make fire, so he breathed a small burst of flame to give them a glimpse of the tunnel ahead. They edged forward as Tsunami's scales began to glow.

The tunnel took a sharp right, then a left, then went down at a steep angle for a few steps. But soon it straightened out, took them around another corner, and ended — at an enormous gray boulder.

Clay's heart thumped hard in his chest. They'd really found it.

He was looking at his prison from the outside.

CHAPTER 12

Tsunami reared up on her back legs and began running her talons along the walls. "Look for something that'll move the boulder," she said.

Clay breathed another burst of fire at the wall on his side. It looked like ordinary flat stone with a few fissures running from the ceiling to the floor. He scraped his claws through the cracks. Nothing happened except his claws tingled painfully.

He tried sniffing around the boulder, then shoved it, but it wouldn't move any more than it had on the other side.

"I hope Starflight's right," he said, pushing away the sinking feeling in his stomach. "I hope we really can open it from this side."

"We can," Tsunami said fiercely. "It'll be a lever or something . . ." She backed away a few steps, peering up at the top of the boulder.

"Or magic," Clay said. "What if it's a magic word? Or some kind of talisman we don't have?"

Tsunami stared at the boulder for a moment, frowning, then shook her head. "They'd need an animus dragon to enchant it, and who even knows if those ever existed in the first place."

The only thing Clay remembered about the lesson on magic and animus dragons was that they had power over objects. He remembered that because Starflight spent the rest of the day sticking his nose in the air and insisting that NightWings were far more magically powerful than any mythical animus dragons.

"If they're so great, why do the NightWings live somewhere mysterious where no one can find them?" Clay had asked.

"Easy," Starflight had said loftily. "It's because we have all these special powers, and we don't want to make regular dragons feel inferior." *Even though they are*, his expression implied.

Clay snorted. "Special powers like what?" he'd asked.

"You know," Starflight had answered, irritated. "Telepathy? Precognition? Invisibility? Hello?"

"You don't have invisibility," Clay had argued. "I mean, you're a black dragon. You're just hard to see in the shadows. That's not a power. I'd be invisible, too, if I were lying in a mud puddle."

"Yeah, well," Starflight had said, "*we* can appear out of nowhere in the dark of night! Swooping down as if the sky has just fallen on you!" He'd spread his wings majestically.

"Still not a power," Clay had said. "That's just you guys being creepy."

"It is *not* creepy!" Starflight had cried, his voice rising.

"It is *magnificent* and *imposing*!" He'd stopped and taken a deep breath. "Besides, we're the only ones with visions of the future, so there."

"Well, I say until the NightWings come down off the clouds, all we have is rumors and a mumbo-jumbo prophecy that could mean anything." Then Clay had draped his nose off the rim of the ledge and peered across at Starflight. "I mean, it's not like *you've* got any special mind powers, other than being way too smart."

"Well, I'll have powers eventually," Starflight had huffed. "Maybe it's something NightWings develop when we're older. You're supposed to be studying, not making fun of me!"

"I wasn't making fun," Clay had protested. It was true he'd been trying to distract Starflight from studying, though. But of course that never worked for long.

Now Clay scraped at the floor under the boulder. He actually missed Starflight. More than that, he was worried about him. How had Kestrel reacted when she couldn't find Clay, Tsunami, or Glory? She wouldn't hurt Starflight or Sunny . . . would she?

Suddenly his claws caught on something. He flattened himself to the stone floor and peered underneath the boulder. A long, sturdy stick was jammed under the rock, holding it in place.

"Here," he whispered to Tsunami. He wrapped his talons around the stick and tried to yank it free. After a few tries, he realized it wouldn't come loose, but it did move from side to side. He tried sliding it sideways, and the boulder began to roll. He stopped quickly and looked at Tsunami.

"What if Webs and Dune are waiting for us?" Clay asked.

"They can't stop us, not all five of us — not if we all fight. The only way they kept us in was by blocking the way out. Once it's open . . . we'll all be free." Tsunami let out a long breath.

"All right," Clay said, gritting his teeth. "Let's do this."

He shoved the stick as hard as he could. The boulder slowly rolled aside with a soft scraping sound. The central cave came into view, and a shiver ran along Clay's tail at how strange it looked from the outside.

A forlorn little shape was huddled by the river, trailing her talons in the water. She turned as the boulder moved, and her gray-green eyes went wide.

"Shhh," Tsunami hissed quietly, bounding across the cave toward her. Sunny leaped up at the same moment and threw her wings open. She pressed her front talons to her snout, beaming.

"You did it!" she whispered.

Clay glanced at the tunnel that led to the guardians' cave. Even if Tsunami was right that Webs and Dune couldn't stop them, he didn't want to stick around and find out. "Where are the others?" he asked quietly.

"I'll get Starflight," Sunny said, heading for the study cave. "Glory — I don't know." She glanced up at the sta-lactites. Clay felt a stab of worry. Was Glory all right? What if something had happened to her while she was camouflaged — would she have stayed invisible? What if she had fallen off a stalagmite or flown into an outcropping and hurt herself? What if —

"Right here," a voice whispered in his ear. Soft wings brushed his, and Glory's long shape shimmered into view. Her scales shifted from gray and black to a warm golden orange flecked with dark blue.

"You're all right," Clay said. In his relief, he twined his tail around hers without thinking.

She tensed, but she didn't pull away immediately like she normally would. Instead she nudged him with her elegant snout. "Of course I am," she said. "I would have been fine on my own, you know."

Perhaps she felt his wings droop, because she added, "But thank you for doing insanely dangerous things for me anyway."

"Anytime," Clay said happily.

Glory stepped back and nodded at where Starflight was staggering out of the tunnel from the study cave.

"Kestrel was pretty furious," she said. "I just had to listen to her from my hiding place. Those two got the brunt of it."

Clay started forward, but Tsunami and Sunny were already on either side of Starflight. For a horrible moment he thought Starflight was limping — that he'd been beaten or burned or terribly injured by Kestrel.

Then he realized that Starflight was moving oddly because he was carrying a giant sack of scrolls on his back.

"Oh, no you don't," Tsunami said, pulling it away from him. "We don't need these. And you've already read them all a thousand times."

"We might need them," Starflight protested, yanking it back. "They'll tell us what's safe to eat and all the different tribal customs and how to fly in bad weather and —"

"*You* can tell us all those things," Clay said. "You're going to anyway."

"But what if I forget something important?" Starflight fretted.

"Ha. You'd be a lot more likable if you ever did forget anything," Glory said.

"The only thing that's important is getting out of here right now," Tsunami said. "Before Webs and Dune wake up."

"And before Kestrel comes back," Glory added.

"What *thrilling* news. Kestrel is part of this? I've been looking for *her* for an awfully long time."

The five dragonets whirled around.

Queen Scarlet was standing in the entranceway. Behind her, the tunnel was blocked by a row of SkyWings in different shades of flame — all of them large, all of them breathing small spurts of fire, and all of them angry.

But none of them looked as angry as the queen of the SkyWings.

CHAPTER 13

"I haven't seen Kestrel in, what, seven years?" Queen Scarlet said in a pleasant voice that didn't match the rage in her eyes. "What a fun reunion this is going to be." She whipped her tail back and forth behind her. "All my least favorite dragons in one place."

Clay was the closest dragonet to her. He took a step back toward his friends and spread his wings. She'd have to go through him to get to them. He hoped she couldn't see how his claws were shaking.

"You followed us here," Tsunami said in a choked voice.

"Oh, I didn't have to," said the queen. "Someone sent up a lovely, helpful smoke signal for me. Led us all right here. What a brilliant idea."

My *idea*, Clay thought, horrified. *This is my fault. I brought the SkyWings down on us.*

"Who — who are you?" Sunny squeaked.

"Now really, this is getting insulting," said the queen. "You're in *my* territory. Apparently you're living under *my* mountain. I am *only* the most important dragon for *hundreds of miles.* How *dare* you not recognize me?" She arched her neck and spread her bejeweled wings.

"Queen Scarlet of the SkyWings," Starflight breathed. He crouched low, touching his head to the floor and crossing his front talons together.

"Now that's more like it," she said, striding into the cave. "Three moons, it's gloomy in here." She glanced around, spotted Starflight's sack of scrolls, and set it ablaze with one burst of fire.

Starflight stared at the burning scrolls, frozen in place. Clay edged sideways, trying to shield him and Sunny and Glory all at once. If only he were bigger!

"My goodness," Queen Scarlet said, squinting. "You're a NightWing!" She batted Clay aside as if he were made of leaves and grabbed Starflight's chin. Clay scrambled up again and took a step toward her, but the clanking of armor and grim expressions of the SkyWings spilling into the cave made him stop.

"A NightWing not yet ten years old," Queen Scarlet said, turning Starflight around and prodding his scales like he was a cow she planned to eat for dinner. "How thrilling! They don't normally let their dragonets out into the world. We might corrupt their superior perfection or something, you know." She breathed smoke into his face, and he coughed. "I've never had a NightWing in my arena before. Thrilling, thrilling! Tell me, what am I thinking right now?"

Starflight's expression was pure terror.

"Too hard?" Queen Scarlet teased. "I'll give you a hint. I'm thinking — now why would a NightWing, a SeaWing, and a MudWing be hiding out under my mountain? Along with whatever those two are that the MudWing is cutely trying to protect?" She flicked her tail at Glory and Sunny. Clay shivered as the queen leaned closer to Starflight. "This wouldn't have anything to do with a certain prophecy, would it?"

"What is going on out here?" Dune grumbled, limping into the cave. He stopped short at the sight of the SkyWings. His black eyes turned slowly toward the queen, and Clay saw fear on his face for the first time ever.

"Webs!" he yelled, and then the maimed SandWing hurtled across the cave toward the queen.

"Stop!" Sunny shrieked. "They'll hurt you!"

Dune didn't seem to hear her. He seized Queen Scarlet and flung her away from Starflight. "Don't touch them," he roared. "You'll never get your claws on them."

The queen twisted in midair and landed on her feet facing him, hissing. "They're mine now," she snarled. She launched herself at Dune.

Webs came pounding into the cave just as the SkyWing soldiers erupted toward their queen. He barely paused before throwing himself in their way. His tail smacked three of them back, and his claws raked the underbelly of another. Clay had never seen him fight before. He hadn't known Webs could be dangerous.

"Stay back," Clay said to Sunny. "And you should hide yourself," he added to Glory.

"Disappear while you try to die for us again?" she said. "No, thanks." She pushed past him and went after Tsunami, who was already fighting alongside Webs. Clay shoved Sunny up onto a boulder and ran to join them.

"Wait, I can help!" Sunny called. "Can't I?"

"These dragonets are sacred," Dune shouted as Queen Scarlet smashed him into a stalagmite. She was smaller than him, but deceptively strong, and his old injuries slowed him down. He staggered up, gasping, with his scarred wing trailing crookedly beside him. "They're the dragonets of destiny. You can't have them!"

"But what if it's *my* destiny to play with them?" she said, lashing her claws at his stump. He howled, and a stream of blood poured from the new wound. "Oh, wait, that's right," she said. "I don't care about destiny. I don't care about prophecies or any of that NightWing silliness."

She scored her talons along his wing, ripping open the scars. "Besides, they made me awfully mad and then ran away. That happens to me far too often, but you know what? I always find the ones who betray me in the end. Even if I have to wait seven years." The queen seized Dune by the neck and pinned him up against the wall. "Right, Kestrel?"

Clay stumbled. The SkyWing he was fighting knocked him over and trapped his tail and wings beneath four massive feet. The battle seemed to freeze for a moment, and from his crushed position, Clay saw Kestrel slide into the cave.

"Poor, poor Scarlet," she said bitingly. "Everyone betrays

you. Well, you've got me now. Let these worthless others go." She didn't even look down at the dragonets.

Clay twisted his head and met Tsunami's eyes. He would never, never have guessed that Kestrel would give herself up to save them. Maybe she really meant it about keeping them alive. Maybe that was the only thing she cared about, no matter how much she hated them.

"Kestrel," the queen tsked. "That sounded like an order. Have you switched from disobeying orders to giving them now?"

"I won't fight," Kestrel said, her voice cold and hard. "I'll come with you. Just leave them. These dragonets have nothing to do with the SkyWings."

"You *will* come with me," said Queen Scarlet. "Funny that you thought you had a choice about that. We've got a thrilling trial planned, followed by an even more thrilling execution. But as for these little dragons . . ." She swept her tail toward Clay and his friends. "You can't really expect me to give up prizes like this."

"They're no prizes," Kestrel snorted. "They're useless, every one of them."

"Plus I'm weird-looking," Sunny chimed in from the top of her rock.

The queen's tongue flicked out of her mouth, and more smoke coiled around her horns. "Oh, they're just the new blood my arena needs. It would be terribly sad to let them go. I would be too, too devastated."

Clay tried to heave the SkyWing off him, but the soldier

who had him pinned was too big. He barely glanced down at Clay's pathetic struggles. *This would be a good time to call up that inner monster*, Clay thought, but no surge of strength or violence or rage answered him.

"Take them all," Queen Scarlet announced. "Except this one, of course." She shook Dune lightly, as if she were shaking the fluff off a dead pigeon. He clawed at her talons, his eyes bulging. "I mean, what use is a crippled dragon who can't fly? I'm surprised you haven't killed yourself already, SandWing. But I can take care of that for you."

"No!" Sunny screamed, leaping at them.

But it was too late. With a chilling *crack*, Queen Scarlet snapped Dune's neck and dropped his body on the stone floor.

"Dune!" Sunny howled. She squirmed past Scarlet and crouched beside him, shaking him with her front talons. His mangled wing flopped, and his scales scraped against the rocks. His black eyes were empty. "Dune, wake up!"

Clay was too horrified to move, even if he could have escaped the SkyWing soldier. *Dune is dead, and it's all my fault. I came up with the smoke-signal plan. I brought the SkyWings here to kill him.*

Who else is going to die because of me?

Kestrel suddenly lunged at the SkyWing soldiers. She grabbed the one who was clutching Webs and ripped him free. "Tell the Talons," she snarled, shoving Webs toward the river.

Before anyone could stop him, Webs pelted down the slope and dove into the water. A huge wave doused the rocks and splashed all the dragons. He vanished below the surface while Clay was still blinking.

Clay remembered the tight gap and the long tunnel he'd swum through. Would Webs fit? Would he make it outside?

"Oooo," Queen Scarlet said, wiping her crest dry with one claw. "The Talons of Peace. I hope they try storming my sky palace to save you. That *would* be thrilling fun. Especially the part where we slaughter them all."

The SkyWing soldiers brought chains forward and started wrapping each of the dragonets in heavy iron. Clay caught Glory's eye. "Hide," he mouthed. She shook her head.

"No way. I'm going with you," she whispered.

The weight of the chains made Clay's wings and head droop as they were all marched through the tunnel and out into the dawn. The sun was slithering up the sky, casting golden light across the mountains.

Clay glanced up and thought he saw a dark figure circle overhead, spot them, and fly away. He guessed it might be Morrowseer, but he wasn't surprised that the NightWing made no effort to rescue them. NightWings never got their claws dirty. They delivered prophecies and told other dragons what to do, but they stayed out of the war and avoided fighting.

Clay's heart ached. They'd come so close to freedom, but now they were far worse off than before. Life under the mountain had felt like prison . . . but he knew it was nothing compared to being trapped in the claws of the SkyWing queen.

PART TWO

IN THE SKY KINGDOM

——— CHAPTER 14 ———

The queen's prisoners were kept in the sky.

For the whole first day, Clay kept his eyes shut. His talons gripped the rock below him so tightly he started to lose feeling in his legs. One glance over the edge — one glimpse of the dizzying drop below him — and he feared he would lose consciousness and fall.

With his wings folded over and clamped in SkyWing metal clips, falling meant death. Horrible, painful, bone-shattering death.

But then, he wasn't entirely sure if that would be worse than Queen Scarlet's plans for them, whatever they were.

His prison cell was at the top of a towering spire of rock. A narrow stone platform gave him just enough room to walk in a circle and lie down. There were no walls. There was no roof. There was only open blue sky and the fierce wind whistling around his ears day and night.

On the second day, a hunk of meat hit him in the face.

Hunger forced his eyes open. An unusual SkyWing dragon was flying in loops around his perch. He guessed she was only a year or two older than him; her horns were full size, but her teeth were still sharp and white, not yet blunted or stained. Veins of gold ran through her glimmering copper wings, and smoke seemed to be coming from her scales as well as her mouth. She stopped and hovered in front of him.

Her eyes were startling, like two small blue flames blazing through the smoke. Clay was pretty sure SkyWings normally had orange or yellow eyes. He wondered if there was something wrong with this one, like Sunny.

Something dead and bloody and charred lay on the stone in front of him. Clay took one look at the blood, remembered the shape of Dune's broken neck, and threw up over the side of the platform.

To his surprise, the other dragon started laughing. "Oh, *gross*," she said. "Too bad the barracks aren't down there. The guards seriously deserve that."

Unwillingly Clay looked over the edge.

His rock-tower prison was one of about a hundred spires, spread out in a huge circle. Nearly every one had a dragon trapped at the top, like him. Like him, they each had thin metal clamps on the outer edge of their wings. In the center of the circle was a bowl of rock, like an empty lake, with sand at the bottom and sheer walls. Above the walls were rows of benches, balconies, and caves for spectators to look down into the arena.

At the bottom of his tower, there was only bare rock. But from up here he could see the heart of the SkyWing kingdom stretched across the mountaintop. Queen Scarlet's vast palace was carved into the gray-and-black rocks of the peak.

Half of it was inside tunnels and caves while the other half was open to the sky and bristling with defenses. Fire-colored dragons crawled across the mountain face, digging and blasting out new palace extensions until they were covered in stone dust and dirt and looked no brighter than MudWings.

The war had slashed this kingdom with sharp talons. Clay spotted collapsed towers, scorch marks along several walls, and a ravine half full of dragon bones. Even as he watched, he saw two SkyWings carry in the corpse of a crimson dragon and dump it in the ravine. They set fire to the body and hovered for a moment over the smoke, their wings brushing against each other. Then they wheeled and flew away, leaving the body to blaze down into ashes and singed bones.

Far off to the east, Clay could see the blue, glittering line of the sea.

He also noticed the thin wires that twisted around his legs and neck. He'd been too terrified and confused to pay attention to what the SkyWings did with him when they first arrived.

The wires stretched from him out to the necks and legs of other prisoners, who all had them as well. One went to his left, to one leg of a moon-silver IceWing on the next column, who was asleep with her tail over her nose. One wire was attached to the dragon on his right, a fuming SandWing whose pacing made the wire shake. The last three wires snaked out across the circle. He couldn't tell where those wires went; they disappeared into a tangled web above the bowl, connecting all the trapped dragons.

So even if Queen Scarlet's captives could fly away, they'd have to all lift off at once . . . and then all one hundred prisoners would be stuck with each other. They wouldn't get very far that way. He wondered what would happen if one dragon fell off his spire. Would the wires drag down all the others as well?

"Aren't you going to eat?" asked the SkyWing who was flapping around him.

"I'm not hungry," Clay said, tucking his head under his wing. He could hear her wingbeats as she circled him a few more times.

"Is it the wrong thing?" she asked. "I don't know what MudWings eat. We've never had one before. You know, because we're on the same side in the war. So that would be rude. Taking them prisoner, I mean. But you're in the Talons of Peace, so the MudWings won't care what we do to you. Come on, you have to eat something."

"Why?" Clay asked, keeping his head buried.

"Because I don't want you to die before I kill you," she said, her tone so matter-of-fact that it took Clay a few moments to register what she'd said. He poked out his snout and stared at her.

"I've never fought a MudWing," she said, deftly avoiding the wires as she looped around him again. "Since we're allies and all. So I'm really curious. I bet it's totally different from fighting SeaWings and IceWings. But Her Majesty will make you fight some of the regular prisoners first, and if you die, then I don't get to fight you."

"And that would be sad," Clay said.

"Right. Not blazing at all. The *most* blazing will be fighting the NightWing, though. Nobody's ever seen anything like that. What if he can read my mind and knows what I'm going to do before I do it?" She tilted her wings and swooped underneath Clay. "At least *he's* eating. Hey, I wonder if she'll make you fight each other. But then I'd only get to fight one of you. Do you think you could beat a NightWing? Probably not, huh?"

"Starflight?" Clay said. "Is he all right? Where is he?" He stood up and peered out at the circle of prisoners. It wasn't so bad as long as he didn't look down.

He could see several blue and green dragons who must be SeaWings, but none of the ones close enough to identify were Tsunami. Most of the trapped dragons were SeaWings, IceWings, or SandWings — they must be prisoners of war. A few were red or orange SkyWings. He guessed those were subjects who had somehow displeased the queen.

Only one prisoner was midnight black, and he was nearly on the opposite side of the circle from Clay. *So far away.* Clay couldn't see his face, but he could tell that Starflight was sitting still, in his helpful "terrified stalagmite" pose, his head drooping.

If only he could *read minds!* Clay wished desperately that he could get a message across the arena. Although he didn't know what he would say . . . maybe just that he was sorry for all the times he'd teased Starflight or hidden his favorite scroll or whined about studying.

"See him?" asked the SkyWing. "He doesn't talk much."

Clay snorted. "Ask him to teach you something — like how the dragons took Pyrrhia from the scavengers during the Scorching. Then you won't be able to shut him up."

"I'll do that," she said, apparently missing that Clay was joking. He squinted at her. The light up here was too bright, and it was even brighter when it reflected off her smoking copper-colored scales.

"Who are you?" he asked. "Are you a guard?"

"Ick, no. I'm Peril," she said proudly. "The Queen's Champion. What's your name?"

"Clay," he said. "What did you mean about fighting me? Why do we have to fight?"

"Wow," she said. "Are you serious? Have you been living under a rock or something?"

"Pretty much," Clay said with a grimace.

"Really?" She tilted her head curiously and thought for a moment. "All right. That's the queen's arena down there." She flicked her long pointed tail at the bowl below them. "There's a battle almost every day for Her Majesty's amusement. If you win enough battles, you go free."

"How many is that?" Clay asked.

"I don't know," she said. "Nobody's ever done it. Her Majesty always sends me in after any dragon has a few wins, and I always kill them." She shifted her wings in a shrug. "I'm really dangerous."

And possibly crazy, Clay thought. *How many lives has she taken? Does she keep count? Does she care?*

"What are you looking for?" Peril asked. Clay had been scanning the prisoners around the circle since spotting Starflight, but he couldn't see any tiny gold dragons or unusual colors. Where were Sunny and Glory?

"The other dragons who were brought in with me . . ." he said. "Do you know where they are?"

"The SeaWing is over there," Peril said, spiraling up above him and pointing to a deep blue dragon halfway between him and Starflight. Clay immediately recognized Tsunami's angry tail lashing.

"Boring," Peril added. "I've fought plenty of SeaWings. Easy, once you know their tricks."

I bet Tsunami has some tricks you've never seen before, Clay thought. "What about the RainWing?"

She tilted her head at him. "There's a RainWing here?"

"You can't fight her," he said quickly. "They have no defenses — it wouldn't be fair."

"I do whatever Her Majesty tells me to," said Peril. "But I haven't seen a RainWing. They didn't bring her to the arena."

"There's a SandWing, too," Clay said desperately. "She's really small and golden, and kind of odd-looking —"

"Haven't seen any dragons like that," Peril said. "But I'll keep an eye out, if you want." She did a slow backward somersault in the air and tipped her wings at him. "I'd better go warm up. Cheer for me!" Peril dove toward the arena.

He watched her glowing copper shape spiral down onto the sand below. A few other dragons were in the arena, sweeping or checking the walls or guarding the seats. Clay noticed that they all hurried to move away from Peril. Wherever she went, dragons fled, as if she had an invisible cloud of poison around her. None of them would even look at her.

Peril didn't seem to care. She strode around the arena as if she knew everyone would clear out of her way. Her head kept turning toward the largest rock balcony, which jutted out of a cave overlooking the arena. Finally she flicked her tail and vanished into a dark opening in the side of the arena wall.

Clay crouched to peer over the edge. He hung on tightly with his talons and fought back the dizzying nausea caused by the view. The smell of the dead rabbit wasn't helping. He wondered if he could hit one of the SkyWing soldiers if he threw the carcass from up here. He couldn't remember the last time he'd eaten — was it before Morrowseer appeared under the mountain? Wasn't that a lifetime ago? — but his normally huge appetite seemed to have deserted him.

As he watched, dragons started filing into the seats below. Nearly all of them were SkyWings, but he spotted the pale yellow and white of SandWings here and there as well. There were even one or two MudWings. His heart jumped. His own kind! Did they know he was up here? Would they demand his release if they found out, even though he was supposedly in the Talons of Peace?

So MudWings and SkyWings were allies on one side of the war. Clay had never been able to remember that before, but he was pretty sure he would now. *If only Starflight had thought of chaining me to a tower above gladiator fights. I might have been an excellent history student then.*

He didn't know how long it took for the stands to fill, but the sun was blazing directly overhead when two of the guards let out a trumpeting roar. All the other dragons snapped to attention. Across the stadium, heads bent, wings tipped, talons were crossed, and silence fell as everyone waited.

Queen Scarlet stepped out onto the large balcony and spread her wings, catching the sunlight in the reflection of her orange scales. The fire-breathing hiss of all the gathered dragons greeted her. Clay knew this sound only as a warning that Kestrel was about to spout flames at him. It took him a moment to realize that the SkyWing dragons were hissing with respect.

He squinted at the dragons around the queen. Several large SkyWing guards took up positions along the balcony, and two of them moved to roll something forward into the sunlight. It looked like a tree with no leaves, a sinuous curving shape with four branches, carved from a single spear of pale gray marble. Looped over the branches, with her tail wound around the trunk, was a dragon the color of deep red rose petals. But as the sunlight hit her, new colors exploded through her scales — constellations of gold sparks, galaxies of swirling violet, shifting pale blue nebulas.

Clay inhaled sharply, and at the same moment he heard gasps and murmurs flutter through the crowd below.

It was Glory, and she was even more dazzling in the sunshine than he'd expected.

A delicate silver chain leashed her to the tree sculpture. It looked flimsy and easy to break, but Glory didn't seem interested in escaping. She stretched her long neck up toward the sun, ignoring the audience, and then coiled herself over the branches again and closed her eyes.

The guards positioned Glory's tree in one corner of the balcony, and the queen stepped forward.

"Well?" she said in a sly, smiling voice that carried across the arena and up to the prisoners. "What do you think of my new art?"

Art! Clay thought furiously. *As if Glory's nothing more than a tapestry to hang on the wall, not a dragon with feelings and ideas and a destiny and friends who care about her.*

But why wasn't Glory fighting it?

And where was Sunny?

Dragons in the lower seats began to applaud, and soon the whole stadium thundered with the beating of wings and talons. Queen Scarlet settled herself on a large flat boulder, looking pleased, and flicked her tail for silence.

"Bring in the combatants," she called.

Peril swept in from the tunnel, waving to the crowd. Clay noticed that the applause was muted, as if most of the dragons weren't really sure they wanted to cheer for her.

Meanwhile three of the SkyWing guards flew up to the prisoner on Clay's right. One of them seized the SandWing's venomous tail and held it out of the way. The SandWing fought, howling angry curses, as the other two unclipped his wires and hooked them to a ring in the center of the ledge.

Clay thought for a moment that the prisoner was going to hurl himself off the edge, despite the bands that were still on his wings. But the guards gripped him tightly and swooped him down to the sands below. They dropped him in a heap in the middle of the arena.

Peril turned to look at him, her eyes glinting.

Clay realized with a sickening lurch in his stomach that he was about to watch a dragon die.

CHAPTER 15

Clay didn't want to watch. But he knew that if he might have to fight Peril one day, he should study her technique. He glanced up at the distant figures of Tsunami and Starflight. It looked like they were watching intently, too, along with most of the prisoners above the arena.

One of the SkyWing guards stood in the center of the arena and clapped his wings thunderously until the audience was quiet. He bowed to the queen and announced, "After four wins, Horizon the SandWing — formerly, and unwisely, a soldier in Blaze's army — has been challenged to a match with the Queen's Champion, Peril. Claws up, fire ready! Fight!"

He sprang out of the arena, leaving Peril and the SandWing facing each other. Horizon shrank back against the far wall, hissing.

Peril stalked slowly toward him, tilting her copper wings to reflect the sunlight. Her long tail snaked across the sand. It still looked like smoke was rising from her scales.

Horizon crouched, then suddenly leaped over Peril's head and fled to the other side of the arena. He didn't try to claw her or strike her on the way past; he didn't even lash out with his poisonous tail. He just ran away.

Why is he so afraid of her? Clay wondered uneasily.

Peril turned in an unhurried way and smiled at Horizon. His black eyes darted left and right, searching for an escape. Suddenly he made a dash for the tunnel.

All at once Peril was in his way, lashing her claws across his chest. It didn't look like more than a scratch from what Clay could see, but Horizon screamed in agony and fell back, scrabbling across the sand.

Peril followed, slashing another scratch along his side. Horizon screamed again. His banded wings flapped desperately, as if he were still trying to fly. Calmly, almost gently, Peril reached out and touched one of his wings, pinning it to his body.

Horizon's screams intensified into one long ear-shattering wail.

Clay couldn't understand it. She was only touching him — nothing more.

Then Peril let go, and as she stepped back, Clay saw the scorched talon print she left behind on Horizon's scales. It looked as if she had branded him, burning his skin without ever breathing fire. Clay squinted and realized there was smoke rising from Horizon's scratches. Did Peril have fire in her claws? How was that possible?

He looked across at Starflight's slumped form, wishing that the NightWing was close enough to explain everything to him.

Suddenly Horizon attacked. He flung himself at Peril, slashing at her eyes and jabbing his tail at her heart.

Peril whirled, avoiding his claws, and knocked him to the sand. His barbed tail bounced off her scales with a spark like miniature lightning, and then burst into flames. Fire engulfed the poisoned tip, and Horizon howled in pain. Clay had never seen anything like it. He'd never heard of dragons setting other dragons on fire just by touching them.

Horizon beat his tail against the sand, trying to put the fire out, as Peril feinted around him. She darted in to give him another scratch, but before she could dart away again, Horizon turned and grabbed her forearms in his talons. He threw his wings around her and buried his face in her shoulder with a high-pitched keening sound.

Peril froze. Smoke billowed off the two dragons and black marks crawled along Horizon's wings until they started disintegrating into ash. He crumpled slowly to the ground, and Peril crouched with him, holding him up with her wings.

A violent shudder went through the SandWing's whole body. He let go of Peril and flopped slowly onto his side on the sand. Disfiguring burns had melted his facial features, and his wings were charred into black strands between large holes. His talons had scorch marks in the center of their palms.

Clay had a sudden, quick flash of memory. Kestrel had the same scorch marks on her talons. Had she fought with

Peril, back when Kestrel lived in the SkyWing kingdom? How had she survived?

Peril stood up, looking down at the dead SandWing. A disappointed murmur was starting to spread around the stadium. Her copper wings wavered, and she turned to glance up at Queen Scarlet.

The queen sighed and stood up. "Well, that was boring," she said. She raised her voice to address all the prisoners. "I hope some of you up there are braver than this pathetic creature."

Clay had never felt less brave. Peril was clearly a whole new category of monster. If Horizon couldn't beat her, perhaps forcing a quick death — even a horrible one — was still a better choice than being killed slowly for the queen's entertainment.

"Don't worry," the queen said to the crowd, shaking out her wings. "We have a special treat tomorrow. Something we've never seen before! Hopefully this time someone will at least *try* to amuse me, unlike *some* dragons." Queen Scarlet gave Horizon's body a stern glare, turning her frown on Peril as well. Peril bowed her head and stared at the sand.

"Dismissed," said the queen with a wave of one talon. She turned and swept away. Clay leaned out as far as he dared, watching Glory sleep while the soldiers rolled her back into the tunnels.

Maybe she was drugged. Maybe the queen had threatened her somehow. Maybe she was sick, or there was something else terribly wrong.

He didn't know who to worry about more — Glory, Sunny who was still missing, or Starflight, who might be thrown into battle tomorrow. Was that what the queen meant by "something we've never seen before"?

Starflight was good at maps and dates and facts and tests, but his claw-to-claw combat skills were tragic.

Clay wasn't at all sure that Starflight could survive the arena.

CHAPTER 16

As the sun began to sink below the mountains, Clay dozed off, still worrying about his friends.

He woke up to the smell of burnt prey and the growling of his stomach. Two of the moons were high overhead, while the third was a dim ivory blur glowing behind a distant peak. His eyes were finally starting to adjust to the bigness of everything. This view was just about the opposite of what he'd grown up with under the mountain.

Clay twisted his head toward the smell of prey behind him and nearly toppled off the ledge in surprise.

Peril was perched on the far side of his stone platform with her tail tucked around her legs and her wings folded in, as if she were trying to make herself as small as possible. Even so, there was only about the length of a dragon tail between them, and Clay could clearly feel the burning heat coming off her scales. It wasn't a warm, basking heat like Sunny and Dune had. It felt like standing too close to an erupting volcano.

"Oh, good, finally," she said. She nodded at a lump of meat on the rock between them. "I brought you something different. Well, I made the guard let me bring it. I hope you don't mind that it's a little crispy." She spread her front talons in an oddly hopeless gesture.

Clay peered at the prey, which smelled like smoky duck. He wanted it, but he was afraid of getting any closer to Peril. What if she burned him, even by accident?

"I'll be careful," she said, guessing his thoughts. "I'll stay really still, I promise." She glanced around at the slumbering prisoners. "I just thought it might be less obvious if I sat here instead of flying around you."

She didn't sound like a monster. Clay couldn't put this quiet dragon together with the brutal killer he'd seen earlier that day.

He scraped the duck toward him, then devoured it in two bites. It tasted like ash and crunched strangely between his teeth.

"Oh dear," Peril said. "That was fast. Do you want another one?"

"I'm all right," Clay said.

She scraped one claw across the rocks. "Do you want me to go away?"

"No," he said, and she looked up, surprised. "Stay and talk to me," he offered.

"Aren't you afraid of me? Now that you've seen what I can do?"

"Of course I am," he said honestly. "But you're still better company than the pigeons. All they want to talk about is nest design and who to poop on."

Peril barked a laugh. She seemed much more subdued than she had been when they first met. He studied her face in the moonlight. "Are — are *you* all right?" he asked.

Peril blinked several times fast. Instead of answering, she said, "That was weird today, wasn't it?"

"What was weird?"

"The SandWing — Horizon — the way he just gave up." She opened and closed her wings, and Clay flinched. "Why would he do that?" Peril went on. "It's poor form. I guess I should have pushed him away to make him keep fighting. Her Majesty was pretty angry."

"At you?" Clay said. "That doesn't seem fair."

Peril blinked again. "Really?" she said. "It doesn't?" She shook her head. "No, the queen is right. It's my responsibility to make the fight exciting if the other dragon won't do it."

"Why do you do what she says?" Clay asked. "Do you — like fighting?" What he really wanted to ask was "Do you like killing?" but he was afraid of what the answer might be. Would *he* like killing, if he'd been given the chance to do it over and over again with no consequences? Was that the kind of dragon he was supposed to be? Would he like it if he had to do it tomorrow, in the arena?

"Of course," Peril said. "I'm good at fighting — and not much else. And she's my queen. I'm her champion."

"Why you?" Clay asked, risking getting closer to his real question: *What's wrong with you?*

"No one else wants me," Peril said matter-of-factly. "No one can even touch me. You saw that. I was born with too much fire. Usually when dragons like me hatch, the SkyWings drop them off the highest mountain peak. That's what my mother was going to do, but Queen Scarlet saved me and killed her to punish her." Her eyes went cold at the words *my mother*.

"Wow," Clay said faintly.

"Yeah," said Peril. "If you want to know everything, I burned up my twin in our egg. I sucked all the fire out of him and scorched him to a crisp." She shrugged, but there was a wobbliness to her voice.

"I attacked the other eggs in my nest when I hatched," Clay said. It felt really strange to say out loud. "At least, that's what the big dragons told me. They said I tried to kill my nestmates. I don't remember it."

Peril tilted her head. "So maybe we were both born to kill other dragons," she said. Clay wished she didn't sound so happy about it. *Maybe she's right. Maybe she's the monster I could be, if I let myself.*

"I don't really want to do that," he admitted. "I like fighting, but the only thing I've ever killed is prey."

"Her Majesty said I might as well follow my true nature," Peril said. "That's how she raised me — letting me be myself, giving me dragons to kill. Maybe you'd feel better if you could be who you really are."

"I hope that's not who I am," Clay said. In the moonlight, Peril's expression changed, and he realized he'd hurt her feelings. "Not — not that —" he stammered. *Nice work, Clay. How are you going to finish that sentence? "Not that there's anything wrong with being a killer"?* Or maybe, *"But it seems to be going great for you"?* "I mean — maybe I was born that way, but does that mean I'm like that forever? I guess I hope I have a choice, is all. I want to be who I *want* to be, not who I *have* to be. Right? Do you ever — I mean, wouldn't you want to be different, if you could be anyone?"

"No," Peril said, clawing at the rock under her talons. "I've accepted myself, and I like myself this way. You should do the same thing." Something clattered far below them, and Peril jumped. "I'd better go," she said.

"Wait," Clay said. "Please. Who's supposed to fight tomorrow? Can you talk to the queen? Tell her not to send in the NightWing. He's not ready for the arena."

"Are you serious?" Peril said. "She'd be furious. She's so excited to see him fight."

"Tell her I volunteer instead," Clay blurted. "Tell her I'm ready, and I promise I'll make it exciting."

Peril was already shaking her head. "I can't. I'm forbidden to talk to you. She was really mad when she found out I visited you before. I guess you're not like the other prisoners."

Clay paused, thinking. That was strange. Why did Queen Scarlet care if Peril talked to him? "But you came to see me anyway?"

She shuffled her talons and looked a little embarrassed. "Yeah, I don't know why. I mean, it didn't seem fair. I like talking to you. Her Majesty never has time to talk to me, and my only other friend is old and tells the same stories over and over again. You're blazing."

So she doesn't obey every order Queen Scarlet gives her. Good to know.

He realized she was looking at him hopefully. "Uh," he said. "You're . . . blazing, too?"

Peril grinned, sharp white teeth flashing in the moonlight. "That's what Her Majesty says. She likes me the way I am and nobody else ever has. Until you."

Yikes, Clay thought. He wasn't sure he *did* like her the way she was. Or that he wanted to be best friends with a dragon who was planning to kill him eventually.

But there was something not entirely awful about Peril — an awkwardness and sadness that he kind of understood. And maybe there was a chance he could talk her out of the whole killing plan. Maybe that was why Queen Scarlet didn't want her talking to him.

In the meanwhile, though, he had to focus on saving Starflight.

"Listen," he said, "could you talk to her about Starflight anyway? What if you acted like you came up with it yourself? A MudWing is still something new, right? So send me in first and save him for later. Besides, if he dies in his first fight, that would be a waste, wouldn't it?" He swallowed the lump that rose in his throat at the idea of Starflight dying.

"You think he would?" Peril said, gazing out at the circle of prisoners. Even with the bright light of the moons, it was hard to see the dark lump of dragon on Starflight's pedestal. "Can't he use his powers? Reading minds and all that?"

Poor Starflight. Clay wondered if a normal NightWing, raised around other NightWings, would already have his powers by now.

He didn't want Peril and Queen Scarlet to know that Starflight was powerless, but he didn't want them to risk Starflight's life because they thought he could do something special.

"They're a little unpredictable," he hazarded. "He's not full grown, you know. He's still learning how to use them. Although, of course, they're very scary when they work." He hoped the SkyWings had no more information about NightWing powers than Starflight's scrolls did.

"Oh," Peril said. "That makes sense." Her tail twitched over her talons as she thought. Clay tried to sidle a bit closer to the edge, away from her blistering heat. "All right," she said finally. "I'll try."

"Thank you," Clay said.

Peril spread her wings to fly away and then hesitated, looking at him. "You wouldn't do that, would you?"

Clay tried to think what she meant.

"Kill yourself like that," she said. "The way Horizon did." She coughed, and a small ring of smoke puffed out of her snout.

Clay had no idea what he would do if he ever had to fight Peril. It sounded even more terrifying than swimming down the underground river. He met her eerie blue eyes and realized that she looked very worried.

"I don't think so," he said truthfully. He couldn't imagine choosing to die that way. And he didn't think he was brave enough to do it either.

"Oh, good," she said. "I'd much rather kill you fair and square. Well, good night." She leaped up into the air and beat her wings, sending a wave of heat over Clay's scales.

He felt very unsettled as he watched her spiral down to the arena.

Peril was the first dragon he'd met outside the mountain, if you didn't count Queen Scarlet. Maybe she wasn't as strange as he thought. Maybe switching between friendly conversation and violence was normal for a dragon.

But somehow he didn't think so.

Was she right about his true nature? If he'd been raised like her, killing dragons and feeding the monster inside him, maybe he'd be less worried all the time. Maybe he needed to accept that part of him, like she had. But would his friends still like him? Would he be more or less worthy of the prophecy that way?

One thing was for sure. Whenever he did end up in the arena, he'd find out how he felt about killing pretty fast.

CHAPTER 17

The next morning, three blood-red SkyWing guards arrived to unchain Clay.

"What's happening?" Clay asked nervously as they unclipped the wires around his legs. He'd gotten used to the feeling that something would catch him if he fell, even if it would probably hurt.

"Private audience with the queen," sniffed one.

"Is that a good thing?" Clay asked. "Or a bad thing? I've never been a prisoner before. Unless, technically, maybe I sort of was, but not like this. This is a lot . . . windier. Plus there's the queen, that's new. Does she normally meet with prisoners? Maybe right before letting them go?"

"Shut up," snapped the guard who had answered him before.

"Right, yes," Clay said. "Only I was wondering about the other dragonets who were with me and if I could maybe see them —"

One of the guards tightened the wire around his neck and hissed, "Another word and there's going to be an unfortunate *accident* on the way down to the throne room."

Clay glanced over the edge and shut his mouth firmly. So far, it seemed to him that most SkyWings were just as grumpy as Kestrel.

With a start, he realized he'd forgotten to worry about Kestrel. The queen had talked to her as if they once knew each other. He craned his neck, looking for her among the prisoners, as the guards flew him down to the arena. But none of the red or orange SkyWings on the spires were quite the right color or size.

He noticed with a shiver of fear that Starflight's perch was empty. He must have been taken away while Clay was sleeping — but why?

As they reached the sandy ground, Clay twisted to look up at Tsunami and saw three more SkyWings surrounding her. They were having a hard time getting close; she lashed and fought and swung her powerful tail at them in a fury.

Oops, Clay thought. *Should I have done that?* He hadn't struggled with the guards at all. He glanced around the arena, wondering if he should try to run now. But his wings were still clamped, and there was only one doorway out of the arena. Since the guards were already dragging him toward it, it seemed a little pointless to break free and then run exactly where they were going anyway.

So he let them lead him into the smoky tunnel, lit with flaming torches and an occasional skylight cut through the rock overhead. The tunnel was wide enough for three dragons to walk side by side, wings spread. It sloped upward through the mountain, into the palace Clay had seen from his prison perch.

At one point they passed a large cave with tall narrow windows cut into the walls, casting bars of sunlight on the stone floor. A pool of water separated the cave from the tunnel. On one wall hung a full-length portrait of Queen Scarlet, staring majestically down her nose. Clay spotted the glint of a few copper scales on the floor and wondered if it was Peril's room. There was nothing else in the cave. It occurred to him that she probably couldn't sleep on animal skins or read scrolls because her touch would burn right through them.

But if fighting was all she was good for, why hadn't the queen sent Peril out into the war? Why was she kept here for gladiator fights instead?

Perhaps Queen Scarlet didn't completely trust the hold she had on Peril. If she were let loose into the world, Peril might realize she didn't have to be a killer . . . or she might decide to kill anyone she liked, without waiting for the queen's permission.

Soon Clay heard clattering and clanking and chattering up ahead, as if a crowd of dragons were busily hurrying about. Then the passageway opened out into a vast hall and he saw that was exactly what he was hearing.

He was standing on a wide balcony with no railing, two levels up from the ground floor. The balcony ran all the way around the hall in a large square, and above it Clay could see five more levels of balconies, and above that, the open sky.

Dragons were hurrying everywhere, glowing in the light. Large windows were cut into the walls all the way up, so the hall was flooded with sunshine. The floors blazed as if little rivers of fire ran through them.

When Clay looked more closely, he saw a design of talon prints, inlaid with gold, running through the stone under his talons. Gold veins were carved into the walls as well, some of them branching into flames or tracing shapes like clouds in the rock.

Clay remembered that the queen must be very wealthy. This showed how powerful she was as well. Even with all this gold at their claw tips, no dragon dared to dig it out and steal it.

The guards shoved him in the direction where the gold talon prints led. Clay followed the trail, gazing at the dragons bustling around the hall. SkyWings flew from level to level, hopping across the great space and dodging wings and tails as they went. Some of them exchanged small message scrolls in midair; others were carrying buckets of water or clean animal skins or platters of food. Everyone seemed either very busy or as if they were trying to *look* very busy.

Clay saw one young orange dragonet winging up to the highest level with a bucket of soapy water clutched in her talons. As she reached the top balcony, her tail tangled with another dragon's and she overbalanced. She lunged for the ledge and dropped the bucket, which plummeted all the way down, whooshing past Clay and the guards.

A moment later, there was a *clang* and then a furious roar briefly silenced the hubbub. All the dragons in the hall glanced down.

A furious and *familiar* roar.

Clay darted to the edge of the balcony and looked down. At the bottom of the hall, under a metal grid, a dragon was trapped like a pinned squirrel. The bucket was rolling across the iron bars. All the suds and water had spilled out over the prisoner.

It was Kestrel. She seized the bars and rattled them angrily as a murmur of laughter rippled around the hall.

Clay didn't get a chance to see anything more. The guards yanked him back and shoved him along the talon-print trail again.

He wondered if that was a special cell for particularly bad prisoners and, if so, what Kestrel had done to deserve it. She'd never talked about her life before the Talons of Peace or why she'd left the SkyWing kingdom. He'd always kind of imagined that she'd been kicked out for being too grouchy. Although now he guessed that would have made her fit right in.

He stopped thinking about Kestrel as the guards pushed him into Queen Scarlet's throne room.

The queen was seated on top of a rock column carved in the shape of clouds, staring down at the dragons on the floor below her. The wall opposite her was entirely open to the sky, revealing a steep drop and jagged rocks below. The gold tracery in the rocks and floor went over the top in here, as if a giant dragon had stumbled around the room vomiting gold all over the place. Clay could barely see at first through the blaze of reflected sunshine.

Then his eyes adjusted and he spotted Glory, laid out along her tree in the sunlight. She had her eyes closed and looked more relaxed than he'd ever seen her. A slow pulse of crimson teardrops wandered through her dark gold and navy-blue scales. Two SkyWing soldiers stood threateningly in front of her, barring Clay's way.

Starflight was kneeling before the queen in a submissive bow. Clay broke away from his guards to crouch beside his friend.

"Are you all right?" he whispered. Starflight glanced up at the queen and gave a tiny shake of his head.

"The NightWing is trying to tell you that it's *rude* to talk to anyone else before the queen in her own throne room," said Queen Scarlet. "First you bow to me, and then you stay put until I'm ready to address you all. Really, what are they teaching dragonets these days? It's so very disrespectful."

"Sorry," Clay mumbled, trying to match the bowing position Starflight was in. Somehow his talons didn't fold in quite the same elegant way. His wings felt like they were sticking out at weird angles. He peeked under one arm at Glory and nearly fell on his head.

Queen Scarlet arched her ruby-encrusted eyebrows at him and sniffed disapprovingly.

Clay tried to stay as still as he could.

An eternity passed. There were no other dragons in the throne room besides the guards around Glory and the three at the door who had brought Clay. There was no sign of Sunny anywhere.

Queen Scarlet studied each of her claws, one by one. Now and then she sharpened them on the rocks beside her.

Finally they heard a commotion in the tunnel outside. Clay couldn't help looking over his shoulder when he recognized Tsunami's voice shouting curses. A whole pack of SkyWings came in dragging the SeaWing dragonet. She had several of the strange wires wrapped around her, binding her talons to her side and trapping her powerful tail. Her head whipped around, snapping at each of them, so they were having trouble moving her more than a few steps at a time.

At last they rolled her alongside Clay, and all the guards jumped back. Clay saw with satisfaction that more than one guard had long scratches and bite marks that looked like Tsunami's work.

"Well, hello," the queen said, looking amused. "We've been waiting for you. I gather you're enjoying your stay?"

"This is an outrage," Tsunami hissed. "How can you treat dragons this way? Especially us! We're the —"

"— dragonets of destiny, yes, very thrilling," said Queen Scarlet. "I understand you've been underground for the last six years, so perhaps you haven't heard: not everyone *wants* this war to end."

Starflight shifted a little on Clay's left side, and Clay could tell he wanted to argue. But the NightWing kept silent.

"Personally, I think the war is quite entertaining," the queen went on. "I pick up lots of contenders for the arena from the battlefield. And it's a terrific distraction for those dragons who might otherwise have challenged me for the throne. No one's even tried in about eight or nine years. Saves me a lot of trouble."

"So it's all right with you that hundreds of dragons have died all across the world," Tsunami spat.

The queen gave her a pitying look. "As if you know anything about that. Have you ever been in a real battle? Have you ever seen hundreds of dragons die? Do you know anything, really, about this war?"

Tsunami's mouth opened and closed a few times. "We've studied it," she said fiercely. "We know it's awful. We know innocent dragons are getting hurt."

"Well, it's easy to say war is awful," Queen Scarlet said, waving one talon. "But it's a lot harder to solve these problems *without* having a war. Especially when you're talking about dragons. Fighting comes naturally to us. You should know — you attacked me when you barely even knew me."

She flicked her tail forward, and Clay saw the ugly red gash in her scales. He felt queasy and guilty. Could they have done something else instead of attacking her? Would everything be different now if they'd found a peaceful way out?

Tsunami looked flustered.

"And who should be the next SandWing queen?" Scarlet asked. "Burn, Blister, or Blaze? I'd love to know if you've already decided that, from the wisdom and wide experience of your safe little underground cave."

"That's not our fault," Tsunami said. "We *wanted* to be out in the world."

Queen Scarlet looked amused again. "That's what you think," she said. "Hilarious. As if you'd have survived this long out here. Your minders *did* tell you what happened to all the other dragonets born on the brightest night, didn't they?"

Starflight inhaled sharply. He and Tsunami exchanged glances, but Clay didn't understand. The guardians had never mentioned any other dragonets born on the brightest night, like they were.

"Tsk, tsk," Queen Scarlet said, seeing the surprise on their faces. "Well, I won't go into details, but it was very sad."

"Excuse me," Clay said. Starflight trod on his foot, trying to shut him up, but Clay jostled him away. "Ow, stop! I have a question! Excuse me, Your Majesty," he said. "Where's Sunny? Is she all right?"

"Oh, the funny-looking SandWing," Queen Scarlet said. "I think Burn will like her very much. She collects curiosities. You should see her palace. It's quite horrifying — full of two-headed lizards and seven-toed dragon talons and stuffed scavengers with the palest skin you ever saw." She shuddered. "That misshapen dragonet will be the perfect present for her."

"You can't give Sunny to Burn!" Tsunami flared. "We have to stay together!"

"I can do whatever I like," Queen Scarlet said. "This is my kingdom."

"What about Glory?" Clay asked. "What's wrong with her?"

"Nothing's wrong with her," said the queen. "She's quite perfect, if you ask me. A lovely accessory for my throne room."

"But why is she all — sleepy?" Clay asked.

"RainWings are naturally lazy creatures," Queen Scarlet said. "Hadn't you noticed? But then, MudWings aren't known for their brains."

Clay stared at Glory. Had her eye twitched? Was he just imagining the slight movement of her wings? Was she asleep, or was she listening? Didn't she care what the queen said about her?

"You have to let us go," Tsunami said. "You can't stop the prophecy and we'll —"

"Shush," said the queen, and one of the soldiers prodded Tsunami with a long stick. "Your spunkiness is starting to bore me. Now listen. In two days, we are having a big celebration for my hatching day. I want all three of you to be thrilling and fierce in the arena for me. But I also promised my subjects that today's fight would be exciting, so if I put one of you into it, it would be very thoughtful if you could win. So. Is the NightWing up to it? Which of you is most likely to win a battle to the death against, say, an IceWing?"

"Me," Clay and Tsunami both said at the same time. Starflight stared down at his talons, looking miserable.

"Adorable," the queen said, narrowing her eyes at them. "But seriously."

"Me!" Clay said. "I'm a great fighter. Put me in." No way was he going to watch while Tsunami got slaughtered. Especially since the others would need her much more than him to have any chance of escaping this place.

"You're delusional," Tsunami snapped at him. "I beat you all the time. I'm the strongest of all of us."

"Not *all* the time!" Clay said. "And a MudWing would be more exciting than just another SeaWing, wouldn't it?" he said to the queen.

"True," she mused.

"Just another SeaWing!" Tsunami raged. "How dare you? You know I'm the best fighter!"

"I love your enthusiasm, dragonets," the queen said, clapping her wings together. "Guards, take these two away." She flicked her tail at Tsunami and Starflight. The SkyWings came toward them, eyeing Tsunami's teeth unhappily.

"As for this one . . ." Queen Scarlet pointed at Clay. Her eyes were malicious yellow slits. "Prepare him for the arena."

—— CHAPTER 18 ——

It wasn't until Clay felt the sand under his talons and heard the roaring of the dragons in the stands that he realized he hadn't quite thought this plan through.

He had no idea what his fighting skills would be like against an unknown dragon. His mind went blank as the SkyWing guards dropped a hissing IceWing onto the ground opposite him. Did he know anything about IceWings?

The sun was high in the sky, and it was much warmer in the arena than up on their prison spires. Clay could see beads of silvery liquid dripping through the IceWing's glacier-blue scales. Above them, Queen Scarlet smirked from her balcony, with Glory sleeping serenely beside her.

The same SkyWing announcer from the day before strutted to the center of the arena and bellowed at the crowd. "After last month's battle with Blaze's army, our queen's dungeons were stuffed with IceWing prisoners of war. Only nine have survived. After two wins, I give you — Fjord of the IceWings!"

Fjord lashed his tail and snarled at Clay.

"And in this corner, an unusual case — a MudWing, but not one of our allies. No, this dragonet was found hiding under our mountains, protected by the Talons of Peace. Is he one of the dragonets of destiny? Not if he loses this battle!"

A murmur of laughter rippled around the seats, but in the closest faces Clay could see expressions of uneasiness and, he thought, concern. He spotted a large MudWing in one of the balconies, frowning down at him. *Try to stop this*, Clay thought at him, praying hard. *Do something! I'm one of you!*

But the MudWing shifted his gaze away, as if he didn't want to watch but couldn't afford to leave.

The SkyWing announcer went on. "If these prophesied dragonets are as wonderful and legendary as they're supposed to be, this should be a showdown to remember. I hope you're prepared to impress us, dragon of the mud. I present to you . . . Clay of the MudWings! Claws up, teeth ready! Fight!"

Clay blinked as the SkyWing flew out of the arena. He'd never been called "of the MudWings" before. It might have been a warmer feeling if he hadn't been surrounded by more than two hundred dragons, including MudWings, ready to applaud his imminent death.

He felt quite far from wonderful and legendary as the IceWing slithered toward him. This was it: kill or be killed. Time to find out if he did have a monster inside, and if it was the useful kind or the kind that would make him hate himself afterward . . . or both.

Fjord's pale blue scales were the color of sky reflected in the snow on the distant mountain peaks. His eyes were slightly darker blue and full of malice. Extra horns like a ruff of icicles stood out around his head. A long claw scratch down his neck had barely begun to heal, with dried blood still sticking to the scales around it. He hissed, darting a deep blue, forked tongue between his icicle-sharp teeth.

"Uh, hello," Clay said as the IceWing drew closer. "Fjord, right?"

Fjord stopped and stared at him, still flicking his tongue in and out. He was only a head taller than Clay, but he looked a lot older and scarier.

"I've never met an IceWing," Clay said, edging back a step. "I've never met much of anyone, really. I mean, I guess I read that you were all the color of ice, but I didn't realize ice came in so many colors. Like, you know, blue. Very surprising. It's cool, though. Oh, ha ha, no pun intended."

"Boooo!" called several dragons from the upper seats. "More blood! More death! Somebody bite somebody!"

"Are you trying to get us *both* killed?" the IceWing growled. "Shut up and let me kill you."

"I'd rather not," Clay said, stumbling back another few steps. A flicker of movement caught his eye, and he glanced up into the sky. Starflight was nearly leaning all the way off his column, flailing his tail and bound wings frantically at Clay. Trying to tell him something. But what?

Something about IceWings. Something they'd learned from the scrolls and lectures.

Something pretty important, judging from the way Starflight was freaking out.

The NightWing was pointing to his mouth. *Fire?* Clay looked at Fjord dubiously. He didn't think IceWings could breathe fire. Wouldn't they end up melting their palaces every time they used it?

Then again, Fjord was definitely doing something with his mouth, and it wasn't smiling.

Clay ducked and rolled out of the way just as a blast of what looked like sparkling smoke shot out of Fjord's mouth. A tiny bit of it brushed his wing tip, and Clay felt a horrible chill rattle through his whole body.

Oh, right. Freezing-death breath. That is *important. Thanks, Starflight.*

Now he remembered the freezing streams of cold air that IceWings could shoot from their mouths. Of course, he couldn't remember anything about how to fight it.

Fire would probably help, though. Clay inhaled, pulling the warmth up from his chest as Fjord's head snapped around toward him. The IceWing opened his mouth to breathe on Clay again, and Clay sent a blast of fire right between his teeth.

Fjord jerked back and scrambled across the sand, batting at his mouth with his clamped wings. The flames had been swallowed instantly by the chill of his scales, but the IceWing looked even angrier than before.

"Sorry," Clay said. "Listen, do we have to fight? What'll happen to us if we —"

Fjord interrupted by racing at him with his front talons outstretched. Clay had to shut up and dart out of the way, barely dodging the sharp claws. Fjord's long, whip-thin tail snaked around and whacked him across the face so Clay was momentarily blinded.

Instinctively Clay threw his wings over his head and lashed out with his back talons. He felt one connect and heard Fjord roar with pain. As his sight cleared, he saw that he'd accidentally hit the scratch on Fjord's neck, which was bleeding again.

Fjord fell back for a moment, touching his neck gingerly with his claws. His tail lashed, and his bound wings beat the air.

How am I going to get out of this? Clay thought. He couldn't feel a monster rising up inside him. Whatever had driven him to attack the other dragonets at hatching was buried too deep. He didn't want to kill Fjord. He didn't want to kill anyone.

He wondered if he should have let Tsunami fight instead. *No, I'm the first-hatched and the biggest. I couldn't let any of the others risk themselves when I could fight for them.* He clawed at the sand and lowered his head to stare into Fjord's eyes. *I have to kill him, don't I? There must be a part of me that can do that.*

He'd always hoped his monster wouldn't be necessary. Some part of him had always figured that the prophecy would somehow come true, the war would end, and all dragon killing could be avoided forever and ever . . . without him ever having to hurt another dragon.

But it's too soon for the prophecy. Our fault, for escaping early.

Still, we had to, to save Glory —

"BOOOOOOOOOOO!" more dragons in the crowd shouted. "A sheep could have won this fight by now! What are you doing? Thinking? Less thinking! More killing! Claw him, claw him, claw him!"

They sound just like Kestrel. Clay couldn't tell if they were rooting for him or for Fjord — or whether they just wanted to see someone die.

Fjord dropped to all fours and ran at Clay again, hissing with his tongue as if he were about to shoot more freezing air.

Kestrel's shouted battle commands flashed through Clay's head. He dropped and rolled under Fjord as the IceWing flew at him. With a quick slash, Clay raked Fjord's underbelly, leaving a trail of blood through the softer scales. He flipped back upright and spun to face the other dragon again.

Fjord shrieked, doubling over.

"YAAAAYYYYYY!" shouted the crowd.

"What is wrong with you?" Fjord yelled at Clay. "That's not how MudWings fight! I was trained in your techniques!"

"Well, I wasn't," Clay said. "Sorry." He wondered whether he fought like a SkyWing instead, the way Kestrel had always wanted. He had a feeling she would say no, he didn't fight like a SkyWing, he fought like a lame wildebeest. But at least it seemed to catch his opponent off guard.

Clay dug his claws into the sand, watching Fjord clutch his bleeding belly. If he attacked now, he could surprise the other dragon and maybe even win. But he felt bad enough, seeing the damage he'd inflicted. He couldn't imagine doing worse — like what? Could he break Fjord's neck? He shuddered, remembering again the *crack* of Dune's neck snapping. That wasn't him, no matter what Kestrel or Peril said.

"All right, dragons." Queen Scarlet's voice cut through the rumble of the crowd, and everyone went still. "Fjord and Clay, we don't have all day. Some of us have kingdoms to run. One of you kill the other one right now, or I'm coming down there to end you both myself."

Fjord snarled and dashed at Clay again. There was no time to think. Clay reared up and grabbed the extra horns around Fjord's head, shoving the IceWing's snout aside before the freezing breath hit him. The cold air blasted toward the lowest row of seats, and several dragons clambered over each other to get away, yelping with alarm.

Fjord's talons locked around Clay's chest, and they grappled across the sand. Clay's wings were pummeled by Fjord's, which were silvery and strangely tough. His talons were full trying to keep Fjord's head pointing away from him. He couldn't fight back as Fjord clawed his shoulders. Bright pain zigzagged through Clay's scales.

"Time to die," Fjord growled. He whipped his tail around to trip Clay's back legs and the two dragons went down in a heap with Fjord on top. The IceWing wrapped his claws around Clay's neck and pressed hard.

Failing again, Clay thought hopelessly as the strength in his arms began to fade. *For the last time.* In a moment he'd have to let go, the IceWing's head would be free, and Fjord would blast Clay with a final killing breath.

Then it would all be over.

CHAPTER 19

Clay closed his eyes. He couldn't bear to see the circle of prisoners up in the sky, knowing that Tsunami and Starflight were up there watching him die.

He heard a faraway yell, and Fjord's head jerked up. Clay opened his eyes again and saw that the IceWing was looking up at the prisoners. So was everyone else in the stadium. He followed their gaze and saw a blue dragon far overhead, thrashing in the net of wires above the arena. The other prisoners were shouting and scrabbling to hold on to their rock towers as the weight of the dragon threatened to drag them all down.

It was Tsunami. She must have thrown herself off her prison cell, trying to get to Clay. But the wires held her fast, and she was fighting like an insect caught in a spiderweb.

"Get up there!" Queen Scarlet roared, and all the SkyWing guards around her lifted off at once.

This is my chance, Clay thought. Fjord was distracted. Now he should kill him. He should. He had to. If he could have killed his nestmates in their eggs, he should be able to kill this dragon who had nothing to do with him.

But he still couldn't. He kept thinking, *Fjord is as much a prisoner as I am. Why should I get to live instead of him?*

This is why the prophecy is doomed — because of me.

So Clay was the only one looking at the ice dragon when a jet of small black droplets spattered against the side of Fjord's face and neck.

Fjord flinched in surprise and automatically reached up with one talon to wipe his face clean. But before his claws reached his snout, both dragons heard a hissing noise. Clay stared in shock as the black drops started to bubble and smoke. The scales underneath them began to melt.

Then Fjord screamed.

It was the worst sound Clay had ever heard. The dragon Peril had killed had screamed in this kind of agony, but to be right underneath the dying dragon, his screams piercing Clay's ears, was so much worse.

One of the drops had landed in Fjord's eye, and that was the first thing to disintegrate, leaving a smoking black cavity in his skull. The side of his face slowly dropped away like ice melting. Fjord lurched off Clay, clawing at his own neck. The spray was eating into his open wound.

Clay covered his eyes, feeling sick. Why couldn't death be clean, painless, and fast, if it had to happen at all?

It finally occurred to him to wonder who had sprayed the IceWing. It must have come from the direction of the queen's balcony. He looked up and saw only three faces up there, staring down at him and Fjord. The rest of the guards were up in the sky, dealing with Tsunami and the other prisoners.

Queen Scarlet, who looked pleased.

Glory, who looked asleep.

And Peril, who looked . . . frightened.

After Fjord finally died, to the sounds of uproarious cheering, Clay was flown back to his tower and locked down again. He could see that extra chains and wires had been added to Tsunami's cell, and the prisoners on either side of her kept shouting angry things about how she'd nearly killed them. But she waved her tail at Clay, and he felt a tiny bit better, though not much.

He hadn't won fairly. He hadn't found the strength in him to kill. He hadn't even wanted Fjord to die. Something — someone else — had killed Fjord for him. And yet there was a ball of wrenching guilt sitting in his stomach. Guilt about Fjord; about Dune; about Glory's weird drugged state; about Sunny, wherever she was; about Starflight, who'd never survive the arena; and about Tsunami, who might, but only if she didn't get herself killed doing crazy things first.

He couldn't eat the pig dropped off by the SkyWing guard that afternoon. He just watched gloomily as it ran around his platform, squealing in terror, until it blundered over the edge. Then he felt bad about *that*, too.

Feeling sorry for prey. Some hero dragon you are.

Clay kept his back to the arena during the afternoon fight, which was between a SeaWing and a scavenger the queen had found in the woods. He'd thought queens would be more careful around scavengers after what happened to Oasis, but now that he saw how pathetic they were, he understood why Queen Scarlet didn't worry about them. The scavenger was allowed to keep his funny little weapons, but they didn't do him much good. The fight was over quickly. Clay covered his ears so he wouldn't have to listen to the munching and crunching and the cheering crowd.

He slept a little that evening, but his sleep was full of nightmares and dying dragons.

It was almost a relief to wake up after dark and find Peril huddled in the same spot as before. Even the heat wafting from her scales was welcome, as the winds were stronger and colder than ever.

"Oh, hi," she said in a rush. "You were amazing today. Although I have no idea what you did. I was looking at the prisoners and then suddenly — well, yikes. That was scarier than me. I mean, I'm pretty scary. But, wow. How did you do that? You don't have to tell me. I mean, you might have to do it to me. You probably will. Which is the scariest thing ever. It was like — I never thought what it might be like, sitting up here watching me kill other dragons. And then I'm the one watching, and thinking, that's going to happen to me. So. But still amazing. Can you tell me? You don't have to tell me."

"Stop," Clay said, worn out with guilt and worrying. "Peril, it wasn't me. I didn't do — that — to Fjord."

She exhaled, and a small burst of fire shot from her nose. "It's all right," she said. "I didn't think you'd tell me. I'd keep it secret, too."

"No, seriously," Clay said. "I think it was Queen Scarlet. She wanted me to win. She must have done something while everyone else was distracted."

Peril looked skeptical. "I've never seen her do anything like that before," she said. "But I guess she might. She definitely doesn't have a problem with cheating." She spread her talons, opening and closing her claws as if offering herself as an example. "I guess she might have found the poison in her treasury somewhere."

"Have you seen my friend Sunny?" Clay asked. He was starting to feel the pain of the scratches across his back and the bruises on his throat.

"Oh! Yes," Peril said. She looked at him sideways with sly blue-flame eyes. "That's why I came. I'll tell you where she is, but I need you to do something for me. And if you won't do it, I won't tell you."

Clay tried to move his aching wings, but they felt stiff and sore. He could tell that dried blood was caked through his scales and the spiny ridge along his back. "You don't have to do that, Peril. I'd help you anyway."

"Sure," she said. "Well. We'll see. It's not an easy thing. And you might get in trouble. I'd definitely get in trouble, if Her Majesty found out." She scratched at the rock underneath her.

"I don't mind," Clay said. "I'm in enough trouble anyway. Is Sunny all right?"

Peril scowled as she answered. "Yes, she's fine. Not a scratch on her. Eating like a queen. Making friends with all the guards. It's a little nauseating, if you want to know the truth."

"That's Sunny," Clay said, exhaling with relief. "What do you want me to do?"

"She told me I wasn't allowed to watch!" Peril burst out. "I'm the only dragon in the whole Sky Kingdom who's supposed to stay away from the arena tomorrow. It's not fair!"

"Why?" Clay asked, his stomach sinking. What new horrible battle did Queen Scarlet have planned? "What's happening?"

"I don't even know!" Peril flared. "It's some kind of trial! Doesn't that sound boring? Why would she keep me away from that? I wouldn't have cared until she told me not to go. Listening to dragons talk about laws is about as exciting as picking sheep fluff out of your teeth. Plus it always ends the same way anyhow. Queen Scarlet just likes the drama of trials and formal executions. Nobody's ever innocent."

"Kestrel," Clay said. "It must be Kestrel's trial. Queen Scarlet said something about that."

"Well, whoever she is, I want to watch," Peril said stubbornly. "So I thought maybe if I hid up here, behind you . . ."

Clay glanced around. The IceWing to his left was asleep. The platform to his right was still empty. If he stood at the edge of his prison and spread his wings, and Peril crouched down, he might be able to shield her from the eyes of the queen.

He tried opening his wings again and winced. The clamp bent the outside of his wing in, as if it were rolled under and pinned up. But he still should have been able to open most of his wing, even if he couldn't fly with it.

"I'm too sore," he said to Peril. "I mean, I'll try. But I can't really open my wings right now, so I don't know if I can hide you."

Peril frowned. "Let me see," she said, pointing to his back imperiously.

He hunched around until his back was toward her. She drew in a sharp breath.

"That sounds bad," he said, trying to twist his neck around to see. "It can't be that bad. Kestrel believes that pain teaches you stuff, so trust me, I've been clawed before."

"Not by an IceWing, I bet," she said. "They have ridged claws so they can grip the ice as they walk. It's like getting clawed four times with each claw instead of once. Can you picture that?"

"Um, sort of," Clay said. "It feels better with you near it."

"It does?"

"Like, the heat, I mean," he said, embarrassed, although he wasn't sure why. "It's better than the wind."

"I don't know how to fix it," she said, sounding frustrated and helpless. He felt her heat draw a little closer. "I guess I could stand here, if that helps."

Clay remembered the poison cave under the mountain and the stinging pain under his scales. He wondered if the same treatment would work here. "There is one thing," he said hesitantly. "If it's not asking too much — I think putting mud on the scratches might help."

"Oh my gosh, of course," she cried. "That's it! I can get you mud! Wait here." She sprang off the tower and flew away.

"Wait here," Clay echoed to empty space. "Because I was going to go where? For a walk?"

He pulled his wings in and tried to huddle against the wind, but it howled at him from every direction, and the tower was even colder now that Peril was gone. The pain felt worse and worse as the moments ticked by and the moons rose higher in the sky. He was shivering badly by the time he saw her spiraling up toward him.

Between her front talons, she was carrying a large rock cauldron, filled with thick brown mud. Clay twisted around to watch her as she landed behind him.

"Where'd you get that?" he asked.

Peril nodded at one of the distant walls of the queen's palace. Clay squinted and saw the reflected glint of moonlight off a cascading waterfall.

"The Diamond Spray River starts at the bottom of that wall," Peril said. "It leads all the way to the sea. At least, that's what I hear. I've never left the Sky Kingdom." She stuck one of her claws into the cauldron. Clay watched curiously as the mud began bubbling and boiling.

"Why not?" he asked. "You must be one of the most powerful dragons here. Why don't you just come and go as you please?"

Peril looked a little shocked. "I would never disobey Her Majesty! That's how my mother got killed." A theory suddenly popped into Clay's head, but before he could explore it, Peril kept talking. "Besides, I have to eat the black rocks every day, or I'll die. The queen makes sure there are always enough for me."

"Black rocks?" Clay asked, puzzled.

"It's part of the curse of having too much fire," Peril said with a shrug. "I'm lucky the queen takes so much care to keep me alive."

"Have you ever tried not eating them?" Clay asked.

"Once, when I was a lot younger," Peril said, shifting her talons awkwardly. "I got mad at Her Majesty because she wouldn't tell me anything about my mother. I wanted to run away. So I stopped eating the rocks to see what would happen, and I got really sick. Like, almost dying sick."

"Oh," Clay said. Her story had a feel of wrongness to it, like scales that didn't overlap properly. It seemed pretty convenient that the queen just happened to have a way to control the most dangerous dragon in her kingdom. But he was hardly an expert on SkyWings with weird, deadly conditions.

"Is that also why you don't challenge her for the throne?" Clay asked. "Because I'm betting you could beat her in a fight."

Peril gave an outraged squawk and nearly hit him with her tail. "I don't want to be queen! What an awful thought! Stop saying treasonous things and turn around."

Clay presented his back to her, opening his wings as wide as he could. Some part of him expected her to plaster the hot mud on with her talons. But he realized she couldn't do that without burning him just before Peril flung the entire contents of the cauldron over his scales.

"Yaa —" Clay clamped his teeth down hard, forcing himself not to yell. The mud was as hot as Kestrel's fire-breath, and at first he felt like all his scales were being burned off.

Then the shock passed, and a moment later the heat became bearable. Clay felt the mud soaking into his injuries, instantly soothing the pain. If only he'd had something like this after all his training sessions with Kestrel!

"Much better," Peril said with satisfaction.

Clay rolled his shoulders. His muscles already felt looser and stronger. "Wow. Does that work for all MudWings?"

"Of course," she said. "How could you not know that?"

"What about other dragons?" Clay asked, turning around to face her. He wondered if this was a trick he could use to heal his friends, if they were ever together and free again.

"I don't think so," she said. "I'm not sure anyone's tried. Because that would be weird. Like, what kind of SkyWing would let you put mud on her scales? Yuck."

"It's the greatest feeling in the world," Clay said. "Well, maybe after flying. And eating. Gosh, I'm hungry."

"I'll just fetch and carry for you all night, shall I?" Peril said.

"Oh, no, you don't have to —" But she was already gone.

Clay sat down and tucked his tail around his talons, thinking.

He had a pretty good idea why Peril wasn't supposed to watch the trial tomorrow. Queen Scarlet had said something about Kestrel disobeying her. Plus there were those burn scars on Kestrel's talons.

And it wasn't too hard to imagine Kestrel trying to kill her own dragonet. Especially once she figured out there was something wrong with her.

Peril thought her mother was dead. How would she react when she found out it was Kestrel — and she was still alive?

CHAPTER 20

Peril brought him three rabbits and two more cauldrons of mud during the night. She stayed at the edge of the rock platform, but the heat from her scales helped keep the mud warm on Clay's back.

It also kept the nightmares away. While he was talking to her, the weight of Clay's guilt felt lighter. Which was strange, he knew: Peril was responsible for a lot more death than he was. But it didn't bother her. He wished he could be so untroubled. If he had to fight in the arena again, perhaps he could take monster lessons from her.

"Won't someone be looking for you?" he asked as the sun started rising over the distant sea.

She shook her head. "I'm supposed to be down in the caves looking for black rocks all day," she said. "As long as I stay up here, behind you, hopefully no one will notice me."

"Not even the guards?"

"They won't feed the prisoners until midday," she said. "The trial is set for dawn. Look, see?" She edged a bit closer to him, peeking around his wing.

Clay looked down and saw dragons filing into the arena seats. They seemed quieter, more subdued than they were for the fights. SkyWing soldiers dragged two large boulders out onto the sand. One of them twisted three large iron rings into the ground in a triangle, then attached thick chains to them.

"Quick, spread your wings," Peril hissed. "Here she comes."

Clay flapped his wings open as Queen Scarlet slithered onto her balcony. He noticed she had traded her gold chain mail for a vest with small black chain links instead, studded with diamonds. She didn't even glance up at the prisoners, although Peril stayed carefully huddled behind Clay's back. Glory was not brought in — no art required at a trial, Clay guessed.

Finally Kestrel was hauled into the ring, hissing and spitting at the guards around her. A chain looped around her snout kept her from breathing fire at them. More heavy chains weighed down her talons and tail so she couldn't lash out.

"It's weird," Clay whispered to Peril. "I've always hated Kestrel, but it still makes me mad to see her like that."

"How do you know her?" Peril asked.

"She's one of the three dragons who raised us, under the mountain," Clay explained. "They didn't like us much, but they were supposed to keep us alive until the Talons of Peace came back to get us for the prophecy." He stopped, swallowing, as he thought of Dune. And Webs — had he survived the underground river?

"At least you had someone. I guess even terrible parents are better than no parents," Peril said. Clay glanced down at Queen Scarlet and wondered if that was true. She'd been the closest thing to a mother that Peril ever had. But what kind of mother made her daughter kill dragons in horrible ways every day?

Maybe Peril would have been better off with no one. Dune and Webs weren't all bad, but Clay wasn't sure he'd have chosen a life with Kestrel over growing up alone.

Then again, if he was right, Kestrel was Peril's real mother. Would Kestrel have been better for her than Queen Scarlet? Not if she was prepared to throw her off the mountain. At least the queen had kept Peril alive.

He hoped that watching this trial wouldn't upset Peril. He wondered if he should warn her about Kestrel being her mother. But what if he was wrong?

"I have real parents, though," he said instead. "Somewhere in the Mud Kingdom, there's a pair of dragons who can't wait to get me back. I'm going to find them one day."

He couldn't see Peril's face, but her silence said a lot. She didn't think he was going to survive this place. Or maybe she thought that if he did, it would be at the expense of her own life.

Something he didn't want to think about.

The SkyWing who did all the arena introductions climbed onto one of the two boulders and spread his blood-red wings.

"That's Vermilion," Peril whispered. "Her Majesty's oldest son. He always argues for the prosecution."

"Why does Scarlet bother with a trial at all?" Clay asked.

"Only SkyWings get trials," Peril said. "Her Majesty likes watching the performance of it — and she thinks it makes her seem like a just and fair ruler."

Clay withheld his snort of disbelief.

The crowd's murmuring died down as another SkyWing climbed onto the other boulder. His scales were a more washed-out red, as if they'd been scrubbed with sandstone for a long time. He moved slowly, dragging his tail behind him like a carcass.

"And that's Osprey," Peril pointed out. "He argues for the defense. Not very well, or he'd lose his head. He's really old and almost blind. He's nice to me, though, because I'll listen to his stories of the old days. He told me he used to have tons of treasure, but a scavenger came to steal it and managed to paralyze his tail before Osprey ate him. So now he can't fly, and he gave all his treasure to Her Majesty so she'd let him live here."

"Tough bargain," Clay said. He felt a wave of heat as Peril rustled indignantly.

"Back in the way-old days before the Scorching," she lectured, "before we had queens and armies, he would have just *died*. Scavengers killed a *lot* more dragons back then. But now, because of our queens, we rule the whole world, and dragons have help when they need it."

"You sound like Starflight," Clay said. "Will there be a test at the end of this lecture?"

"He wouldn't talk to me, by the way," she said. "Not even when I asked him to tell me the history of the Scorching, like you suggested. He just buried his nose under his wings and ignored me."

"Wow," Clay said, looking across at the slumped black dragon. "He must be really depressed."

Peril was quiet again. Clay wished he could call across to Starflight and tell him they'd find a way out of this. If he really yelled, Tsunami might be close enough to hear him, but he didn't think Starflight would. And besides, hollering escape plans across the arena probably wasn't the best idea.

In any case, the trial was about to begin. Queen Scarlet beat her wings, and all the dragons turned their attention to her.

"Loyal subjects," she said. "This dragon, Kestrel, once of the SkyWings, stands accused of the highest treason — disobeying *me*. Vermilion speaks for the prosecution."

"Your Majesty," Vermilion said, bowing and crossing his talons. "The facts are clear. You gave an order. Kestrel disobeyed you and fled the kingdom. She has been living under your mountains for the last seven years, aiding and abetting the Talons of Peace, who also refuse to follow Your Majesty's orders. She deserves a long, painful execution. There is no need to drag this trial out."

The dragons in the seats made their hissing fire-breath sounds and flapped their wings. Kestrel glared at the queen. Smoke seeped from her bound mouth and nostrils.

"Well said." The queen nodded to Vermilion. "Now

Osprey may speak for the defense. Or not, if he'd prefer to sleep through this trial, too."

The crowd laughed appreciatively.

Osprey stretched his neck toward the queen, then toward Kestrel, as if he were trying to get close enough to see their faces from his boulder.

"Your Majesty," he said in a voice creaky with age but still loud enough to carry to the prisoners up above. "I do have one or two words to say in this prisoner's defense."

Queen Scarlet's tail lashed slowly behind her as she stared down at him. "Certainly," she said. "That's what you're here to do. Go ahead."

Osprey cleared his throat, coughing out a black puff of smoke. All the dragons were leaning forward to listen. Clay could feel Peril's heat dangerously close to his scales as she tried to peek under his wings.

"Consider first the charge of disobedience. Kestrel did not do as you ordered — but then, didn't you reverse the order after she was gone?"

What? Clay could barely follow the old dragon. Was this not about Peril?

"Osprey," Queen Scarlet hissed. "Speak plainly, or do not speak at all. And let me point out that one of those options would be much smarter than the other."

"Forgive me, Your Majesty," the old dragon said, straightening his wings. "I must speak. Kestrel was one of your most loyal soldiers. She was sent through the breeding program, on your orders, and brought forth one egg. Upon hatching, it turned out to hold twin dragonets."

Behind Clay, Peril gasped, nearly loud enough for the dragons below to hear her. Clay flapped his wings, trying to cover the noise, but no one looked up. All eyes were on the trial.

"We know all this," said Queen Scarlet, yawning. "Skip ahead to the part where we execute her."

"The dragonets were defective," Osprey went on stubbornly. "One had too much fire. The other did not have enough. As per SkyWing custom, you ordered Kestrel to kill them both and stay out of the breeding program for the rest of her life."

"That doesn't make sense," Peril whispered behind Clay. He ducked his neck to look at her. She met his eyes, shaking with confusion. "I'm the only twin SkyWing hatched in the past ten years, but he can't be talking about me. My brother was dead when we hatched. *I* killed him. Then my mother tried to kill me, and Queen Scarlet stopped her."

"Or maybe that's just what she told you," Clay whispered back.

The queen rose to her full height and spread her wings so the sunlight caught on the rubies embedded around the edges. "Quite reasonable," she said.

"But Kestrel tried to escape," Osprey pressed on. "She took her two dragonets from the hatching cave and tried to flee with them down the mountain."

"So you agree she disobeyed me," said Queen Scarlet. "Then I think we're done here."

"You caught her at the Diamond Spray River," Osprey said. "And there you issued a new order. You told her you would forgive her disobedience on one condition. She must choose one of the dragonets to die, and then you would spare the other's life, and Kestrel's own."

"No," Peril whispered.

"Then she did obey you, didn't she?" Osprey said. "She killed the dragonet with too little fire, right there at the river. With her own claws."

"And then I changed my mind again," Queen Scarlet said. "I am the queen. I can do that."

"You told your guards — I know, for I was one of them — to kill the other dragonet and take Kestrel back for trial. She tried to grab her daughter and fly away, but the heat of the dragonet's scales burned her talons before she was a wing-beat into the sky, and she had to drop her. She fled, leaving her only living dragonet at your mercy."

There was a heartbeat of silence.

"Sounds guilty to me," Queen Scarlet said cheerfully. "We'll execute her tomorrow. And while we're at it, let's execute him, too, for boring me." She pointed at Osprey.

"No!"

Clay nearly fell off his tower as Peril exploded past him. He flapped his wings for balance as she shot toward the sands. His front right leg flailed free, and when he glanced down, he saw that Peril had accidentally burned through the wire as she flew away.

"It can't be true!" Peril cried, landing on the sand beside Osprey. "Tell me it's not true!"

Kestrel reared up with a muffled roar. From the look on her face, Clay could tell she'd thought Peril was dead this entire time.

"Oh, yes," Queen Scarlet said maliciously to Kestrel. "Didn't I mention she's still alive? And working for me?" She turned her fierce yellow eyes on Peril. "You're not supposed to be here."

"You lied to me!" Peril shrieked. "You said she was dead!"

Queen Scarlet sighed. "Look at the trouble you've caused," she said to Osprey. "Peril, dear. Would you have wanted to know your mother was alive somewhere, raising other dragonets and wishing she'd killed you instead of your brother?"

Peril hesitated.

"She could have escaped with your brother," Scarlet pointed out. "You're the one who burned her when she tried to save you. She thought she chose wrong. That's why she didn't come back for you."

Kestrel roared unintelligibly through the chains.

"Haven't I kept you alive all these years?" Scarlet went on. "Finding you the black rocks, feeding you, making you my champion? Don't you appreciate all the things I've done for you? Aren't I a better mother than her anyway?"

"I want to stand for her," Peril said, almost too softly for Clay to hear.

Smoke hissed from Scarlet's nose, billowing up around her horns. "What?" she said slowly.

"I call upon the tradition of the Champion's Shield," Peril said. "It says the queen's champion may stand forth for any dragon sentenced to execution. If I can defeat the next dragon you set me to fight, you must let her go free." She looked into Kestrel's eyes for the first time. "I want to stand for my mother."

CHAPTER 21

Queen Scarlet's yellow eyes were small slits between orange scales. "Now where," she hissed, "did you hear about *that* particular law?"

Peril shifted on her talons. "I read about it."

"I bet you did," Scarlet said. "With claws that burn right through paper when you touch it. Someone's been telling you things too big for little dragon ears."

"No!" Peril said too quickly. "Nobody —"

The queen was airborne before Peril could choke out another word. Queen Scarlet snatched Osprey up in her talons and shot into the sky.

"Stop!" Peril yelled. "It's not his fault!" She leaped into the air and beat her wings, chasing them.

Clay watched the queen rise higher and higher above the arena. Osprey writhed in her claws, his tail hanging heavily below him. Scarlet had nearly reached the height of the wire net when suddenly she opened her talons and dropped the old dragon.

He plummeted like a stone. Clay had never thought about

how a dragon needs his tail for balance while flying. Osprey's wings were slow to extend, and when they did he lurched horribly, dragged down by the useless weight of his tail.

Peril darted at him, talons outstretched, but he twisted away from her and she stopped, helpless. If she caught him, the burns would kill him just as much as the fall would, perhaps even more painfully. Clay saw her claws reach out again anyway, but it was too late.

Osprey flapped his wings in one last burst of energy, but he couldn't right himself. He hit the sand at an awkward angle. Every dragon in the arena heard the ripping and snapping of bones breaking and wings tearing as he tumbled. He collapsed near the arena wall. Peril landed beside him.

Queen Scarlet fluttered delicately back onto her balcony perch. "I hope this has been a lesson to any other dragons who were thinking of teaching my champion bad habits," she said, glaring around the arena.

"He's not dead," Peril said, clawing at the sand.

"He will be soon." Queen Scarlet waved a dismissive claw. "Now. I won't argue with the Champion's Shield. The champion has asked to stand for the prisoner. I will choose her opponent, and they will battle at the end of the games tomorrow. If she wins, Kestrel goes free. If not, well, I'll have a dead champion, but at least we'll get to execute Kestrel right afterward. All in all, a wonderfully bloody day for me and Queen Burn to look forward to."

The cold wind whipped around Clay, piercing the

wounds on his back and whistling through his scales. Burn was coming here. Tomorrow. And when she left, she'd be taking Sunny with her.

"All right," Peril said, staring down at Osprey's last dying spasms. "Tomorrow, then." She reached for Osprey's talons and stopped, her claws hovering over his, agonizingly close but not touching.

"Of course we'll have to lock Kestrel back up," said Queen Scarlet. "We wouldn't want her to try escaping again. You understand."

"Fine." Peril turned and looked at Kestrel. They faced each other as Vermilion dismissed the crowd, and dragons began to pour out of the arena, buzzing with excitement.

When most of the crowd was gone, Kestrel pointed to the chains around her mouth. She wanted to talk to Peril.

"No," Peril said as one of the guards stepped forward. She stared into Kestrel's eyes. "You killed my brother. You *left* me here. And it's your fault my friend is dead. I may not want you dead, but I don't want to know you."

She turned and left the arena. The guards dragged Kestrel away under Queen Scarlet's triumphant smile.

Clay's head was spinning. He tried to catch Tsunami's eye, but she was storming around her platform, clawing angrily at the air. Across from him, Starflight was sitting up and looking at the sky.

Clay tried to think. If Peril succeeded in freeing Kestrel, surely Kestrel would try to free the dragonets as well. Maybe she'd go to the Talons of Peace for help.

But by then it might be too late, at least for some of them. Certainly for Sunny, who would be on her way to the SandWing stronghold in Burn's clutches. And perhaps for Starflight, who would have to fight in the arena tomorrow. Maybe even for Tsunami and Clay himself, if they had to fight, too.

No, they couldn't wait for Kestrel. They had to escape before the games tomorrow. Clay wondered if Peril would help them, now that she knew how the queen had betrayed her.

He waited hopefully for her to come back, but the day wore on with no more activity in the arena below. The hot sun baked the mud on his back until it began crumbling away into dust, while the wind yanked at his tail and his wings like a dragonet playing with prey. And Peril never came.

When the guard dropped off another pig at midday, Clay tried to ask him to take a message to Peril. But the guard snorted fire at him, scaring the pig right into Clay's talons, and flew away without responding. The only good news was he didn't notice the broken wire attached to Clay's front right talon.

By the time the sun started drifting down over the western peaks, Clay was getting anxious. Was Peril all right? What if Queen Scarlet decided to get rid of her before she could fight for Kestrel?

Heavy wingbeats in the distance distracted him from his worries. He looked up as a score of SandWings appeared from the west, outlined by the red glow of the setting sun. The largest was in the lead, with the others fanned out in a V formation behind her. They swooped toward the queen's palace, staying in perfect lines, and vanished beyond a distant wall, where Clay guessed the landing field for visitors was.

Burn was here.

She was the biggest and meanest of the three rivals for the SandWing throne. She held the SandWing palace stronghold. From what Clay could remember, she was the most likely to win the war — and the most likely to kill anyone who got in her way.

Dune had warned them that she was the most dangerous dragon in Pyrrhia, even meaner than Queen Scarlet. They knew the story of what she did to the SkyWing egg before they all hatched. Scarlet was bad enough, but Burn was the worst possible dragon to get her claws on the dragonets of destiny.

It seemed like only a few moments had passed when Clay saw the lead dragon come winging back over the wall toward the arena. As she flew closer, he could see her muscles rippling in her back like wind over sand dunes. Her poisonous tail was coiled up above her and her black eyes were staring straight at Clay.

He found himself crouching lower as she swept overhead. Her neck whipped around to keep her eyes on him as she flew in a circle, around and around just above him. He didn't know what to do. He couldn't read her expression at all.

After a minute, she hissed at him with a forked black

tongue. She darted away to circle over Tsunami's head, and then Starflight's. Even Tsunami seemed cowed by this silent inspection. All three dragonets stayed still and watched her, until Burn flew away again and disappeared into the palace.

We have to get out of here, Clay thought. *Now. Tonight*. He couldn't imagine what those dark eyes would see in Sunny. He had a horrible feeling Burn would "collect" the little SandWing by killing, stuffing, and mounting her on the wall.

But it was impossible. This was worse than their situation under the mountain. There, at least, they'd been together. Clay wasn't the clever thinker of the group. He couldn't come up with bright ideas and brilliant escape plans all by himself.

He realized Peril hadn't kept her end of the bargain by telling him where Sunny was. So even if he could get down from his prison, he'd have no idea how to find Sunny in the vast SkyWing palace.

Had Peril forgotten about him? Or was she angry for some reason?

Clay paced, fretting, and the loose wire whacked at his other talons. He peered down at it. The sun was just a golden sliver against the mountains, and the moons were only starting to climb the sky, so he didn't have much light.

He held up his free talon to the last of the sunlight. The wire had a curious clasp that held it in place around his leg as long as it was mostly taut. But now that the wire was loose at one end, he could see how to slide it out by worrying it with one claw. The other end had once been attached to Horizon, the SandWing prisoner Peril had killed. Now it was clipped to a ring in the center of the empty rock platform, which was why no one else had noticed that it was swinging free.

After a few moments of poking the clasp, Clay was able to work the wire off his leg. He was left with a stretch of wire about the length of his own tail. It was made of a hard sinewy metal that gleamed silvery-pink in the last rays of the sun — the same stuff in the bands on his wings. He could guess that it was fireproof, or other prisoners would have blazed through the wires long before him. Which meant Peril's scales must be significantly hotter than regular fire, to blaze through the wire so easily.

Clay glanced around. Most of the prisoners were curled up to sleep for the night. It was only sunset, but there was not much else to do up on the rock columns. There were no guards in sight. There must be some kind of welcome banquet happening for Burn. Hopefully all the SkyWing soldiers would be there, feasting and laying bets on the gladiator fights scheduled for tomorrow. And hopefully Peril would be in her room, the closest cave to the arena. If he could just get her attention . . . if he could only talk to her, maybe she'd find a way to save them.

He wrapped one end of the wire around each of his front talons and tried sawing it across the wire that extended from his neck out into the web. He'd hoped it would slice through or something useful like that, but both wires looked undamaged when he stopped.

But as he slid the wires across each other, an eerie note echoed across the arena, like the lone cry of a bird or the last hum of a harp string.

That was kind of cool, Clay thought. He wondered if he could make different notes. He tried sliding the wire farther away from him, then closer to his neck, and then he tried the other three wires attached to his legs. The sounds were different — higher, lower — but still with that eerie, melancholy quality to them.

Maybe Peril will hear this and come talk to me, Clay thought. But how would she know it wasn't just the wind or owls calling?

A song. The only song he knew was the one Tsunami sometimes sang to annoy the guardians — about the dragonets coming to save the day. *Still. Maybe that'll tell her it's me calling*.

He tried the wires again until he found the notes he wanted. It was fully dark now, with only a distant glimmer of moonlight creeping up the mountains. He couldn't see the prisoners across the arena from him at all, but he hoped Starflight and Tsunami would be listening.

Clay concentrated, sliding the wires in order.

Oh, the dragonets are coming. . . .

He paused. It was too slow. When Tsunami sang it, the song was fast and fierce, so you could imagine a hall full of dragons roaring it at top volume. But Clay couldn't get between the wires quickly enough to get the notes right and keep that tempo.

He tried again.

They're coming to save the day. . . .

The notes echoed around the arena, soft and mournful. How would Peril ever recognize it? It sounded like ghosts of ancient dragons whispering from under the sands.

Maybe if he kept practicing.

They're coming to fight . . . for they know what's right. . . . the dragonets . . .

Clay stopped. The last "hooray!" would sound particularly ridiculous as an ancient ghost whisper. This was hopeless.

"Oh, the dragonets are coming. . . ."

Clay leaned forward. Was that an echo coming back to him?

But . . . he could clearly hear words in it. . . .

"They're coming to save the day . . ." He swiveled his head to the left. That was definitely a voice — a second voice.

And neither one was Tsunami, because these dragons could actually sing.

"They're coming to fight . . . for they know what's right . . . the dragonets . . ."

Now there were at least six voices, all as soft and haunting as the notes from the wires. They slowly faded out, leaving off the last hooray just as Clay had done.

The prisoners were singing.

Clay set his wires together and began to play again. This

time one voice after another joined in. As the arena began to fill with moonlight, Clay saw the prisoner to his left, the IceWing, with her silvery head stretched toward the sky, singing.

He picked up the pace a little the fourth time around, although the notes still had that eerie, plaintive sound. Even if this didn't get Peril's attention, the singing filled him with a wild, hopeful feeling. It seemed like every prisoner in the sky was singing now. He was pretty sure he could even hear Tsunami's croaky voice and Starflight's pure tenor.

This song meant something, even to dragons hardened on the battlefield and in the arena. They believed in the dragonets and the prophecy. For the first time, Clay's dreams of doing something big and legendary and helpful seemed like they belonged to this world instead of his imagination.

They were on their sixth time through the song, all of them singing wholeheartedly, when a blast of fire shot through the arena doors below and Queen Scarlet stormed onto the sand with Burn right behind her.

"Stop that infernal noise right now!" Burn roared.

The singing broke off at once. Clay quickly hid the wire in a fold of his wing, although he didn't think the queens could see the prisoners very well, up in the dark.

"You," Queen Scarlet growled, pointing at Tsunami. "And you." She pointed at Starflight. "And — well, probably not you, but get down here anyway," she snarled at Clay.

SkyWing soldiers spilled out of the tunnel and soared up to the three dragonets. Clay realized they were about to discover his missing wire. He lunged away from the two who'd come to get him, flapping and whacking their heads with his wings.

"Here, stop it or we'll drop you," one of them snarled.

"But he's a —" the other one started.

"Shhhh," said the first. "You heard the queen. We don't call them that."

It was enough. In the confusion and the dark, they each thought the other had unclipped that leg, and they flew him down to the sand without catching their mistake.

Tsunami and Starflight both gave Clay concerned looks, and he realized he must still have a fair amount of blood and mud crusted to his scales.

"Bring them this way," Queen Scarlet snapped, stomping into the tunnel with Burn. Clay reached out and brushed wings with Tsunami as they were shoved along. Whatever happened next, at least he was with his friends now.

CHAPTER 22

They stopped at Peril's cave. Peril was resting her head on one of the narrow window ledges, staring out at the sky. She turned and gave Queen Scarlet a cold look.

Clay noticed that the full-length portrait of the queen was gone from the wall. A pile of ashes smoldered on the floor under the spot where it had been. He saw the queen's eyes dart to the empty wall, and more smoke curled from her nose.

"Out," she said to Peril.

"This is my room!" Peril snapped back.

"I'm the queen here," Scarlet said. "You do as I say. Go sleep in the arena. If anyone else tries to sing, fly up and burn out his tongue."

Peril's tail lashed furiously. A moment passed, and then she stormed toward the door. The two queens had to scurry out of her path in a very undignified way, and Clay saw a few of the SkyWing guards hiding smiles.

The wave of Peril's heat swept over them, and she hurried off down the tunnel, barely glancing at Clay as she went by. He stared after her, worried. *Maybe she is mad at me. But why?*

"In here," Queen Scarlet said, shoving Starflight into Peril's cave herself. He stumbled trying to jump over the pool of water and ended up with his back legs splashing around for a moment. Tsunami shook her guards away and hopped over the pool, and then Clay followed.

"You will not interrupt my feast again," Queen Scarlet hissed. "I'm sure you're very amused with yourselves."

"Why don't you kill them?" Burn asked. She was much bigger than Scarlet; her head scraped the top of the tunnel, and her talons were twice the size of Clay's. She wore no precious jewels or chain mail, but her claws and teeth were stained red from all the blood she had shed, and a vicious scar was burned along her left side, below the wing. There was no white to her eyes at all; they were orbs of pure, menacing black.

"Because that wouldn't be fun," Queen Scarlet answered. "I want to see them fight. We have a whole day of entertainment planned for tomorrow. It's my hatching day! I want it to be thrilling."

Clay was starting to hate the word *thrilling*.

Burn gave the SkyWing guards a glare, and they quickly shuffled up the tunnel, out of earshot. She lowered her voice so only Scarlet and the dragonets could hear her. "But if they *are* the dragonets of the prophecy, then the best way to break the prophecy is to kill them."

"Well," Scarlet said. Her tongue flicked in and out of her mouth as she regarded Starflight. Clay could tell she still wanted to see a NightWing in combat. "Perhaps. But that didn't work so well for you, did it? Everyone knows about the SkyWing egg — all the SkyWing eggs, in fact."

Clay's ears pricked. *What did that mean?*

Burn's tail thumped the floor hard enough to shake the ground below Clay's feet. "On the contrary, that worked perfectly. They don't have a SkyWing, do they? Only four dragonets — the prophecy is already incomplete."

Clay and Tsunami exchanged glances. *She didn't tell Burn that Glory is one of us. She wants to keep her new "work of art" for herself.*

"And yet our ignorant subjects are always yowling about the dragonets who are going to save the world," Scarlet said. "They believe in it, no matter what they've heard about broken eggs. If we kill the dragonets now, out of sight, it does us no good. Even if we hang their bodies from the palace walls, no one will believe it's them."

Burn bared her teeth in a snarl. "The world doesn't need a prophecy. It needs me as queen of the SandWings."

"But listen," Scarlet said smoothly. "If we put the dragonets in the arena, everyone can watch them die. They'll see how weak they really are. They'll lose all their faith in the dragonets, and more important, in the prophecy. It'll all be over. Much more powerful than just making them disappear." The SkyWing queen cast a sly look at her guest. "Don't you agree?"

"And what if they win?" Burn demanded.

"They won't," Scarlet said. "But of course killing them ourselves is a solid backup plan."

"Excuse me," Tsunami interrupted. "You know we're right over here, right? Don't you want to hatch your evil plans somewhere more secretive?"

Clay thought the combined force of the queens' glares would knock her over, but Tsunami just glared back.

Scarlet opened a pouch slung under her wing and scattered several round black rocks across the mouth of Peril's cave, on the tunnel side of the pool of water. She opened her mouth and breathed on them, and the rocks all burst into flames. In moments, the dragonets were trapped by a wall of fire.

"Sleep well, so you'll be thrilling in the arena," Queen Scarlet said. "I thought I'd get to play with you for longer, but I guess you all have to be dead by sunset tomorrow." She sighed. "Nobody lets me have any fun."

Clay listened to the heavy thump of the queens' talons fading away up the tunnel. He turned to look at his friends just as Tsunami cannoned into him.

"Ow!" he yelped, but he didn't fight her off as she twined her tail with his and wrapped her wings around him.

"I'm so glad you're alive," she said. "You incredibly huge idiot."

"So am I," Clay said. "But I'm more glad you two are alive." He reached out a wing and drew Starflight into their hug. The NightWing rested his head for a moment on Clay's shoulder, and Clay felt worried all over again about what would happen to Starflight in the arena.

"We need to figure out how to get out of here," he said.

"First we're cleaning you up," Tsunami said, stepping back and shooing Starflight out of the way. "Into the water. Go!"

"That's not important," Clay said. "I feel —"

Tsunami pushed him into the pool.

Clay surfaced, coughing and sputtering. The pool was almost as deep as he was tall. He could stand on the bottom and hold his head above the surface if he kept his neck extended. The water was cold, but with the black-rock fire so close, it was slowly heating up.

"See?" Tsunami said. "Much better." She leaned over the edge and rubbed the scales on his back, cleaning off the dirt and blood. Clay decided it wasn't worth arguing with her.

"That was pretty smart," Starflight said to Tsunami. "With the song. I have no idea how you managed to pull a melody out of your ear after being completely tone-deaf your whole life."

She blinked at him. "I didn't do that. I thought you did!"

"It was me," Clay admitted. He drew out the wire and slid it across the floor. Starflight picked it up and peered at it.

"How did you break that?" Tsunami said. Clay really liked the tone of awe in her voice. He wished he could say he'd done something clever.

"I had help," he admitted. "That dragon who was just here — Peril. Her touch can burn through it. She did that by accident."

Starflight reached up and fingered the bands on his wings, looking thoughtful.

"That dragon is psychotic," Tsunami said. "Didn't you see her decimate that SandWing? And she's Kestrel's daughter, which kind of makes sense."

"Yeah," Starflight said. "No wonder Kestrel always hated us. I bet the Talons of Peace thought she'd *want* to be on dragonet-minding duty after what she'd lost. But we just reminded her of her dead children every day."

Clay shivered. He hadn't thought of it like that. "Peril's not completely crazy," he said. "She's kind of nice when she's not killing someone. She brought me mud for my back. And she said she found Sunny."

Starflight's head shot up. "Where?"

"Can she get to her?" Tsunami demanded. "Can she set her free?"

"I don't know if Peril will help us," Clay said, rolling his shoulders in the water. "I haven't talked to her since the trial. I'm afraid she's mad at me."

"I'm not mad at you." Peril stuck her head through the wall of fire and looked down at Clay in the pool.

Tsunami jumped back with a hiss of alarm. Starflight crouched and froze, watching Peril with large eyes.

"Oh, good," Clay said to Peril. He wondered how much of their conversation she had overheard. Would she help them even if she'd heard Tsunami calling her names? She certainly wasn't giving Tsunami the friendliest look. "Where have you been?"

"I didn't want to put you in danger," Peril blurted. She flapped her wings, and the fire whooshed higher around her.

"Come inside," Clay said. "It's weird talking to someone on fire."

He ducked his head underwater, and Peril hopped over the pool into the cave. Tsunami and Starflight both backed up to the windows, staying as far away from Peril as they could.

Clay climbed out of the pool and spread his wings so Peril's heat could dry them off. She coiled her tail in close to her and dipped her head at him, ignoring the other two.

"I was afraid the queen would hurt you like she hurt Osprey," Peril said miserably. "I shouldn't even be talking to you. If she finds out I like you, she'll do something awful to you just to punish me."

Tsunami gave Clay a sharp look he didn't understand.

"Can you help us escape?" he asked Peril hopefully.

"I wish," she said. "That would make her madder than anything. But I can't get you through that fire." She flicked her tail at the wall of flames.

"Could we use the water to put it out?" Starflight asked. He flinched as Peril turned to look at him.

"No — those rocks have to burn down to embers. They can't be put out any other way."

"What about Sunny?" Clay asked. "Is there anything you can do to free her? We have to rescue her before Burn takes her away."

Peril's blue-flame eyes narrowed. "You talk about this Sunny a lot. Is she really that important?"

"Yes!" all three dragonets answered at once. Peril's tail twitched. Clay had no idea why she looked so displeased.

"Peril," Tsunami interjected. "Listen. Sunny is like a little sister to us. To all of us."

Starflight looked down at his talons.

"Think about your brother," Tsunami went on. "Wouldn't you have saved him if you could?"

Peril's expression shifted, and she nodded. "A sister. Yes. I understand. All right, I'll help."

"Where is she?" Starflight asked. "Is she all right?"

"She's in a kind of birdcage," Peril said, "hung over the feasting hall. Everyone will be celebrating out there all night tonight, but tomorrow, while they're watching the arena, I can sneak in and get her."

"Oh, thank you!" Clay nearly twined his tail around hers, but he remembered at the last second not to touch her.

"What about Clay and Starflight?" Tsunami asked. "I can survive the arena, but they can't."

"Um, I can survive the arena, too," Clay said. "Hello, I already have."

"And how did you do that, exactly?" Tsunami asked. "I happen to know you don't have secret venom in your claws."

"I know what to do!" Starflight cried, jumping to his feet.

"In the arena?" Tsunami said skeptically.

"No, right now," he said. "I know how we can get out of here."

CHAPTER 23

Starflight pointed to the flames rising from the black rocks. "Peril, the fire doesn't hurt you, right?"

She shrugged. "It tickles a little, that's all."

"And the fire is coming from the rocks. What if you picked up the rocks and moved them? You could put the fire somewhere else and open the doorway for us, couldn't you?"

Clay's heart was beating fast. Peril tilted her head at Starflight. "He *is* smart," she said. "Just like you said. I guess I could do that." She sounded like she wasn't entirely convinced. "If you're really sure you want to escape tonight."

"Of course we are," Tsunami said, springing to her feet. "Let's get out of here."

"But Sunny —" Starflight said.

"We hide somewhere and wait until Peril can free her tomorrow," Tsunami said.

"And Glory," Clay said. "We have to save Glory, too."

"Glory?" Peril's brow creased in a frown.

"The RainWing. Queen Scarlet's new artwork," Clay said.

"Oh," Peril said. "Her. She's very beautiful." She narrowed her eyes at Clay, which confused him.

"Let's run away *now* and worry about that *later*," Tsunami said. "Is there somewhere we can hide?"

Peril snapped her wings open. "Below the waterfall. There's a cave only I know about." She turned, nearly smacking Clay with her tail, and hopped over the pool into the fire. Clay watched in amazement as she wrapped her claws around two of the black rocks and picked them up. She stepped into the tunnel, and the fire from the rocks went with her, blazing around her talons.

Carefully she piled the fire on the rock floor outside until there was a gap big enough for the dragonets to jump through. Tsunami went first, and then Clay, and then Starflight. When they were all out in the tunnel, Peril rebuilt the wall of fire across the cave entrance.

"There," she said with satisfaction. "Now she'll have no idea how you got out."

"Can you get these off our wings?" Starflight whispered, pointing to the bindings. Peril gave him a hard look.

"Maybe," she said. "But maybe I'll wait until I know you won't leave without saying good-bye."

"We wouldn't leave without our friends," Clay promised. She scowled.

"Which way to the waterfall?" Tsunami asked.

Peril nodded up the tunnel and slithered off, leading the way.

"Stop making her mad," Tsunami hissed in Clay's ear as they followed.

"Me?" he said, genuinely surprised. "What did I do?"

"Well, you're a handsome idiot," she said affectionately. "And I'll tell you later."

Which didn't clear things up at all.

Shortly before they reached the central hall of balconies, the tunnel turned left and began to rise. Peril signaled for them all to move quietly, and they crept toward the sound of dragons shouting, singing, and smashing things.

Peril glanced over her shoulder at Clay, who was concentrating on moving his talons carefully over the rocky, gold-laced floor. "Hey," she whispered. "Once you're free . . . what are you going to do?"

"We'll go find our parents," Clay whispered back. "I've never been to the MudWing kingdom. I can't wait."

"Really?" Peril said. "You'll go straight there? Just the five of you?"

"Absolutely. As soon as poss —" Clay started, and then Tsunami trod heavily on his tail. He squelched a yelp of pain and made a face at her. When he looked up again, Peril had hurried ahead.

Clay guessed they had climbed two levels, circling behind the balconies, when they reached an open doorway as tall as five dragons and just as wide. They hid around a corner of the tunnel and peeked out.

The doorway led out onto a flat half-circle plateau

between the cliffs, packed with SkyWings and SandWings and lit by floating globes full of fire. Most of the SkyWings were wearing gold or copper or precious jewels that sparkled in the firelight. The SandWing desert dragons looked rough and common next to them, and many of them stood awkwardly as if they would rather be charging into battle than making polite conversation at a party.

Statues of Queen Scarlet in different regal poses were scattered about the floor, some carved from marble, some of gold, others of smooth black rock with rubies for eyes. Tables around the outside were piled high with food, and several kinds of prey were also running frantically between the dragons' claws. A low rock barrier kept the prey from escaping into the tunnel, and all around the plateau were steep cliffs going either up or down, so they were trapped.

Clay saw a SkyWing pause mid-conversation, smash her talons down on a mountain goat, pop it in her mouth, and continue chatting with the SandWing opposite her. He also spotted a couple of scavengers among the prey. Instead of running around like terrified chickens, one was trying to climb the cliff; the other was crawling under one of the tables to hide. It made him wonder if scavengers were smarter than they looked.

Now that he could see the feast was out in the open air, he realized how the dragons out here had heard the prisoners singing. He'd been wondering how the sound had carried down the long tunnels, but from here the arena was only a short dragon hop across a couple of cliffs.

Queen Scarlet lay on a tall golden throne, looking down at the other dragons. Another, shorter throne was set up next to her for Burn, although Burn's enormous height brought their heads to almost the same level. Burn kept shifting and scowling as if the fancy curved seat was uncomfortable.

Starflight grabbed Clay's shoulder and pointed at a large birdcage hanging over the center of the space. It was held aloft by wires like the ones on the prisoners' legs, strung between tall poles on either side of the plateau. Occasionally a dragon or two would fly up and circle the cage, peering in, and then fly back down to the floor.

Crouched inside the cage with her wings over her head was Sunny. Her golden scales glowed dully in the firelight, as if she were just another piece of treasure.

"Stop," Tsunami whispered as Clay started forward. "I know. I want to go get her, too."

"But if we do it right now, it's suicide," Starflight agreed. "Better to let them think we'd leave without her. If they know we care about her, they'll use it against us." His tail lashed in frustration.

"But she's all alone," Clay whispered. If only she knew they were there, not too far away. He stretched a little farther out, looking for Glory, but he couldn't see her. Perhaps Scarlet was hiding her from Burn.

"You guys cross first," Peril said. "Crouch low and run, and hopefully they won't spot us." She sent Tsunami darting across first, and the others followed one at a time. Clay found himself wishing he had darker scales that could melt into the shadows like Starflight's. They huddled around the next bend, waiting for Peril.

"Sorry," she said when she caught up a few moments later. "I had to wait for the queen to look away."

From here the tunnel branched in several directions. Peril took the one leading down under the cliff where the feast was. The torches were spaced farther apart as they went along, so the tunnel grew darker and darker. Soon Clay could hear roaring up ahead, and this time he knew for sure it was a waterfall.

They emerged on a narrow ridge halfway up a tall, craggy cliff. By the light of the moons, they could see straight down to a glittering, winding river far below. The waterfall pounded ahead of them, loud and fierce, and the wind carried bursts of cold spray into their faces.

Starflight pressed himself back against the cliff. "Are you sure you don't want to unbind our wings now?" he said, closing his eyes.

"You'll be fine," Peril said. "It's easy to climb down from here. I've done it when my wings are tired. See? The cave's right there."

Clay peeked over the edge and saw a small gap in the cliff far below, like a tiny gash in the wall behind the waterfall. It was definitely a journey he'd prefer to do with functioning wings. But if they had to keep Peril happy . . .

"I see some claw holds," he said. "And we can rest on that boulder halfway —" He stopped. Over the roaring of the waterfall, he could hear wingbeats. Someone was coming.

He spun around. "Hide," he said, frantically pushing Peril toward the tunnel. "If they find you helping us, the queens will kill you, champion or not."

She stopped in the mouth of the tunnel, staring at him. Clay turned and saw Tsunami and Starflight wearing matching shocked expressions.

"How did you do that?" Peril whispered.

"Do —" Clay started, and then he felt the heat in his talons. He had touched Peril's scales without even thinking. He looked down, expecting to see dark scorch marks and claws crumbling to ash. But his talons were only glowing a warm red, and even as he looked at them, the redness and the heat faded away until his talons felt entirely normal again.

"Stop gawping," Tsunami ordered, shoving him at the tunnel. "Everybody run."

"I don't think so," said Queen Scarlet's chilly voice behind them. Clay turned slowly and saw the SkyWing queen descending from the cliff above, her bejeweled wings spread wide.

"Thank you, Peril," the queen said nastily. "You may be excused."

Clay didn't understand. *Thank you for what?* Peril gave him an agonized look and fled up the tunnel.

Queen Scarlet smiled at the dragonets as SkyWing soldiers began to rain from the sky. "Going somewhere?"

~ CHAPTER 24 ~

The queen was not pleased to find her wall of fire still in place when the dragonets were hauled back to their cell. She sighed disapprovingly.

"So you've figured out what MudWings hatched from blood-red eggs can do," she said. "I suppose it was only a matter of time."

Clay glanced at the others in confusion as the guards used long shovels to scrape the rocks aside. What did she think he'd done? Tsunami and Starflight looked grim, as if they understood a lot more than he did.

"Find the ten most sober guards," Scarlet instructed Vermilion. "Post them out here. These dragonets are done ruining my party." She glared at the three of them as they were pushed into the cave once more and the fire wall was scraped back into place. "It's really very selfish of you," she snapped. "My hatching day only comes once a year. I've been planning this for months. So stop being awful, or I will take Burn's advice and kill you right now."

They waited until she was gone and the spiny backs of ten very grouchy SkyWing guards filled the passageway outside. Then Tsunami pulled Clay and Starflight to the far corner, where the wind whistling through the narrow windows would cover their conversation.

"I don't remember anything about that in the scrolls," she whispered to Starflight.

"There was one reference to a legend from before the Scorching," Starflight whispered back. "But I didn't think it meant anything. The guardians never said there was anything special about a red egg. I don't think they're even all that rare."

"What are we talking about?" Clay asked.

"You, you great lummox," Tsunami said, poking him with one talon. "And your no-good, evil girlfriend."

"I — who?" Clay said.

"Peril," Starflight explained. "The one who betrayed us to Queen Scarlet instead of helping us escape."

Clay was finally catching up. "You think she did that?" he said. "Why would she do that?"

"Because she wants to keep you here, obviously," Tsunami growled. "This is what happens when you're too nice to psychotic killer dragons."

"I'm still confused," Clay said. "How do red eggs come into it?"

"Don't you remember the prophecy?" Starflight asked.

Clay winced. It was the one thing the big dragons had tried to drill into their heads over and over again. But it never seemed to stick in his.

"For wings of earth, search through the mud," Starflight

quoted, *"for an egg the color of dragon blood."* He stopped and looked expectantly at Clay. There was a pause.

"What, me?" Clay said.

"Tell us about the legend," Tsunami said impatiently to Starflight.

"It was something about how MudWings hatched from dragon-blood eggs can walk through fire," Starflight said.

"Oh, that's all?" Tsunami said, her voice laced with sarcasm. "Well, that doesn't sound at all useful. Certainly not worth mentioning."

"Hey, if I had my scrolls with me, I'd have all the information we could possibly want," Starflight pointed out.

"Wait, that can't be right," Clay said. "Kestrel burned me plenty of times in combat training."

"But you have no scars," Tsunami said. "She tried to set you on fire way more than the rest of us, and you always healed in, like, a day."

"It still *hurt*, though," Clay said. He remembered that really clearly.

"The mud," Starflight jumped in. "Dragons draw strength from their natural habitats. SeaWings are most powerful in the ocean. I bet you had to encounter mud before your full immunity from fire could develop." He paused, thinking, and his expression turned hopeful. "Maybe my powers will be activated by moonlight or something."

"If that's true, the Talons of Peace were especially stupid to keep *you* underground," Tsunami said.

"We've been on those columns at night for the last couple of days," Clay said. "Do you feel any different?"

Starflight glanced at the stars glittering outside the window. "No," he admitted after a moment. "But maybe I just don't know what it's supposed to feel like."

They sat for a moment quietly.

"Do you really think Peril betrayed us?" Clay asked.

"She definitely did," Tsunami answered. "She doesn't want to lose you."

"Oh," Clay said. "That's so sad. I guess she doesn't have any other friends."

"Clay!" Tsunami said, exasperated. "Don't feel sorry for her. She just betrayed us. And by the way, she clearly likes you as more than a friend." Clay blinked in surprise, and she nudged his wing with hers. "Hey, I get it. You're lovable or whatever. But you can't forgive her for this. She'll only get more possessive if she thinks she can get away with it."

"You should stay away from her," Starflight agreed, shaking his head. "She can't be trusted."

"I guess she's not going to rescue Sunny either," Clay said sadly.

"No," Tsunami agreed. "We'll have to do that ourselves."

"Tomorrow," Starflight added. They all looked out at the guards stationed in the tunnel. Even if Clay moved the fire rocks, the three of them were no match for that many fierce, bad-tempered warrior dragons. They were trapped for the rest of the night.

"We'll figure out something," Tsunami said.

Clay was exhausted. He hadn't slept much, and then only badly, since his fight with Fjord. He curled up on the floor, and the other two flopped over him — the way they all used to sleep, in a pile of dragonets, before Kestrel insisted on the sleeping caves and rocky ledges for beds.

The warmth and weight of the other two was just what Clay needed. Despite his fears about the morning, his guilt over trusting Peril, and his sadness at her betrayal, he was asleep within moments. And he didn't have a single nightmare.

——— CHAPTER 25 ———

The roaring of dragons woke them the next morning. The three dragonets barely had time to scramble to their feet before guards began pouring into their cave. The black rocks had burned down to embers, which the SkyWing soldiers swept into the pool easily with their tails. Several of them grabbed Tsunami and pushed her toward the arena; the rest herded Clay and Starflight up the tunnel.

"Wait!" Clay cried. "Where is she going? Why can't we go with her?"

"Listen to him. *Oh, please hurry up and kill me*," mocked one of the SkyWing guards.

"Don't worry, it'll be your turn soon enough," said another, and they all cackled unpleasantly.

Clay and Starflight were shoved up a flight of long, wide, black stairs and emerged blinking into bright sunlight.

They were standing on the queen's balcony, overlooking the arena. Queen Scarlet was already there, lounging on her throne. She smirked at them.

"I thought you'd appreciate the best view in the house

for this." She nodded at the arena, where Tsunami was snapping and clawing at the guards around her.

Fat chains were wound around their necks, and Clay and Starflight were bolted to rings on the balcony floor. Burn stood next to Scarlet, ignoring the throne provided for her. She glowered at all the dragons equally. Clay got the feeling she preferred actual fighting over watching other dragons fight.

He jerked back against his chain as Glory was rolled forward into the sunlight. She was still lying in relaxed loops around the tree, with waves of emerald green and peacock blue drifting through her scales. Her eyes were closed, but as she rolled past, Clay was sure they opened a tiny bit, just enough to see her friends chained nearby. At least, he hoped that's what he saw.

Burn's black eyes were fixed on Glory as well.

"Oh, that's my new toy," Queen Scarlet said airily. "Pretty, isn't she? I bet I'm the only queen with my very own RainWing."

"Waste of food," Burn muttered, but her expression was envious.

"She doesn't eat much," Scarlet said. "She's more like an exotic plant than a dragon. Water, lots of sunshine, a little fruit, and a monkey here or there. Worth it until I get bored of her anyway."

"Hmmm," said Burn.

The seats were filled with hundreds of dragons — all the dragons in the Sky Kingdom, it seemed to Clay. They roared and stamped their feet, demanding bloody entertainment.

Vermilion fluttered down into the center of the arena. "Fellow dragons," he called. "Loyal SkyWings and visiting MudWings and honored SandWing guests. We have a full slate of thrilling games today, so let's begin!" He turned to gesture to Tsunami just as she broke away from her guards and charged at him. With a yelp of terror, Vermilion shot into the sky, barely escaping her talons.

The dragons in the audience roared with laughter. Tsunami hissed at Vermilion as he looped in circles above her.

"Looks like someone's mistaken me for her opponent today," Vermilion announced with a nervous laugh. "Sorry to disappoint you, SeaWing, but there's a much more dramatic fellow we'd like you to meet." He gestured to the sky. Several guards were wrestling with a pea-green SeaWing on one of the spires.

"Down on the sands, we have one of the so-called dragonets of destiny," Vermilion bellowed, staying up in the air. "Are they really so great and powerful? This is how we find out. I give you . . . Tsunami of the SeaWings!"

The sound of beating wings and hissing fire-breath filled the arena. It was louder than Clay had expected, as if the watching dragons were really rooting for her. He could pick out some of the voices in the crowd.

"It's really them! The dragonets of destiny!"

"Well, you saw what the MudWing did to Fjord! What was *that*?"

"Did you hear the mountain singing last night?"

"Such a fabulous party . . ."

". . . must have been an omen."

". . . ghosts in the peaks . . . the dragonets are here . . ."

". . . wearing the same ruby medallion! It was too embarrassing."

". . . hope she wins . . ."

Clay glanced at Queen Scarlet, who had smoke billowing in rings around her horns. She flicked her tail at Vermilion as if to say, *Get on with it*.

"AHEM," said Vermilion. "Some of you may remember a dragon a few months back who refused to fight."

"BOOOOOOOOO!" the crowd chanted obediently.

"Indeed," said Vermilion. "Tried to start a regular prisoner revolution, didn't he? Tried to get all the dragons to stop fighting. Well, clearly he had to be taught a lesson, or we'd all be lying in our caves right now, bored out of our skulls. Am I right?"

"WOO HOOOO!" the crowd agreed.

"So what's the best way to punish a SeaWing?" Vermilion swooped over the crowd, trying to look as if he was perfectly comfortable in the air instead of on the sands where he usually did his announcing.

"Chop off his head!"

"Stuff grass in his gills!"

"Drown him!"

Vermilion sighed. "All good suggestions," he said. "But no. The best way to punish a SeaWing — is to take away their water. *All* their water. For months."

Tsunami looked up at the queen's balcony and met Clay's eyes. Her scales were pale with horror.

The writhing SeaWing landed hard on the sands, dropped by the guards. He was twice as big as Tsunami, with talons as sharp and curved as fishhooks. Dried blood flecked his mouth as if he'd been trying to drink from his own veins. His scales were dull and crusted, and his dark green eyes were bloodshot and rolling wildly in his emaciated skull.

He looked completely insane.

"Dehydrated, mentally unstable, and ready to fight at last. It's Gill of the Seawings! Claws up, tails ready! Fight!"

Gill didn't wait for Vermilion's order. He tore across the sand toward Tsunami as soon as he'd recovered his balance. His mouth was open as if he thought he was roaring, but no sound came out. His tongue, purple and swollen, lolled to the side.

Tsunami leaped over his head and ducked into a roll as she landed, carrying her halfway across the arena. She spun to face him as Gill turned and charged her again.

"He's fast," Starflight whispered to Clay. "He's desperate."

"Tsunami's fast, too," Clay said. But he wondered if she was feeling everything he'd felt, down on the sands. Facing her first battle to the death, was she hesitant to kill another dragon? Because Gill wouldn't hesitate at all. He couldn't be distracted like Fjord. He'd been driven mad with thirst, and he'd tear Tsunami apart without knowing what he was doing.

The big green dragon reared up with his wings spread and tried to slam himself down on Tsunami's back. She slashed at his underbelly with her claws. Bright red blood spurted over her blue scales. Gill's talons slipped off her back, and he crashed face-first into the sand as she shot out of the way.

He was up immediately, lunging after her. His claws seized her tail and he yanked hard, lifting her off her feet. She wriggled in midair and sank her teeth into the webbed skin between his talons.

Gill did his soundless roar again. There was something unearthly about watching dragons fight in silence. It made Clay feel like his scales were crawling across his back.

Gill dropped Tsunami and she whirled quickly, smashing her tail into his legs. The big SeaWing went over like a toppling boulder. The thud of his body landing shook the whole stadium.

Tsunami pounced on his head, pinning his wings with her back talons. She seized his horns in her front claws and shoved his face into the sand. His tail thrashed, bucking her up and down, but Tsunami's weight was too much for him to throw off.

"I've won," Tsunami shouted. "You can all see that. We can end this now, without killing anyone. I ask you all to let me let him live!"

There was a stunned silence across the arena. Clay glanced at Queen Scarlet, wondering if she would stand up to argue with Tsunami. But her expression was smug, as if she knew exactly what would happen next.

"KILL HIM!" several SkyWings shouted at once. "Snap his neck! Pull out his teeth! Oooo, gouge his eyes! Something gory! Death! Death! Death! Death!" Suddenly all the dragons were shouting at her in unison.

Tsunami lowered her head, breathing hard. She seemed to be studying Gill, perhaps wondering if there was any way to bring him back from the madness.

"She doesn't have a choice," Starflight said. "It's her life or his. If she lets him go, he'll kill her right away. She has to know that."

Yes, but knowing that doesn't make it any easier, Clay thought.

"Perhaps our 'dragonet of destiny' doesn't have the stomach for battle," Queen Scarlet called snidely. "Maybe war is *too scary* for her. Perhaps she'd like to go back into hiding instead?"

Tsunami lifted her chin and stared straight into Queen Scarlet's eyes. With a wrench of her talons, she snapped Gill's neck in one clean break. The expression on her face said, all too clearly, *I'm imagining this is you.*

— CHAPTER 26 —

"Disappointing," Queen Scarlet said to Burn, as the crowd of dragons erupted in cheers.

"Catastrophic," Burn growled. "Look, the idiots love her now."

Dragons were leaning over the top of the arena walls to throw small jewels at Tsunami. A couple of little emeralds bounced off her scales as she dropped Gill's head and stepped back from his limp body.

Tsunami gave the cheering dragons a disgusted look, but that didn't stop them.

"Don't worry, I have a plan," said Queen Scarlet. She rubbed her front talons together. "But now it's time for the NightWing! My hatching-day present to me!"

Starflight's terrified eyes locked with Clay's. All his know-it-all superiority vanished in a heartbeat.

"Wait!" Clay cried as the guards started to unchain Starflight. "Let me fight for him instead!"

"These dragonets," Scarlet said, waving a claw at Burn. "Constantly pushing and shoving to save each other. It's just the weirdest thing." She signaled to the guards with one talon, and they hauled Starflight off to the tunnel. Clay leaned his full weight against his chains, trying to break free, but they held fast.

"You're not spoiling this for me, MudWing," Scarlet said. "I've been dying to see the NightWing fight. He's so very sparkly and good-looking. I think after he's dead I'll cut off his wings and hang them on my throne room walls. Wouldn't that be magnificent and thrilling? All those silver scales sparkling like diamonds against obsidian. I *love* it."

Burn growled low in her throat. "This is a frivolous palace," she muttered.

"Careful how you speak of your allies," Scarlet said. "Remember you need us."

Burn shifted her wings and kept her mouth shut.

No one had chained up Tsunami after her fight. She was still standing in the arena, her back turned to the SeaWing corpse, which was already beginning to smell of dead fish.

Then Starflight was shoved out of the tunnel, and Clay realized what Scarlet's plan was. Hope fluttered inside him. Tsunami would never kill Starflight. Not in a million years. Not even to stop one of his endless lectures about the science of fire-breathing.

"The rarest of all dragons," Vermilion called from the safety of a ledge opposite the queen's balcony. "A real live NightWing. Is he the dragonet of the prophecy? Let's see what happens when two of them have to fight each other. Tsunami of the SeaWings and Starflight of the NightWings! Claws up, teeth ready! Fight!"

Tsunami and Starflight stood looking at each other. Tsunami's sides were heaving, and she was covered in Gill's blood. She looked a bit scarier than usual, and Starflight clawed the sand nervously, as if he wasn't entirely sure she *wouldn't* snap and kill him.

Slowly Tsunami walked over to Starflight. He opened his wings, and she leaned into him, resting her head on his shoulder.

"BOOO . . . ooo?" called a solitary voice from the crowd, dropping off as no one joined in.

"Awwwww," went a few dragons in the upper seats, far enough from the queen that they wouldn't be recognized.

"This is getting worse and worse," Burn hissed through gritted teeth.

"Aren't you going to fight?" Queen Scarlet called. Tsunami and Starflight didn't even look up. "That's very annoying," the queen added. "Go on, you've been stuck with each other for years. You must be ready to kill her, NightWing. Doesn't she drive you mad?"

Clay looked over at Glory, wishing she'd smile at him. She'd joked often enough about ways to shut up both Tsunami and Starflight. But her eyes stayed closed.

"No?" Scarlet leaned forward. "Oh, fine, be the worst gladiators ever. Vermilion! Release the scavengers!"

Vermilion flapped his wings, and a huge cage came rolling out of the tunnel. The queen's son flew to the top of it and bit down to sever the cord that held the door. The door fell open, and four scavengers burst onto the sand, waving claws and squeaking ferociously.

"Scavengers? To kill the dragonets of the prophecy? Are you mad?" Burn snarled.

"Well, it only took one to get your mother," Scarlet observed. Burn's head whipped around, her venomous tail arching up toward the SkyWing queen.

"Oh, calm down," Scarlet said with a snort. "It'll be fun. I've got more things waiting in the wings to kill them if this doesn't work. This is the only NightWing I'll probably ever get in my arena, and I want to see him fight *everything*."

Clay leaned forward, worried. They'd never practiced fighting or hunting scavengers. Scavengers only attacked dragons with treasure, and the dragonets didn't have anything. He wondered if Starflight had read about their fighting techniques in any of his scrolls.

Then again, scavengers were still prey, only a little fiercer and pointier. The guardians would often release animals in the caves for the dragonets to chase, so they could learn hunting skills. Were scavengers really any different from lizards or goats or ostriches?

Tsunami pushed Starflight back against the wall and spread her wings in front of him, baring her teeth at the scavengers. Three of them ran right at her; the fourth took one look and bolted for the tunnel entrance.

Well, it wasn't normal for prey to run *at* a dragon. So perhaps scavengers were a little different after all.

Tsunami cuffed aside the first scavenger with a swipe that sent it flying into the seats. All the closest dragons lunged for it, clawing and shouting and climbing over each other to catch it. The scavenger landed, screaming, in one SkyWing's outstretched talons, and the dragon promptly ate him.

The other two scavengers skidded to a stop and back-pedaled out of Tsunami's reach. She flicked her tongue at them.

Meanwhile, the scavenger who had tried to run came hurtling back out of the tunnel, herded by a trio of large SkyWing guards holding long spears. He pelted across the sand, letting out one long shriek of fear, until he crashed into the opposite wall and fell over. He didn't get up again.

"This is going well," Burn muttered. "The NightWing isn't even doing anything."

"The other two scavengers are female," Scarlet pointed out. "They sometimes last a bit longer."

One of the scavengers pointed, and they split up, circling Tsunami from different directions. They approached slowly, each holding out a silvery claw. Tsunami eyed them until she couldn't watch them both at once. Then she turned and lunged at the one on her left.

That one darted under her talons and stabbed at her underbelly. Tsunami yelped and reached to grab the scavenger, but it had already scurried away.

At the same time, the other scavenger shot behind Tsunami's back and threw herself at Starflight. The NightWing tried to bat her away like Tsunami had done, but she swerved around his claws. Suddenly she was climbing up his front leg and before he could shake her off, she scrabbled onto his back.

Clay tensed. He'd never seen a move like that. Definitely not something a cow would try.

Starflight tried to twist his head over his shoulder to bite at the scavenger, but she moved fast, clinging to his scales like a salamander going up a rock. He shook his head furiously and reached up to claw her off. She wriggled aside, and he accidentally clawed his own neck. A thin trail of blood trickled from his scales.

"Not very impressive," Queen Scarlet sniffed. "I suppose they can't read scavenger minds. Not enough going on in there."

Clay clenched his talons. That scavenger was getting close to Starflight's snout. If she stabbed that claw into one of his eyes . . .

"Tsunami!" he yelled.

Tsunami was halfway across the arena, chasing the scavenger who'd attacked her. Tsunami was faster, but the scavenger kept changing directions and running underneath her. At Clay's call, Tsunami whipped around and saw Starflight's danger.

She raced toward him, but before she got there, Starflight suddenly gritted his teeth and slammed his head to the ground. The scavenger was flung forward over his horns, landing hard and rolling into the wall. Almost instantly she was up and staggering away from his teeth, which snapped on empty air.

Starflight didn't chase her. He stood rubbing his head,

watching the scavenger stumble on the churned-up sand. When Tsunami started past him, he reached out and stopped her. Tsunami's own scavenger ran by and helped Starflight's scavenger lean against the wall. The two scavengers glared around at the stadium full of dragons. Loud angry squeaking noises came out of both of them.

"You're right," Scarlet said with a sigh to Burn. "This isn't nearly as thrilling as I thought it would be. Let's go straight to the IceWings!" she shouted across to Vermilion.

He signaled, and guards took off from all over the stadium. Clay watched in dread as they scattered to the IceWing prisoners. He counted at least eight IceWings up there. He vaguely remembered something from one of Starflight's lectures about how IceWings hated NightWings from some long-ago war.

"Finally a smart idea," Burn hissed.

"Let me fight, too!" Clay pleaded. "Put me in there with them!" He knew three dragonets had no chance against eight IceWings, but he would rather be down there with his friends than stuck on the balcony, unable to help.

Suddenly a cloud seemed to pass over the sun. The fluttering of wings made all the dragons look up as a wave of darkness flew overhead. One piece of the darkness separated from the rest and spiraled down into the arena, ducking under the web of wires.

As he descended magnificently onto the sand, wings outstretched, Clay recognized him.

Morrowseer had arrived at last.

CHAPTER 27

Clay was torn between relief and anger. What had taken the NightWing so long?

A hush fell over the arena. The SkyWing guards hovered up in the sky, halfway through unchaining the IceWings. All the dragons stared at Morrowseer, whose vast black form seemed to fill the whole arena. His darkness sucked up all the light around him.

He pointed to Starflight and addressed Queen Scarlet. "This dragonet is ours."

Just him? Clay thought. *What about the rest of us?* He was afraid if he spoke up, the queen would kill him before Morrowseer had a chance to save them. But maybe he could get into Morrowseer's thoughts. . . .

"Ours who?" Queen Scarlet said. "We found him with some Talons of Peace revolutionaries. Are you telling me the NightWings have finally chosen sides?"

Burn chimed in with a snarl. "Are you allying yourselves with an underground peace movement instead of a real queen?"

Morrowseer glanced up at the sky, where a flight of black dragons was circling. "No," he said in his deep rumbling voice. "I come only to claim this dragonet as ours. We will take him and go."

"Oh, *will* you?" said Queen Scarlet. "On whose authority? Would your mysterious queen like to appear and discuss the matter with me?"

Morrowseer's eyes glittered dangerously. "Do not anger the NightWings, sky dragon. Give us our dragonet."

And the rest of us! Clay thought as loud as he could. *Over here! Dragonets of destiny! Four more besides Starflight! All totally key to the prophecy!* Maybe Morrowseer had forgotten they were there. But he could read minds — couldn't he hear Clay shouting for help?

Queen Scarlet stamped her foot. "No! I want to see him fight IceWings! It's my hatching day!"

For a moment, as everybody paused, Clay was afraid that Morrowseer would give up and fly away. Then the black dragon's tail twitched, just the tiniest bit, and all at once several NightWings came plummeting out of the sky.

Clay watched in awe. *He must have called them with his mind.*

Without a word or a visible signal, the NightWings fanned out across the circle of prisoners. The SkyWing guards dodged out of the way, looking terrified. Each pair of NightWings fell on an IceWing prisoner, talons slashing. Within moments, all the IceWings were dead. Their silvery corpses flopped across their cells. Bluish-red blood dripped slowly down the sides of the rock spires.

That wasn't fair, Clay thought. *The IceWings were all chained up — they couldn't fight back. If the NightWings are so tough, why not free all the prisoners instead of killing more dragons?* He looked down at Morrowseer again and thought he saw the dragon's scornful gaze pass over him. *Oops. I mean, thank you, NightWings! We're very glad you're here. ALL FIVE OF US!*

So much smoke was pouring out of Scarlet's nostrils that it was hard to see her eyes. Beside her, Burn's tail was lashing. She looked ready to jump down and attack Morrowseer herself.

The large NightWing smiled coldly. "There," he said. "We've taken care of your IceWing problem. Now we'll be going." He beat his wings once, lifting up into the air, and then swooped down on Starflight.

"Wait!" Starflight cried as Morrowseer's talons closed around him. "What about my friends?"

YES! Clay screamed in his head. *WHAT ABOUT US?*

Morrowseer didn't even look down at the dragonets. He soared off into the sky, carrying Starflight away with him. The rest of the NightWings circled once more and then followed him south.

Clay felt like he'd been pummeled by a SeaWing tail. A rescuer had come down from the clouds . . . and decided not to rescue them. He met Tsunami's eyes. Hers were bitter and angry.

She was not the only one. "Guards!" Queen Scarlet roared. "I will have one thing go right today," she fumed.

"Fetch my champion. And clean up that mess down there."
She swept one wing toward the arena.

Burn looked too angry to speak. The queens watched in
silence as SkyWings hurried onto the sand and started dragging off the bodies of Gill and the scavenger. The two
scavengers still alive were shooed back into the cage and
rolled away. Guards threw chains over Tsunami, who sub-
mitted without fighting for once, perhaps too shocked and
angry to muster the energy.

All around the stadium, a shocked stillness hung over
the watching dragons. Clay guessed it had been a long
time since they'd seen anyone win a showdown with
their queen.

"As you all know," Scarlet said suddenly, her voice regal
and commanding as if mystery dragons hadn't just swooped
out of the sky to steal her toy, "yesterday my champion,
Peril, offered to stand for the accused prisoner, Kestrel, in a
Champion's Shield. She will now fight a dragon of my choosing, and if she wins, Kestrel goes free. If she loses — then I
suppose I'll have to get a new champion."

She paused, expecting a reaction from the crowd, but
nothing happened. Queen Scarlet frowned. "Oh, right," she
said. "You think Peril *can't* lose. Well, it so happens that we
have a special guest here today — a dragon whose scales are
impervious to fire. Isn't that . . . *thrilling*?"

Clay barely had time to register this before guards
seized him.

As he was being dragged into the tunnel, he caught a glimpse of Queen Scarlet's face and realized she knew exactly what she was doing.

She knew he and Peril were friends. Or had been, before her betrayal anyway.

The queen was forcing Peril to choose between him and her mother.

And now Clay had to choose between killing Peril . . . and death.

CHAPTER 28

Sand that was sticky with blood clumped between Clay's talons. The sun beat down, bright and hot in his eyes. He paced around the arena, thinking. Was there any way out of this?

He couldn't count on Peril sparing his life, that was for sure. She'd betrayed him once. Surely she would do it again, if it was to save her mother.

He heard her scales scraping along the tunnel and turned to face her as she entered the arena.

She stopped, and it was like every emotion in the world hit her face at the same time. "I should have guessed," she said, furious and low, so only Clay could hear. "The only dragon here who can touch me. No wonder she wanted me to stay away from you."

"I guess you should have," Clay said. Peril flinched.

"There you go, Peril," Queen Scarlet said. Behind her, Tsunami was dragged onto the balcony, wrapped in chains and glowing with anger. "That's the dragon you have to kill before I set your mother free. Have fun!"

Peril slid toward Clay, and he fled to the opposite wall. She hesitated, then put on a burst of speed and chased after him. He waited until she was a heartbeat away, then lunged forward and body-slammed her to the ground.

The crowd roared with surprise and delight.

She lay there gasping as he got up and ran to the other side of the arena again. *She's not used to her opponents being able to hit back*, he thought. Fiery heat blazed where his shoulder had touched her, but it faded quickly.

He turned with his back to the wall and crouched, waiting for her to get up. Slowly she rolled to her feet and paced toward him. This time she stopped a short distance away.

"I'm sorry," she said plaintively. "I know you're mad. I made a mistake. I just — I thought you were trying to get away from me."

"Well, I am now," Clay said.

"I don't want to kill you," she said, clawing the sand in frustration.

"Buuuuut you have to," he finished for her.

"I had a whole plan," she said. "A plan where I saved you after Kestrel, and you liked me best of all."

"Peril, that's insane," he said. "I don't care if you save me. I want you to save my friends. That's what's important to me."

She snarled suddenly. "*I'm* your friend! You don't need them!" She leaped at his head, and he shoved himself upward, throwing her over him and into the wall. He was across the arena again by the time she was able to crawl to her feet.

"I'll stick with the friends who aren't trying to kill me, thanks," he called.

"I'm not — well —" She stamped her talons again. "It's not fair! The others can have any dragon! I only want you!" Her wings snapped open and she leaped up, then dove at him with her claws outstretched.

Clay snatched a talonful of sand and threw it in her eyes. She shrieked and blundered sideways in the air. He leaped to grab her shoulders and flung her to the ground. He rolled her onto her back and sat on her, looking down into her face.

"I know I don't know much about anything," he said. "But I think it doesn't have to work like this."

"It does," Peril said, struggling to push him off. Her talons shoved ineffectually at him. "Dragons kill each other all the time. In war, in here, anywhere, for no reason at all. That's how we are. Especially you and me. We're the same. We're dangerous."

"That's not how I am," Clay said. "No matter what happened when I hatched. I can't feel this killer inside me that's supposed to be there. Maybe that's what the prophecy is about. Maybe the dragonets are supposed to show everyone how to get along without a lot of killing."

He noticed that the closest dragons in the audience were leaning in, listening intently. He hadn't been speaking for the whole stadium to hear, but at least a few had.

Queen Scarlet wasn't among them. "Hurry up and do it, then," she called from her balcony. "You have her at your mercy. Use your venom! That was thrilling, and I didn't even get to see it the first time!"

Clay and Peril stared at each other for a moment.

"Did she just say what I think she said?" Clay asked.

"But if the venom didn't come from her," Peril said, "then where —"

Clay whipped around to face the balcony as Glory suddenly reared up in a blaze of sunflower gold and cobalt blue. She snapped her thin chain like a reed and launched herself off the marble tree. Her mouth was wide open, hinged like a snake's. She hissed, and a jet of black liquid shot out of her two longest fangs.

Burn shoved Queen Scarlet in front of her and shot into the sky. Glory's venom hit Scarlet on the side of her face.

The SkyWing queen began to scream.

The stadium erupted in pandemonium. All the dragons tried to take to the sky at once, crashing into one another and clawing viciously to get away from Glory and the screaming queen.

"Wait!" Peril grabbed Clay as he jumped away from her. She reached up and touched the bindings on his wings. They broke apart instantly, and his wings stretched free for the first time in the Sky Kingdom.

"Thank you," he called, lifting off.

The guards on the balcony had all scattered after Burn, so when Clay landed next to Glory, there was no one left but him and her and Tsunami, and Queen Scarlet, who was beating her own head with her wings and staggering toward the edge.

"Glory!" Clay cried. "You're awake!"

"Of course I am!" she flared, tugging on Tsunami's chains. "You couldn't tell I was faking? I was waiting for the right moment to do something. Did you seriously think I was asleep this whole time?"

"Uh —" Clay said.

"You looked pretty asleep," Tsunami said.

"Well, that's great," Glory said. "For the first time in my life, I pretend to be as lazy as everyone thinks RainWings are, and you actually believe it. I'm glad my friends have so much faith in me."

"Hey, you never told us you could do *that*," Clay said, pointing to her venom-spitting teeth. Beyond them, Queen Scarlet crashed into her throne and screamed even louder. Her gold chain mail was starting to melt into her scales.

"I never could before," Glory said. "Are you going to help me with this?"

Clay grabbed the marble tree and tried to lever it under Tsunami's chains.

"So how *did* you do that?" he asked.

"Oh," Glory said, "well, there's a logical scientific explanation and *seriously, right now you want to have this conversation*?"

"You scared off Burn, but she won't stay gone for long," Tsunami pointed out.

Clay gave the sky a worried look. "Peril!" he shouted. "Get over here!"

"No!" Tsunami said. "Not her! Keep her away from me!"

"We need her help," Clay insisted as Peril landed beside him. "Their chains and bindings," he said to Peril. She hesitated. "Please," he added. "If we're really friends."

"All right," she said, glancing at Queen Scarlet. She touched the chains around Tsunami, and they broke apart, collapsing with great clanking sounds to the balcony floor. Clay held his friends' wing bindings away from their scales, and Peril burned right through them.

"Now we get Sunny," he said, leaping into the sky.

The air was full of beating wings, red and gold and desert pale, whacking into each other and knocking one another off course. Peril shot ahead of him, clearing a path as dragons panicked out of her way. Clay saw her tail accidentally brush a SkyWing's leg. The other dragon howled, clutching the burn, and tumbled into the side of the mountain with smoke rising from his scales.

Tsunami and Glory were close behind Clay as they soared up to the feasting hall, over the cliffs. Wind billowed under his wings, and despite his fear of Burn, he felt that same fierce joy grip him at the freedom of flying. After days of being terrified he might fall, it was exhilarating to know that now he couldn't — that he had the whole vast crystal-blue sky to move in.

Peril reached Sunny's cage first. Clay saw Sunny peering through the bars, trying to figure out what all the noise from the arena was about. Then her gray-green eyes landed on Clay, and her face lit up with joy.

"I knew you'd be all right!" she cried as the three dragonets each nosed her through the bars. "I knew I shouldn't have worried. I just kept thinking about the prophecy and how we can't die because we have to stop the war."

Tsunami snorted. Peril hovered in front of the cage and sliced through the bars with her claws. The metal sizzled and steamed for a moment, then dropped to the ground below.

Sunny flung herself out the door into Clay's arms. She pelted him happily with her unbound wings.

"Wait," she said, looking around. "Where's Starflight?"

"We lost him," Glory said.

"What?"

"Stop that," Tsunami said, hitting Glory with her tail. "Glory means Morrowseer came and took him away. He's fine. Better than us, especially once the dragons stop panicking and start looking for us. Let's head for the river." She banked around toward the cliff, scattering clumps of rusty blood-red sand from her wings.

"But — he just left?" Sunny asked. She caught one of Clay's talons and stopped him in midair. "Without us?"

"He didn't have a choice, Sunny," Clay said, clasping her claws in his.

"Clay, wait," Peril said. Her copper wings shivered, and she clenched her talons as if she were about to split in two.

"My mother. If Queen Scarlet isn't dead, the first thing she'll do is kill her."

"She's right," Clay said as Tsunami and Glory came winging back to see why they hadn't moved. "Tsunami, we have to get Kestrel out."

"Why?" Tsunami challenged. "What do we care? Kestrel was awful to us."

"We care anyway," Sunny said softly. "We can't help it. Even you."

"I don't," Glory said. "She was going to kill me. Remember?"

Clay did remember. He remembered every cruel word, every vicious bite. But he also remembered Kestrel offering herself to Queen Scarlet in their place. And he remembered the scars on her palms, and the look on her face when she saw that Peril wasn't dead.

"She didn't raise us to care about her," Tsunami argued. "Kestrel was just keeping us alive, and if that's what she wants, the best thing we can do is run away right now."

"I'd like to be something more than alive," Clay said fiercely. "I'd like to be the kind of dragon she doesn't think I am — the kind they write prophecies about. That dragon would rescue her no matter how awful she is."

Tsunami lashed her tail, nearly knocking Glory sideways. Even though she was covered in blood, her blue scales shone through in the sunlight like buried sapphires. She glared at Peril for a long moment.

"Fine," she growled at last.

"Not me," Glory said. "Do what you like, but I'm not a big mushy ball of forgiveness like you are, Clay." She met his gaze calmly, but her scales were rolling red and black like embers inside thunderclouds.

"Then take Sunny, go to the cave at the bottom of the waterfall, and wait for us," Tsunami said.

"Can't I help?" Sunny asked. "I think I could —"

"Yes, by not getting yourself killed," Glory said. She tipped her wings at Sunny, and flashed away over the edge of the cliff. Sunny hesitated, then squeezed Clay's talons and followed her.

"This way's the fastest," Peril said. She beat her wings, soaring up the cliff that overlooked the feasting grounds. Tsunami made a face at Clay and followed her. Clay could still hear the shouts and roars coming from the arena. He couldn't tell if the queen was still screaming. Dragons filled the air; none of them seemed to be searching for the dragonets yet, but he knew it wouldn't be long.

As they flew up, Clay passed a narrow shelf of rock with a scrubby bush clinging to it. To his surprise, a scavenger was hanging from the cliff face a few lengths above the shelf. It was one of the prey scavengers from the party; it had somehow managed to climb up this high without being spotted. It was still struggling up the rocks, gasping for breath and shaking with exhaustion. Clay glanced up at the distance to the top of the cliff and realized how much farther it still had to go, especially for such a tiny creature.

He didn't know why he felt sorry for it. Scavengers were delicious nuisances, nothing more, according to everything he'd been taught. But he was going that way anyway . . . and it had tried so hard . . .

Clay dropped back, scooped the scavenger up in his talons, and flapped after Peril and Tsunami again. The scavenger gave a yell and started shoving at Clay's claws, but it carried no weapons and, as far as Clay could tell, scavengers had no natural defenses of their own. This one was smaller than the others he'd seen, with a thatch of black fur on its head and smooth skin nearly as brown as Clay's scales.

It wriggled and beat at his talons frantically for the few moments it took to reach the top of the cliff. Up here the view was mountains in all directions. Clay didn't know what a scavenger's natural habitat was, but this was the best he could do. Peril and Tsunami were already vanishing into a large hole that was the open roof of the main palace hall. Clay set the scavenger down gently behind a tall boulder.

"And stay away from dragons from now on," he said sternly, although he knew the scavenger couldn't understand him. The scavenger stared at him, its mouth opening and closing. *Not even clever instincts*, Clay thought. Why wasn't it running away?

Not his problem anymore. He nudged it with his claw, turned, and dove into the roof hole. Down at the bottom of the hall, he could see Peril and Tsunami spiraling onto the grate over Kestrel's head.

From here he could also hear the clamor in the tunnels.

Most of the SkyWings were outside, hiding in the sky around the mountain peaks. But the heavy thump of dragon feet and clattering of claws and teeth echoed through the hall.

Burn only had to collect her soldiers — a shield between her and Glory's venom — and then she'd come searching for the dragonets.

—— CHAPTER 29 ——

Clay landed beside Tsunami on the grate and then jumped back as Kestrel's yellow eyes glared through the bars at him.

"What are you doing here?" she snarled.

"Rescuing you," Tsunami snapped back. "Against my will."

"Stand back," Peril said, reaching for the metal latticework. She laced her claws through the thick bars, and the sharp smell of melting iron filled the air.

Clay had never seen Kestrel look so uncertain before. She watched Peril with an uneasy expression, flicking her forked tongue in and out. Peril kept her own eyes fixed on the bars. They were much thicker than the delicate birdcage Sunny was in, and took longer to burn through.

"I thought you were dead," Kestrel said finally.

"I thought *you* were dead," Peril answered without any warmth in her voice.

"I heard Scarlet had a lethal new champion," Kestrel said. "I didn't know it was you."

Peril shrugged. "I guess I didn't need you. I turned out all right without you." Clay and Tsunami exchanged glances.

"All right" wasn't exactly how Clay would have described Peril.

"Queen Scarlet took care of me," Peril went on. "She found me the black rocks I needed and gave me a purpose and a place to live."

"Black rocks?" Kestrel broke in. "What black rocks?"

"Hey!" A pair of SkyWing guards came charging out of the nearest tunnel. "Stop!"

One of them made the hissing fire-breath noise and shot a bolt of flame at Tsunami. Clay flung himself in the way and felt the fire blast his scales. Hot pain flashed through him, and then faded a moment later. He shook himself as the red glow ebbed from his scales and looked up into the guard's shocked face.

Tsunami lunged at the other guard, slashing his side and then slamming her tail into his head. He staggered back, then threw himself on her with his large wings beating back her defense.

At the same time, Clay's guard attacked him. They grappled, and he felt her talons rake the wounds that were still healing on his back. He threw her off with a fierce heave. She skidded into the wall just as the last bar snapped, and Kestrel rose, huge and angry, out of her cell.

Clay had forgotten how big Kestrel was. Her red scales were scraped and chipped in places where the chains had pinned her down. Her talons looked blunted, as if she'd been clawing at the walls of her prison.

"Kill them and let's go!" she roared.

Peril darted toward the guard who had Tsunami pinned. He let go of her, but it was too late. Peril's talons caught him and sliced through his neck, leaving black scorch marks behind that bubbled and smoked. He tried to scream, and she raked his throat again, burning through the flesh and scales like they were paper.

Clay felt sick to his stomach. He was glad he hadn't eaten anything in a while. He looked down at the guard he'd been fighting. Her orange eyes were watching Peril in terror. She was only a soldier, fighting for her tribe and her queen.

"Run," he said to her. He hauled the SkyWing guard up and shoved her at the tunnel. She didn't hesitate; in a flash of red and gold, she was gone.

He turned and saw Peril's face. She knew he'd been protecting the guard — a total stranger — from her. She knew now for certain how he felt about what she did.

"Stupid worm," Kestrel hissed from behind him. "She'll raise the alarm. Queen Scarlet will catch us in moments."

"Queen Scarlet is probably dead," Tsunami said sharply. "And don't talk to Clay that way. Just — follow us and stop talking." She launched herself up toward the sky. Clay met Peril's eyes again. Her claws opened and closed, reaching toward him, and then she pulled them back.

"Come on," he said to her, trying to put understanding in his voice that he didn't feel.

They lifted off after Tsunami, copper and brown and red wings glowing as the sun reached them. Clay burst into the air and banked sharply toward the waterfall. He could feel Peril's heat close on his tail.

The rocky cliff flashed by beside them as they dropped toward the base of the waterfall. Tsunami led them closer to the bellowing water, whisking through the spray. Clay closed his eyes for a moment, turning his face into the mist of droplets.

The sounds of the palace faded behind them, swallowed by the waterfall's roar, as they plummeted farther and farther. This waterfall was taller than the one Clay and Tsunami had encountered on their way out of the mountain. It bounced over outcroppings of rock, divided into smaller cascades, poured in long, straight sheets and then shot out in bursts like dragons of water lashing out with their claws.

At the bottom Clay saw a glittering ice-clear lake, with the Diamond Spray River crawling out the other side, through sloping hills east and south, toward the sea. Stubby trees and ragged scrubland, brown and green, edged the lake at the base of the mountain.

Tsunami angled toward the dark gap in the wall near the bottom of the waterfall. As they drew closer, Clay saw a glint of gold as Sunny peeked anxiously out.

They touched down on the muddy banks of the lake, in a thick copse of trees beside a small cave nearly hidden by the roaring wall of water. As Peril landed, the grass around her talons shriveled to ash. She looked down at the blackened earth and curled her tail in close to make her imprint as small as possible.

"Kestrel!" Sunny cried. "You're all right."

"No thanks to you five," Kestrel growled, lashing her tail. "You wanted so badly to be free. Now do you see why we had to protect you?" One of her wings snagged on a tree branch and she wrestled it loose, growling.

"You're welcome," Tsunami snapped back. "We could have left you in the Sky Kingdom. I would have."

Clay couldn't resist the mud squelching between his claws. He threw himself to the ground and rolled, letting the warmth coat his arena-dusty, aching scales.

"Good grief, Clay, yuck," Glory said. She edged toward the lake and spread her wings to catch the sunlight.

"Careful." Tsunami reached to pull her back. "If they're looking for us, they'll definitely spot a bright purple dragon from the air."

Glory flared her ruff at Tsunami. "I am not *bright purple*. Queen Scarlet called this my violet mood, thank you very much."

"Oh, sorry," Tsunami said. "I meant to say they'll definitely spot a *moody violet* dragon from the air."

"You are the epitome of hilarious," Glory said. "Anyway, I can take care of that." Her wing scales shimmered as if they were drawing in the sunlight, and then the purple color started to break up like water being poured into paint. Soon she was the color of the muddy ground below her. "Happy?" she asked Tsunami.

"I want to know what my cool power is," Tsunami muttered. "You've got camouflage scales and venom-spitting teeth. Clay is immune to fire. Starflight apparently has big dragons waiting in the sky to save him whenever things get scary. What do I get?"

"Clay is immune to fire?" Sunny asked. "What? And did you say venom-spitting teeth?"

"Yeah," Clay answered. "I'm afraid you'll have to be nicer to Glory from now on, Sunny."

Sunny flapped her wings in outrage. "I'm always nice to — oh, you're teasing me," she said as he choked with laughter. She smushed a giant talonful of mud into his face. Clay ducked away and noticed Peril watching with drooped wings and a sad expression.

"See, we can take care of ourselves," Tsunami said to Kestrel. "You didn't even know what Clay and Glory could do. You didn't think we were good for anything, but it was your own fault for keeping us underground and treating us like eggs."

"Oh, we did everything wrong," Kestrel said scathingly. "Go ahead and blame us, but we did as the Talons of Peace asked. You would probably all be dead if we hadn't."

Tsunami lifted her chin. "We're not going back to the Talons of Peace," she said.

"We're not?" Sunny squeaked. Glory gave her a scornful look.

"Oh?" Kestrel said. She bent her head to avoid the branches and gave Tsunami a sharp orange glare. "What is your magnificent plan, if I may ask?"

"We're going to find our homes," Tsunami said. "And our parents. We're going to see this war firsthand, instead of reading about it in scrolls. And then we'll figure out for ourselves *if* we're going to do anything about it."

"But, Tsunami," Sunny whispered, tugging on her wing. "The prophecy! We have to!"

"Shh," Clay said. He drew her back, away from the wrathful look on Kestrel's face, just in case there was any fire-breathing about to happen.

Privately, he agreed with Sunny. They couldn't just ignore the prophecy. Something had to be done about the war, and everyone was waiting for the dragonets to do it. He kept thinking of the prisoners, singing the song of the dragonets as if it would save them.

But he also agreed with Tsunami — they couldn't do anything until they were out in the real world, figuring out what *could* be done. On their own, without the Talons of Peace keeping them away from their families and everything that made stopping the war important.

There was a pause as Kestrel and Tsunami glared at each other. Smoke puffed from Kestrel's nose, drifting away on the air. Clay glanced at Peril, but her eyes were fixed on her mother.

"Fine," Kestrel snorted unexpectedly. "What do I care? I'm done with you. I've done everything that was asked of me, and all I have to show for it is a pack of ungrateful lizards. Go find your precious families. I don't care what happens to you."

"Oh, Kestrel," Sunny said, climbing over and hugging Kestrel's leg. "You don't mean that. You know we appreciate everything you did for us."

Clay caught Glory and Tsunami rolling their eyes at each other.

"You're on your own now," Kestrel said. She pried Sunny off and stepped back toward the lake. "And good riddance. Peril, are you coming?"

Peril hesitated.

"I thought you were coming with us," Clay said. Peril's eyes brightened.

"Over my charred, dead body," Tsunami growled, whacking Clay with one of her wings.

"Why not?" Glory said, her eyes on a passing butterfly. "Maybe Peril's the missing dragonet you all need for the prophecy . . . your 'wings of sky.'"

Clay blinked at her. "Wow. Do you think so?"

Tiny scarlet flame shapes flickered around Glory's ears, and she shrugged.

"Oh, could I be?" Peril breathed.

"No!" Kestrel spat.

"The largest egg in mountain high," Glory quoted. "If you hatched with a twin, your egg must have been huge." Her eyes stayed on the butterfly instead of looking at the other dragonets.

"That's true!" Peril said. "Maybe I'm part of your destiny!" She looked at Clay hopefully.

"Not a chance," Kestrel said. "Peril and her brother

hatched over a year before you misbegotten worms. The prophecy speaks of five dragonets hatching together on the brightest night. Face it, your SkyWing died in the egg. I saw the broken shell and the murdered dragon who carried her."

Clay looked down at his muddy talons. Kestrel was right. He hadn't remembered the exact words of the prophecy. There was no way Peril could be the fifth dragonet.

"Sorry," he said to her. Her copper wings slumped. "You can come with us anyway," he offered.

"I can't," she said. "I have to go back for the black rocks."

"Tell me about these black rocks," Kestrel ordered.

"You must know," Peril said. "I need to eat them every day in order to live."

Kestrel lashed her tail, uprooting one of the bushes without noticing. "More of Scarlet's lies," she spat. "You don't need anything like that."

"But — I stopped taking them and got sick," Peril said.

"Poison in your food," Kestrel said. "One of Scarlet's favorite tricks."

Peril looked up at the palace on the mountain. Smoke curled from her copper scales and her claws dug into the ground.

"Come with me," Kestrel said roughly. "I'm not much, but I'm better than Scarlet." She reached toward Peril and then saw the scorch marks on her own palms and pulled back. Peril ducked her head, huddling into her wings.

"Where are you going, Kestrel?" Sunny asked.

"None of your business," Kestrel answered.

Sunny sat back, looking hurt. Kestrel took a step toward the lake and rubbed her talons against a rock to sharpen them. She glanced back at Sunny.

"But I suppose," she said, "when you realize you need me, you can send me a message through the dragon of Jade Mountain. Not that I'll come running, mind you. You deserve all the trouble that's coming to you."

"Before you go," Tsunami said, "tell us what you know about our eggs and where they came from."

Kestrel snorted. "Well, there's no surprises with you. Webs stole your egg from the SeaWing queen's own hatchery."

"Tsunami!" Sunny gasped. "You're royalty! Just like in the story!" Tsunami twitched her tail, looking surprised and thoughtful.

"Morrowseer brought us Starflight's egg," Kestrel said. "Dune found Sunny's egg in the desert, hidden near the Scorpion Den. And our big, strong hero came from somewhere around the Diamond Spray Delta, near the sea, where the lowest-born MudWings crawl."

Clay turned to look at the river that flowed from the lake. His heart started pounding with excitement. His home — his family — they were closer than he'd imagined.

"What about me?" Glory asked.

Kestrel shifted her wings in a shrug. "I have no idea. Webs scrounged you up somewhere after we lost the SkyWing egg. I never cared where, because I knew you weren't important."

"Oh, go away!" Tsunami burst out. "Everything you say is hurtful and mean."

"Everything I say is true," Kestrel said.

"I don't think you'd be good for me," Peril said, staring up at her. "I never imagined you like this."

Kestrel hunched her shoulders. "I am the way life has made me. Take it or leave it." She spread her wings. "Because I'm going now, and you can come with me or not."

"Remember," Clay said to Peril, "she tried to save you. She's not the kindest dragon, it's true, but look. She cared about you enough to do this." He took one of Kestrel's talons and opened it so Peril could see the scorch marks burned across her palms. Kestrel snapped her teeth at him and yanked her arm back.

Peril shook her head. "I'm not ready," she said. "Maybe one day we'll find each other again."

Kestrel's tail whipped back and forth, churning up the ground. "Well. Suit yourself." Her orange eyes shifted balefully from one dragonet to the next and landed on Clay. "Listen, MudWing. For all your noble talk, you're not going to be any use to the others if you can't fight and kill to defend them. Just think about that."

Her words stung, like they always did. His hopefulness wilted a little. Clay felt Sunny nudge him sympathetically.

Tsunami took a threatening step toward Kestrel, but before she could say anything, the large red dragon spread her wings and launched herself into the sky. She banked over the lake and flew off to the west without looking back.

── CHAPTER 30 ──

Clay met Peril's eyes. "Some reunion," she said, glancing down at the blackened earth below her.

"You can still come with us," he offered. "Even if you're not in the prophecy."

"No," she said slowly. "I don't think . . . I don't think I deserve to."

He tilted his head at her. "What does that mean?"

"It's like you said," she said. "You're the kinds of dragonets they write prophecies about. You're heroes and saviors and I'm — well, I'm the opposite of that. I'm the bad guy."

"I'm not a hero," Clay said. "You're the one who got us out of the Sky Kingdom."

"Only because of you." She shook her head. "I thought I was born a killer, but it turns out I wasn't. Queen Scarlet made me that way . . . or I let myself become that way. It's like I chose it without knowing I chose it. But you *were* born that way." Clay winced, and he felt the other dragonets staring at him. "You knew what you were like, and you chose to be something else. I guess I feel like I can't be one of you unless I can do that, too."

She blinked, her blue-fire eyes taking in each of his friends. "I'm going back to the Sky Kingdom. That's where I belong, and I need to know if Queen Scarlet is dead."

"Don't you want to leave?" Clay asked. "Don't you want to see the world outside the Sky Kingdom?"

Peril stirred the ash below her talons. "Not until I feel like the world can be safe from me," she said.

"Can we speed up the touching good-bye?" Tsunami asked. "Because we've got company." She nodded grimly at the top of the cliff.

Two flights of dragons were lifting off in graceful spiral formations. One group gleamed red and gold; the other shimmered with pale white heat. The unmistakable shape of Burn soared over them both. After a moment, they split apart, and dragons fanned out in every direction. Their wingbeats filled the sky. Their long necks whipped from side to side as they searched.

The hunt for the escaped dragonets had begun.

"What do we do?" Sunny asked in a hushed voice.

"We should get to the delta," Tsunami said. "We can find Clay's family there. Maybe they'll help protect us."

"And then we'll be at the sea," Sunny said, "so we can find yours, too. And maybe Starflight will find us there? Do you think he's looking for us?"

"Doubtful," said Glory. Sunny's face fell. "He's with his wonderful NightWings now. And I hate to point this out, but there are about two hundred dragons overhead who actually are looking for us. The minute we stroll out from these trees, they'll be on us like fur on a squirrel."

"Well, I have an idea," Clay said hesitantly, "but you're not all going to like it."

"Oh, good," Glory said. "My favorite kind of plan." Clay tried to smile at her, but she wouldn't meet his eyes.

What have I done now? Clay pointed to the river. "We swim to the delta."

Glory made a face. Her claws rippled from brown to pale blue and back again.

"I'm not a very good swimmer," Sunny said anxiously. "But I guess I could try."

"They'll see us from the air," Tsunami pointed out.

"Not Glory," Clay said. "She can camouflage herself in the river. And if she rides on your back, she'll hide you, too."

Glory and Tsunami both looked less than thrilled at that suggestion.

"Then we roll Sunny in mud and put her on my back," Clay went on. "I'll stick to the shallows, and from the sky we should look like part of the riverbed."

Peril jumped in. "I'll wait till you're gone and then fly off in a different direction. Maybe I can lead them away for a while. It's not like they can touch me or do anything to me, once you're safe." She glanced at Clay and then away again.

"All right," Tsunami said. "It's our best shot. Let's do it, then, and quickly." She slid into the lake with Glory.

Clay turned to Peril. "Are you sure?" he asked. "What if Burn takes her anger out on you?"

"How, exactly?" Peril asked. "There's only one good thing about me, and it's that no dragon can hurt me. Except you, I guess." Her wings wavered.

Clay took her talons in his, feeling the heat draw into his scales. "That's not the only good thing about you, Peril." He twined his tail around hers and wrapped his wings around her.

She leaned into his shoulder. "You make me hope that's true," she said.

"Clay," Tsunami called. "We have to go."

Clay pulled away, and Peril stepped back, rubbing her talons where they had touched him. "Be careful, all right?" he said.

She nodded. "When you end the war, come back and visit me."

Sunny lay down in the mud, letting Clay cover her scales. Her golden glow disappeared under the thick layer of brown. He made sure to submerge her tail and pack mud into the gaps between the spines along her back. When he was done, she didn't exactly look like a MudWing, but she certainly didn't look like Sunny anymore.

"I feel all heavy and goopy," she said. But her weight was barely more than a cow's as she climbed onto Clay's back and clutched the spiny ridges. He lifted her easily and slid toward the lake.

The other two were already floating in the water, waiting. It was eerie, seeing only the blurry outline of his friends. With her wings spread, Glory hid most of Tsunami's shape, although bits of blue wings and tail stuck out here and there. Clay hoped it wouldn't be enough to spot from the sky.

Sunny wriggled to look over her shoulder at Peril. "Thank you for helping us," she said.

"After betraying us first," Tsunami muttered. Glory shoved her head back under the water.

"Good luck," Peril said.

"You too," Clay said. "Bye, Peril."

As Clay slid into the lake, he felt her eyes staring after him. He hoped she would be all right.

They paddled along the lakeshore cautiously, trying not to send out too many ripples. The still, clear water flowed around Clay's talons, icy cold. He felt the stirring of a current as they reached the mouth of the river, and then they were swimming downstream, following the Diamond Spray River away from the mountains.

Clay felt like his scales were being washed clean of the dust and pain of the arena. His wings stretched free and his friends were close again. Maybe they weren't safe yet, but at least now he had a chance of protecting them.

The Sky Kingdom was behind them.

Ahead of him were the Mud Kingdom swamps and the Diamond Spray Delta, and his parents, and home, at last.

PART THREE

AN EGG THE COLOR OF DRAGON BLOOD

CHAPTER 31

The dragonets swam and drifted, drifted and swam, all the rest of that day and into the night. When it was fully dark and they hadn't seen any blasts of fire overhead for some time, they crawled out onto a mud bank to eat and rest.

It turned out hunting was a lot harder in wide-open grassland than it was in an enclosed cave. Clay cursed the guardians several times as two rabbits and a coyote slipped through his talons. But he finally caught and killed some kind of large, warty pig with leathery skin, which he dragged back to share with the others.

Sunny came bounding out to help him lift the carcass. "Tsunami caught some fish, too," she said. "And I dug up these awesome wild carrots but nobody else wants to eat them."

"Carrots?" Clay said, wrinkling his snout. "Who would eat those on purpose?"

"I *like* them," Sunny said. "And these are all earthy and crunchy. I bet you'd like them if you tried them."

"Nope," Clay said. "We're free now. I'm only going to eat what I want to eat from now on." *As long as it's slow enough for me to catch it*, he thought ruefully.

It was too dark to see much of the landscape around them other than the twisted shadows of trees here and there, but the light of the moons outlined the jagged mountains looming against the sky. Dark shapes wheeled over the peaks like bats. Burn had not given up searching for them, and probably wouldn't anytime soon, Tsunami pointed out.

"Why does she want to kill us?" Sunny asked. "We haven't done anything to her."

"She doesn't trust prophecies," Tsunami said. "Especially ours. It says two of the sisters will die — of those 'who blister and blaze and burn' — but it doesn't say who. She'd only like it if it said really specifically that Burn was going to have a great victory. Right now it's too vague and cryptic for her. She'd rather get us out of the way and fight the war on her own terms."

"So when we pick who wins, it definitely won't be her," Sunny said with a shiver.

"Maybe Blaze," Tsunami said, gnawing a piece of meat. "Starflight says she's dumb, but at least the SandWings like her."

"I like the sound of Blister," Glory said. "There's nothing wrong with a smart queen. Not that I get a say or anything."

Clay glanced at her, surprised, but Tsunami answered before he could ask what that meant.

"Blister isn't just smart, though," Tsunami said. She rested her head on her front talons. "If we can believe the scrolls and everything the guardians told us, she's cunning and manipulative and doesn't care what she has to do to become queen. Even if it means destroying the other tribes and the rest of the world along the way."

The dragonets fell silent. The enormity of the sky above them made Clay feel very small. It seemed crazy to think they'd get to choose the next SandWing queen, let alone end the war. Who would listen to them? Certainly not the rival queens themselves. How could five dragonets make anything happen?

Sunny stared up at the moons hopefully. Clay knew how she felt — he wanted Starflight to suddenly drop out of the stars and land beside them again, too. He hadn't thought he'd miss his know-it-all friend so much, but it felt wrong not to have him there.

Especially when he probably could have answered some of their questions, like where Glory's venom had suddenly come from. "Do you think all RainWings can do that?" Clay asked after Tsunami and Sunny fell asleep, curled up together. Glory was lying apart from the others with her tail curled over her nose, staring fixedly at the mountains.

"How should I know?" Glory demanded. "Has anyone ever told me anything about RainWings — except that they're lazy and, by the way, in case we haven't mentioned it a thousand times, not part of the prophecy?"

"Are you mad at me?" Clay asked. It seemed like she'd barely spoken to him since their escape.

Glory closed her eyes and didn't answer. Which seemed kind of like a yes to Clay.

He didn't let himself sleep for long, although he was

exhausted. They all wanted to keep going while it was still dark. When he forced his eyes open, two of the moons were dipping behind the mountains while the third was glowing high in the sky. The river lapped and gurgled softly nearby, and the mud was warm under his scales.

Then he noticed that Glory was gone.

His heart plunged. He thought, *No, I'm not losing anyone else.*

Clay shook the others awake. "Where's Glory?" he whispered.

"I knew it," Tsunami growled, leaping to her feet. "I knew she was angry about something."

"About what?" Sunny asked with a bewildered look at the darkness. "Isn't she glad we escaped?"

"Maybe she didn't feel welcome," Tsunami said, "thanks to this clodhopper." There was a pause, and then she flicked Clay with her tail. "That's you, dopey."

"Oh." Clay had been trying to figure out what a clodhopper was. "What did I do now?"

"Gee, let's think," Tsunami said. "Oh, oh, wouldn't it be amazing if psychotic Peril was our 'wings of sky.' Maybe she's the fifth dragonet we've been waiting for our whole lives. Let's just toss aside Glory, like Morrowseer wanted us to, and replace her with the first SkyWing who comes along."

"I didn't want to replace Glory," Clay said, appalled. "I just — I thought Peril might fit in with us — but *all* of us! I never wanted Glory to leave! Besides, wait." He clutched his head. "It was Glory's idea. *She* said Peril might be our SkyWing."

"Yeah, well, you weren't supposed to get so excited about it," Tsunami said.

"What?" Clay sputtered. "That's not fair. It's like I'm in trouble for failing some kind of secret test only girl dragons know about."

"*I* didn't know about it," Sunny objected.

"No, you're in trouble for choosing that vicious SkyWing over Glory," Tsunami snapped back.

"I never did!" Clay nearly yelled. "I wouldn't do that. Nobody told me it was one or the other."

"That's true," Sunny interjected. "I never thought anyone meant we'd have Peril instead of Glory. I thought we'd all go fulfill the prophecy together."

"Of course you did," Tsunami said to her. "We always know what you're thinking."

Sunny's back spines flared up. "Do we?" she said in a voice as close to a growl as Clay had ever heard from her.

Tsunami had already turned back to Clay. "Glory's probably on her way to the rain forest right now. I bet she figures we're better off without her."

"But that's not true," Clay protested. "She's one of us. The prophecy doesn't say we can't care about anyone else. She's the reason we did all this, why we escaped in the first place — doesn't she know that?"

"Good grief," Tsunami said. "Is that supposed to make her feel better? All of this is her fault?"

"No, not like that," Clay said. "I mean, I'd do it again. I'd do all of it again, and more, and anything, to make sure she was all right. I'd do the same for any of you." He looked down at the mud squishing through his talons. "We have to follow her. Forget the delta and my family and all that. We'll go to the rain forest and find her, right now."

Frogs chirruped in the darkness around them. Sunny looked from Tsunami to Clay and back.

"Told you so," said Tsunami.

"Yeah, OK," said Glory's voice. "You were right. For once." Clay felt her wing tips brush against his, and her scales slowly shimmered back into sight in the moonlight. "Thanks, Clay. That was sweet."

"You were there the whole time?" he said, jumping back.

"I was trying to decide if I should leave," Glory said. "I thought you wanted me to, but Tsunami said you didn't. I'm sorry, I was just — really mad."

"Well, now *I'm* really mad," Clay huffed. "That was a mean trick."

"It was Tsunami's idea!" Glory said. "Be mad at her."

"Oh, thanks," Tsunami said.

"I'm mad at both of you!" Clay stomped over to the river. "Come on, Sunny, let's go plan a clever, rotten trick of our own."

"Clay," Glory called after him, but she didn't sound terribly worried. *She knows I'll always forgive her*, Clay grumbled to himself. *They know I can't help it.*

"We should keep swimming anyway," he heard Tsunami say to her.

Sunny caught up to him at the edge of the river.

"That *was* mean," she said. "I don't think we should trick each other like that."

"Next time we stop, we should shake mud all over her," Clay suggested.

Sunny wrinkled her snout at him. "I'm serious! You've always said we have to stick together. You always stop the others from fighting. You should tell them that means we have to trust each other, too. And you should tell them to be better listeners. You know, to everyone."

"I think they know that," Clay said, adding another layer of mud to her scales. He was also pretty sure Glory and Tsunami would laugh at him if he started lecturing them on how to be better friends.

Sunny sighed and climbed onto his back. They slipped into the water again, and he felt the ripples of Glory and Tsunami doing the same close behind them.

The river seemed to get warmer as they swam south and east, toward the sea. After a while, the sun peeked over the horizon ahead of them, and they saw the glitter of vast ocean in the distance. The land rolled down like unfurling dragon wings, through scrub-covered hills of pale brown and dark green.

Clay forgot to worry about hostile dragons in the sky; he forgot to worry about where Starflight was; he forgot to be angry at Glory. His wings beat to the rhythm of his heart, faster and faster, pushing him through the water. The Mud Kingdom was so close. His own dragons, the world he'd always imagined.

The sound of a waterfall up ahead didn't worry him either. He dodged the rocks jutting out of the river and called to Sunny to hang on. As the speeding current swept them over the ridge, he spread his wings and vaulted into the air.

For a moment he was all joy, riding the wind. Ahead of him he could see the river branching into a hundred small streams as it wandered through marshes into the sea. And he could see the homes of MudWings — tall mounds made of mud, several dragons high and several more wide, jutting out of the marshes like fat brown teeth.

Then Sunny clutched his neck with a gasp of horror, and Clay looked down.

Right below them, between the ridge and the marshes, was a battlefield littered with dead dragons.

CHAPTER 32

Clay stayed in the air, circling the battlefield slowly. The river below the waterfall was muddy and dark with spilled blood, and it didn't run clear again as far as his eye could see. He wasn't getting back into that water.

The ground was churned up into mud, but not welcoming mud — here it had blood and bones ground into it, with broken wings sticking out from large sodden lumps, like tree branches smashed by a storm. The dragon bodies were so covered in mud that they all looked like MudWings, but here and there Clay saw the bright shimmer of icy blue and the near white of desert-sand scales. One IceWing had been dropped at the base of the cliff not far from the waterfall, and the spray cast a small rainbow over his shredded silver wings and bloody scales.

"This battle must have just happened," Sunny said. "In the last few days, I mean. Look, some of the fires are still burning." She leaned over his shoulder and pointed to the orange flames that dotted the muddy ground, belching ugly, foul-smelling black smoke into the sky.

Clay swooped lower over one of the fires and saw brown-scaled limbs sticking out of the burning wreckage. He spiraled back into the sky, trying not to throw up. Those were the corpses of MudWings burning.

Glory and Tsunami caught up to him, flying separately. Glory had abandoned the color of the river for a muted green, like grass dotted with morning dew. Tsunami's gills flared, and her gaze darted around the battlefield. They both looked as sick as Clay felt.

"Who do you think won?" Tsunami asked.

"Who *won*?" Sunny cried. "Nobody. No one could look at this place and think, 'hooray, we won.' They just couldn't." Her voice was subdued and sad and furious all at once.

"Blaze's army must have attacked the MudWings," Glory said. "See, there are IceWings and SandWings — that's Blaze's alliance."

"I bet the MudWings sent a message to Queen Scarlet asking for help," Tsunami growled. "And I bet she decided to let them fight alone rather than interrupt her hatching-day festivities."

Clay could see evidence of the IceWings' freezing breath, even now, when most of the ice would have melted. Some of the bodies below were intact, but twisted into horrific positions of agony, their mouths agape as if they'd been frozen mid-scream. Several patches of dirt glittered with tiny ice crystals, where blasts of cold air had missed and frozen the ground instead. And on some of the corpses, body parts had been sheared off in sharp, clean lines, where half a leg had been frozen and then fallen away.

"We're not going to find help here," Clay realized.

Sunny pushed herself off his back and wheeled around in front of him. "Why not?"

"The MudWings won't trust the four of us, all together like this," he said. The others gathered around him, beating their wings to stay in place.

"That's true," Glory said slowly. "Especially you, Tsunami. The SeaWings are on Blister's side."

"I should go in alone," Clay said. "If my parents are still alive —" He stopped, distracted by a flash of white below. His stomach heaved as he realized it was a bone with the flesh scorched off, sticking out of an unrecognizable pile of mud.

"— you'll have a better chance of finding them without a couple of MudWing enemies tagging along," Tsunami finished. "But we don't know what's waiting for you in there. They might take you prisoner, too, like Queen Scarlet did."

"This isn't where the MudWing queen lives," Glory said. "She's farther south, in the swamps. We're on the outskirts of the Mud Kingdom here. Not that that makes it safer, I guess."

Clay remembered Kestrel saying something about "lowest-born" MudWings living around the delta. But he didn't care if his parents were peasants or clodhoppers or any of those words. He didn't need a royal family; he just wanted his family.

"If I don't come back by sunrise tomorrow," he said, "come looking for me."

"What if you need us before then?" Sunny worried.

"I can go with you," Glory said suddenly. "If they figure out I'm a RainWing, nobody will care — we're not in the war anyway. But I can also do this." She hovered for a moment, fluttering her wings, and then brown spilled across her scales. Amber and gold glinted in the cracks and along her underbelly, and the rising sun seemed to melt her to the warmest color of earth.

"I think you're still too pretty to be a MudWing," Clay said doubtfully. She was too long and graceful, and the ruff around her ears wasn't very MudWing either, although she could fold it back until it was hard to spot. And if she kept her tail straight instead of curling it like a RainWing's . . .

"Nonsense," Tsunami said. "You're just as pretty as Glory, Clay." Sunny nodded vigorously.

Clay wrinkled his snout at them. "I'm not sure how to take that."

"Me neither," Glory said. "Let's just go, before the MudWings spot us all hovering suspiciously over this battlefield."

"We'll wait by the waterfall. Be safe." Tsunami wheeled up and around. Clay watched her sleek blue form fly away with Sunny hurrying after.

"Thanks for coming with me," he said to Glory. She shrugged, and he remembered he was supposed to be mad at her. Why couldn't he keep things like that in his head?

As they flew down into the marshes, Clay wondered why no one had come to bury or burn the dead on the battlefield. He couldn't imagine leaving any dragon lying out there like that, not even enemies.

"There," Glory said quietly, tilting her wings. Clay saw a small circle of seven MudWings on the ground near one of the mud towers. They seemed to be practicing a formation — turning and lashing out and defending their flanks without losing their positions.

He took a deep breath. This was it. Time to meet dragons of his own tribe.

Wind that smelled of the sea whistled around his ears as they swooped down. Reeds bent and ducked away from the breeze of their landing. Clay felt his claws sink into wet, marshy dirt, and a shiver of joy ran along his spine.

The MudWings heard them land and whirled around, teeth bared. Clay threw open his wings and held up his front talons, trying to look harmless.

All seven brown dragons stared at him and Glory for a moment as if confused. Then the biggest one shifted her wings and made a dismissive noise deep in her throat. At once they all turned their backs and returned to their formation practice.

Clay blinked at them as the dragons shifted left and darted forward one at a time, clawing at an imaginary assailant. The biggest dragon grunted orders now and then, although they sounded more like suggestions than commands. "Watch your tail on the outside — save some energy for the next thrust — don't forget the signals from the inner wings," she called.

It was as if they'd forgotten Clay and Glory were there. He gave Glory a helpless look.

"Maybe we should find someone else to ask," he whispered.

"AHEM." Glory cleared her throat loudly. "Excuse me."

The biggest dragon glanced at them, arching her brows. "Carry on," she said to the rest of the soldiers, then slithered over to face Glory. Her thick bulk slid easily over the mud, giving her a sinuous grace even though she was as solidly built as Clay. She had patches of mud and grass plastered over several recent wounds on her sides and neck, and one of her horn tips was broken off.

"Look, I'm sorry there's only two of you left," the MudWing said bluntly, "but we're not looking to add anyone. We've only lost one in three years, and that's because we're focused, we practice every sunrise, and we don't bring in unsibs."

"Unsibs?" Clay echoed. The MudWing gave him a puzzled look. Glory trod on his foot. *Act like you know what they're talking about*, Clay reminded himself.

"We're just looking for someone," Glory said. "A MudWing couple who lost an egg six years ago."

"A MudWing couple?" said the other dragon, sounding confused. Clay felt drops of morning dew dripping on him from the leaves overhead. He stirred the mud with his tail and tried to look like he stood in swamps every day. He wanted to fling himself to the ground and roll around like a new-hatched dragonet, but he had a feeling that might seem odd and undignified.

"There was a red egg," Glory tried. "It was stolen from around here somewhere."

"Stolen!" hissed the MudWing. "I'd like to see any dragon try that!" Her talons flexed open and shut ominously, squelching in the mud. Glory took a step back.

"Or taken, anyway," she said. "Maybe by a dragon named Asha?"

The MudWing's back ridges relaxed. "Oh, Asha," she said. "That's right. Her sister Cattail had a blood egg about six years back. But I can tell you there wasn't any stealing involved. Indeed." She snorted.

Clay's chest felt ready to burst. Cattail! His mother had a name! "Is she all right?" he asked. "Cattail? Is she still alive?"

"Somehow," the other dragon snorted. "That troop has no discipline. And their bigwings hasn't been the same since Asha left. They're down to four now."

It was like a different language. Clay desperately wanted to ask what a bigwings was, but he didn't dare.

"Where can we find her?" Glory asked.

The MudWing raised a claw and pointed at a gap between the mounds. "They'll still be asleep, but that troop usually bunks in the sleephouse with the hole in the side, at the end of the dry path."

"Thanks," Clay said as she turned back to her formation. She didn't answer, her focus already back on the other soldiers.

There was a raised dirt path winding between the tall dragon mounds and swamp grasses. Clumps of reeds shushed and swished in the breeze and gnarled trees dotted the marsh. Most of the trees were covered in hanging vines, although when Clay looked closer, he could see that some of the vines were actually thick coils of crimson and olive-green snakes. The deep croak of bullfrogs warbled through the air.

As they followed the path, Clay peered into one of the giant mud puddles, trying to spot a particularly loud bullfrog. Suddenly a pair of eyes blinked open in the middle of the mud. Clay jumped back, nearly knocking Glory into the marsh on the other side of the path.

"Watch it!" she hissed.

"There's a dragon in there," he whispered. Now he could see two ears like his sticking up behind the eyes, and two nostrils poking out of the mud in front. The eyes regarded him narrowly for a moment, then closed. The dragon sank below the mud again.

"There's one over here, too," Glory whispered back. Clay turned and saw that what looked like a submerged log was actually the long, ridged back of a dragon, lying just below the surface of the mud. His nose rested on a rock, his eyes were closed, and he was snoring softly.

"Gosh, they look comfortable," Clay said.

Glory shuddered. "I could never sleep in mud. My

dreams would be full of quicksand and mosquitoes and goopy muck that would never wash off."

Now that they were looking, they saw more submerged dragons in every mud pool. The sun was climbing the sky. As the rays spread across the swamp, some of the dragons began to rise up from the mud, opening their wings and basking in the warmth. Others emerged from the mounds through low doorways hacked out of the muddy bases.

None of them took any notice of Clay or Glory, which struck him as odd. The dragons seemed uninterested in strangers in their midst. He noticed that they stayed in their troops, each somewhere between five and nine dragons, talking only to the other MudWings in their own group. One group of six all came out of the same mound and then formed a circle around it, stretching their wings and necks and tails in unison.

Another group of eight dragons bubbled up from the shallows of a muddy lake and took to the sky, one at a time, following the biggest in a large swoop around the swamp. After a few moments of circling, the leader dove into the reeds and rose up again with a crocodile thrashing in his talons. He landed on an island of dry ground, and all eight dragons began to rip up and eat the crocodile together.

"The scrolls never said anything about this. We didn't have any really good scrolls about MudWing life. But maybe they're like army troops," Glory guessed. "You stick with your own soldiers. Maybe that's what makes them such strong fighters, because they have these little loyal units within the army."

"Maybe," Clay said. He liked how close the dragons within each group were. But it made him nervous that no one had greeted him and Glory or asked who they were or anything. Still, once his mother knew who he was, surely he'd be welcomed with open wings.

He twisted to look around the village and finally met a pair of eyes — the only ones looking his way. They were a shade of pale amber, and they belonged to a small MudWing with a healing mud patch stuck across his nose. His horns were not yet full grown, but he wasn't a very young dragonet either. He was staring at Clay curiously, boldly. Clay smiled and waved a wing at him.

The little MudWing blinked and darted back into his mound.

The path led under one of the trees heavy with snakes and away from the center of the village, toward an area of the swamp where there were fewer, more isolated mounds. After a short walk, the path ended at a lake filled with swaying reeds. Next to the lake was a lopsided mound with a crumbling hole toward the top, as if a dragon had punched through the mud in a rage at some point.

Clay found himself holding his breath as they got closer. Was this where he should have hatched? It was much warmer and wetter than the cold, bare cave under the mountain. But there was a heavy smell of rotting vegetation and no sign of life from the last mound. They paused outside of it, glancing at the stagnant reed-choked water in the lake.

"This must be what that dragon called a sleephouse," Glory said. "So I guess your mother's in there?"

"Cattail," Clay said quietly, trying out the word.

They sat on the path for a moment. "Aren't you going to go in?" Glory asked.

Clay didn't really love the idea of sticking his head into a dark mud tower full of strange dragons. "I'm sure someone will come out soon —" he started, and just then a wide, flat snout poked out of the doorway. A pair of yellow eyes glared at him.

"It's a pair of dragonets," growled the MudWing. "Chattering like crows while we're trying to sleep."

"Well, get rid of them!" roared a voice from inside the mound.

"I'm sorry," Clay stammered. "We didn't mean to be loud. We're looking for Cattail." He hoped fervently that this wasn't his father.

The dragon squinted at him, then withdrew into the mound. They heard grumbling and grunts and wings flapping, as if the MudWings inside were scrunching around to let one of them climb over the others.

At last a thin brown dragon scrambled out into the open. She shook out her wings, which had dappled patterns of paler brown scales, and frowned down at Clay and Glory.

"Yes?" she said. "What do you want?"

Clay's talons felt rooted to the ground. He couldn't believe it. After all of his imagining and wondering and hoping, here he was — finally face-to-face with his own mother.

CHAPTER 33

Clay could only open and close his mouth silently. Glory rolled her eyes and jumped in.

"Are you Cattail?" she asked. "Asha's sister?"

The dappled dragon gave a little hiss and ducked her head. "Yes," she said. "Who are you?"

Glory poked Clay hard with one of her talons. He blurted, "I'm Clay. I think I'm your son."

Cattail stared at him. Her eyes were brown like his, but with a ring of yellow around the black slit of a pupil. He waited, his heart pounding. He'd imagined this moment a thousand times. In *The Missing Princess*, this was when the joy and feasting began.

"So?" Cattail said.

Clay guessed she hadn't heard him right. "I think you're my mother," he said.

"Those would seem connected," said Cattail. "And?"

"You don't understand," Glory said. "This is the dragonet you lost six years ago."

Cattail's claws slowly stirred the mud underneath her. "I haven't lost any dragonets." She didn't look confused or worried or pleased. Mostly she looked like she was putting up with this conversation until they let her go back to sleep.

Clay had no idea what to say.

"Listen," Glory said. "Maybe we got this wrong. Clay hatched from a blood-red egg that was taken from somewhere around here six years ago by a dragon named Asha. He's come back looking for —"

"Oh, that egg," Cattail said with a yawn. "Asha got all excited about that. Don't know why; the village has a red egg every few years or so. But I didn't lose it."

"What happened to it?" Clay managed to ask.

"We sold it to the Talons of Peace," Cattail said. She gave them a look that was suddenly sharp and furtive. "Does this mean they want the cows back? Because they can't have them. I know we were supposed to breed them, but we ate them, so too bad."

"You *sold* me?" Clay cried. He felt like long claws were slashing through his chest.

"Why not?" Cattail asked. "There were six other eggs in the hatching. They didn't need you." She pulled a stray duck feather out from between her talons. "Asha didn't tell you any of this?"

"Asha's dead," Glory said. "She died trying to keep Clay's egg safe."

"Dead?" Now Cattail finally looked upset. "I *told* her not to leave us! Our bigwings will be furious." She flicked her tongue out and in with a growl. "I guess it serves her right, choosing the Talons over us."

"She was trying to help fulfill the prophecy," Glory snapped. "At least the Talons care about something besides themselves." Clay would have laughed if he hadn't felt so crushed. That was the nicest thing Glory had ever said about the Talons of Peace.

"That's Asha, all right," Cattail said. "She was always softhearted and mushy about crazy things. She loved mooning around little dragonets, telling the story of that prophecy. She left a lot of blithering, obsessed dreamy-eyed dragons behind in this village, let me tell you; they still won't shut up about destiny and peace and all that."

Dragons did not cry easily, and Clay had never shed tears in his whole life, no matter how much Kestrel had hurt him with words or claws. But now, suddenly, he had a glimpse of what their life could have been like if Asha had lived. She would have been one more dragon under the mountain to take care of them — but this one kind and affectionate, idealistic and hopeful. A guardian who would have given them faith in the prophecy and themselves. A counterbalance for Kestrel's harshness.

He had never spent much time thinking about Asha, the dragon who brought in his egg, but now his chest ached with sadness that she was dead and he had never known her. He realized that he was dangerously close to tears, and he could just imagine how his mother would react to that.

"What about my father?" Clay asked, steeling his voice. "Didn't he try to stop you from selling me?"

Cattail threw her head back and laughed, a high croaking sound like a thousand bullfrogs yelling at once. "You really don't know anything about MudWings, do you?" she said when she could catch her breath again. "I don't even know who your father was. And he certainly doesn't care. We have breeding night once a month and then everyone goes back to their own sleephouses. No, dear, there's no father here for you."

"And no mother either, apparently," Glory said coldly.

But Cattail just nodded, untroubled. "That's right," she said. "I wish you luck, but there's no room in our troop for clingy little dragonets."

Her voice was matter-of-fact. Clay could see that she wasn't trying to be mean, but it still hurt worse than anything he'd ever felt — more than Kestrel's taunts and attacks, more than the IceWing's claws in his back, more than seeing Sunny in a cage or knowing Peril had betrayed them. He felt all his dreams thudding like stones inside his stomach.

He'd always believed there was someone out in the world waiting for him. He'd imagined finding his mother and father and how it would be just like the story. None of the scrolls they'd studied had talked about MudWing families, but he knew NightWings and SeaWings had mothers and fathers, so he'd always assumed all the dragon tribes were the same way.

It had never occurred to him that no one would even know who his father was. And he certainly hadn't expected his own mother to care so little, or to send him away as soon as she met him.

Another thing Asha could have warned me about, he thought bitterly. If she'd lived, she could have told him how things were in the Mud Kingdom and saved him a lot of useless dreaming.

"Come on, Clay," Glory said, tugging on his wing. She steered him back toward the mud village. Clay's scales felt as heavy as boulders. His tail dragged slowly behind him.

"You tell the Talons," Cattail called after them, "that we made a deal! No matter what happened, they can't have those cows back!"

"Do you want to try talking to anyone else?" Glory asked as they reached the village. "Maybe she's wrong, and your father would want to know you."

Clay shook his head. "There's no point," he said. "I don't have a place here."

Suddenly Glory stopped with a hiss. She pointed to the clearing ahead and darted under the nearest low-hanging vines. Clay hurried after her.

A burly SandWing was stamping his feet in the center of the mud village, trying to shake off the wet mud that clung to his claws. He was missing an ear and a couple of teeth, and he grimaced at the two MudWings in front of him.

"What?" he bellowed. "Speak up!"

One of the MudWings raised his voice. "I said we haven't seen anyone like that."

"You sure?" said the SandWing. "There'll be four of them. A MudWing, a RainWing, a SeaWing, and a kind of SandWing-looking thing."

The MudWing wrinkled his snout. "No," he said. "I assure you we would have noticed a SeaWing, a RainWing, or a . . . 'SandWing-looking thing' strolling through our sleephouses."

The SandWing snorted, as if he doubted that was true. "Well," he said, "if you do spot them, let Queen Burn know right away."

Both of the MudWings bowed their heads politely. "Of course."

Glory and Clay ducked farther under the tree as the SandWing took to the sky. "We've got to get out of here," Glory whispered.

"I forgot the MudWings are on Burn's side," said Clay. "We're lucky Cattail didn't know Burn was looking for us. She would have turned me over in a heartbeat." He didn't feel lucky, though. He felt perfectly miserable.

"Let's go around the village," Glory said, slithering back toward the waving reeds. Almost at once, she sank in a pool of mud up to her belly. "Oh, *urrrrgh*," she groaned.

Clay saw a snout poke out of the swamp a short distance away. The dragon gave them a suspicious look.

"Remember to act like a MudWing," he whispered, sliding into the mud beside Glory. "Mmmmmm, mud!"

"Yaaay," Glory said unenthusiastically. She floundered a few more steps into the reeds, spattering mud all across her wings.

This was going to be a long walk at that pace. Clay checked the sky. "All right, he's out of sight. We can fly back to the others."

He wriggled out of the mud onto a dry island and hauled Glory up beside him. They both shook their wings to get the biggest clumps off, and then they leaped, quickly clearing the trees. Clay spotted the river winding toward the cliff to their left and banked in that direction. He was ready to leave the Mud Kingdom behind him forever.

"Hey!" a voice shouted behind them. "You, dragonets! Stop!"

CHAPTER 34

Panic shot through Clay and he sped up, flapping his wings frantically. Glory soared up beside him.

"Stop!" she whispered. "If we run, they'll know there's something wrong."

Clay knew she was right, but it was almost impossibly hard to swing around and fly back toward the MudWing village and the voice that had called after them.

Five dragons were hovering in the sky, watching them intently. As they drew close to each other, Clay realized that they were dragonets, not yet full-grown. The biggest one was a bit smaller than Clay, with warm golden-amber eyes and a recent claw-mark wound on his tail. The smallest was the dragon with the patch on his nose who had stared at Clay in the village.

"Hey," Clay said to them. He hoped he sounded casual and nonthreatening. "We were just leaving."

The MudWing dragonets glanced at each other. The biggest one said, "We heard you were asking about a blood egg from one of Cattail's hatchings."

"That's right," Glory said.

"Do you know what happened to it?" the smallest MudWing blurted. "Did it hatch? Who came out? Where's the dragonet?"

Glory poked Clay with her tail before he could respond. "Who's asking?" she said.

"I'm Reed," said the biggest dragonet. "This is Sora, Pheasant, Marsh, and Umber." The smallest one, Umber, had his eyes fixed on Clay again. The other three kept checking the sky with nervous expressions.

"I'm Clay, and this is Glory," Clay answered. Pheasant tilted her head at Glory.

"That's not a normal MudWing name," she said. *Oops,* Clay thought.

"I didn't choose it," Glory said with a shrug that lifted her up and down in the air currents.

"Did one of you hatch from the blood egg?" asked Reed. "Are you our missing sib?"

"Sib!" Clay said suddenly. "Siblings! That's what everyone keeps talking about!" He launched himself forward and gripped Reed's front talons. "Is that what you mean? Were we in the same hatching?"

"I knew it!" Umber yelped. "I knew he had a familiar feeling! I told you!" He bundled into Marsh and nearly knocked them both out of the air.

"You're our brother," Reed said with a grin that warmed Clay to the tips of his claws. "You should have been with us all along."

"He's not just our brother," Pheasant pointed out. "Look at him. He should be our bigwings."

The grin faded from Reed's face as he studied Clay from wing tips to talons. "That's true," he said.

Clay wanted to bring that grin back. He didn't understand what was wrong. He pointed to a clear island in the marshes below. "Let's talk," he said.

His brothers and sisters couldn't believe how little he knew about MudWing life, but they were happy to explain it all to him, their words tumbling over one another. The five of them coiled together naturally in the tall grass, tails and talons and wings entwined, with Umber climbing up their backs and standing on heads to make himself heard.

They told him that MudWing dragons laid their eggs in warm mud nests protected by walls of hot rocks. They were so safe that the mother never needed to check on them, and the dragonets were usually born when she wasn't even there. The firstborn was always the biggest, and his or her first task was to help the other dragonets out of their eggs by cracking their shells from the outside.

As they came to this part of the explanation, Glory gasped. She turned to Clay. "That's what it was!" she said. "When we hatched — the guardians didn't know anything about MudWings, so they thought you were attacking us. But you were trying to help. Your instinct told you to get the rest of us out of our shells. Clay, you know what this means? You weren't trying to kill us at all."

Clay felt like he was filling up with warm summer clouds. Kestrel was wrong, all wrong about him, and she always had been. His strength wasn't for killing and violence; it was for protecting his brothers and sisters. He wasn't destined to be a monster. He wasn't a killer deep inside somewhere.

He was a bigwings.

He crossed his tail over Glory's and smiled at her, too happy to speak.

"So from then on, the bigwings takes care of all the others," Pheasant said, nudging Reed with affection. "Some of them can be pretty bossy or too weak, but we got a good one." She stopped, realizing what she'd said. "I mean . . . you would have been good, too, I'm sure. . . ."

Reed tugged up a clump of marsh grass and started shredding it without looking at Clay. "And then we all stick together," he said. "For always. We learn to hunt and survive together, we grow up together, and we live together for the rest of our lives. And when we're at war, we all fight as a group. Every MudWing troop is a hatching of siblings. Except for the ones who've lost too many, and then they try to find unsibs to form a new troop with."

Pheasant glanced around at the others — wriggling Umber, silent Sora, nervous, twitching Marsh — as if she would rather die than replace them with unsibs who weren't her own brothers and sisters.

"How many have you — have we lost?" Clay asked.

"Two," said Reed. "You, and our sister Crane, two days ago in the battle by the cliff." He nodded in the direction of the waterfall. Clay's insides twisted as he realized one of the dead bodies he'd flown over had been his own sister.

"That was our first battle," Sora said softly.

"It was awful," Umber added.

Reed sighed heavily. "I was not the bigwings I wanted to be."

"You were!" the others all protested at once. "You were amazing, Reed," Pheasant said firmly.

"We'd *all* be dead if it weren't for you," Marsh agreed. They all had the same expression as they looked at Reed. Clay could see it was trust — faith that their bigwings would take care of them, no matter what happened.

"But it's all right now," Reed said. "Because you're back, and you should be our bigwings." He glanced sidelong at Clay, and in his amber eyes Clay could see all the worries he'd ever felt himself . . . all the fears for his friends, all the things he'd done and would do to protect them, all the ferocity of how much he cared about them.

Clay cared about his real brothers and sisters, too, although he'd only just met them. He felt instinctively like they were extensions of his own claws and wings. This was the family he'd always wanted.

And if he stayed, it would tear them apart.

He could see it in their eyes — they wanted him and were afraid of him at the same time. If he became their bigwings, what would happen to their loyalty to Reed? What would happen to Reed himself, forced to follow him but desperate to protect them his own way?

Clay didn't know anything about MudWing life, or troop formations, or even how to hunt in a swamp. How could he lead them into battle? It would never be like the closeness they had with Reed, no matter how hard they all tried.

There was only one way to protect his siblings, he realized. If he was really their bigwings, he had to leave them — and leave Reed as their bigwings, the way he'd always been. He would keep them safe better than Clay ever could, and their sibs would not be forced to choose between them.

Glory was looking at him, too.

Clay shook his head. "No," he said to his brothers and sisters. "Reed is your bigwings. You trust him and you need him. I couldn't replace him, even if I tried."

His brother raised his head, pride warring with disbelief on his face. The other dragonets looked relieved and sad at the same time.

"Besides," Glory said, "he can't stay with you. He's *our* bigwings." She brushed Clay's wings with hers. He was glad he couldn't change colors like her, or he felt like he might have turned crimson from nose to tail.

"Are you sure?" Reed said to Clay. "You could still join us, bigwings or not. There's more fighting ahead, and we could always use another strong dragon at our side."

Clay was tempted. He wanted to know his brothers and sisters, and it would be so easy to slip into this life and become a warrior, with no prophecies to worry about and no angry SandWing queens hunting him. But he remembered the charred corpses on the battlefield, and he thought about his friends and how they'd try to go on without him.

"I'm afraid I have a destiny," he said ruefully. "We're going to try to stop the war."

Umber's eyes went wide. "Like the prophecy?" he breathed. "That's *you*?"

Pheasant looked at Glory doubtfully.

"That's us," Clay said, touching Glory's talon.

"Apparently," Glory added. "More or less."

"We'll try, anyway," Clay said. "But maybe after that, once the war is over . . . maybe then I could come back?"

"You're one of us," Reed said. "You can come back anytime."

"I hope you do," Umber said. The others nodded.

Clay looked from face to face, wondering how many of his brothers and sisters would survive the next battle.

He wondered if he could stop the war in time to save them all.

CHAPTER 35

Tsunami and Sunny did not seem at all surprised to hear the explanation of Clay's attack on their eggs.

"Of course," Tsunami said. She had hunted while they were gone, and she nudged a dead wild duck in Clay's direction. "I never thought you *were* trying to kill us."

"As if you would ever!" Sunny agreed.

"Well, *I* didn't know that," Clay said. They had found a small grove at the top of the cliff, far enough away from the waterfall and the battlefield that they couldn't smell the burning dragons anymore. He dug his claws into the duck, suddenly famished.

"So what now, bigwings?" Glory asked, clawing up a pheasant for herself. "I'm never going to get tired of calling you that."

"We'll be like the MudWings," Clay said proudly. "We stick together. No matter what happens. We're a team, and we look after one another. Which means the first thing we have to do is find Starflight. The NightWings can't just take him away. He's one of us, and we'll search the whole world until we find him. It's time for us to get our friend ba —"

He stopped as a heavy thump shook the ground and wings flapped to a stop behind him. The others were staring over his shoulder.

"That better not be who I think it is," said Clay.

"Found him!" Glory said gleefully.

Clay turned around. Starflight stood, blinking, in the waving grass just outside the trees. The sunlight picked up glints of purple and deep blue in his black scales. Up in the sky, the black bulk of Morrowseer was winging away.

"Oh, bye!" Tsunami shouted after him. "Thanks for everything! You've been SO HELPFUL!"

Sunny flung herself at Starflight with a cry of joy. "You found us!" She batted his wings with hers. "I hoped you would." He returned her hug, smiling shyly at her.

"Hello," Clay said to Starflight. "You couldn't have waited until after my noble speech? Maybe a day or two, so we could at least pretend to look for you?"

"Morrowseer saw you flying up from the marshes," Starflight said. "He said to tell you some other dragon could have spotted you, too, and we should be more careful."

"Well, great," Tsunami said. "That's such useful advice. Glad he's so concerned, now that we've managed to save our own selves about a hundred times and everything. Any other survival tips? Or prophecy-fulfilling suggestions?"

Starflight ducked his head, looking uncomfortable. "I'm sorry he took me," he said. "I wanted him to bring me back right away, but he wouldn't. He said they couldn't afford to lose any NightWings, even —" He swallowed. "Even peculiar little ones."

"What the heck does that mean?" Clay asked.

"You're not peculiar!" Sunny said. "I'm the one that's peculiar and little."

"Well, he is a bit," Glory said. "But we don't mind."

Tsunami looked thoughtful. "Couldn't afford to lose any NightWings?" she echoed. "Is there something wrong with them? Did you notice?"

"No." Starflight glanced up at the sky. "He didn't take me to the secret NightWing kingdom, if that's what you're wondering. I didn't even get to meet any of the dragons he'd brought with him. We just stayed up in the mountain peaks, waiting. I guess he wanted to see what would happen to you guys."

"Not that he was going to do anything about it," Glory muttered.

"So he doesn't care what we do next?" Clay asked. "He's not making us go back to the Talons of Peace?"

"I'm not sure he's really happy with the Talons of Peace right now," Starflight said.

"Then we can do whatever we want," Clay said. "I say we visit Tsunami's mother, who, by the way," he said to Starflight, "is the queen of the SeaWings, according to Kestrel."

"Seriously?" Starflight said, staring at Tsunami. "Like in the scroll? Coral's supposed to be a great queen. Not crazy like Scarlet."

Tsunami looked uncharacteristically nervous. "Do you think she'll be happy to meet me? What if she's like Clay's mother — no offense, Clay."

"I *know* she'll be happy to see you," Starflight said. "Don't you remember what it said in *The Royal Lineage of the SeaWings, from the Scorching to the Present*?"

All four dragonets groaned.

"Remind me why we wanted him back?" Glory asked Clay.

"This is important and fascinating!" Starflight said, stomping his feet. "Listen! Queen Coral doesn't have an heir. Not a single one of her female dragonets has lived to adulthood. Rumor has it there's a curse on her hatchings. *That's* why she'll be glad to meet Tsunami — you're the lost heir to the Kingdom of the Sea."

Tsunami puffed out her chest. "Me? Really?"

"Oh my gosh! Tsunami! You could be queen of the SeaWings one day!" Sunny cried.

Tsunami grinned. "Wouldn't that be great? I've always thought I'd be a good queen."

"Boy, I don't know," Glory said. "I mean, if you want to be queen one day, you'll have to be bossy, controlling, full of yourself . . . oh, wait."

Tsunami whacked her lightly with her tail. "Behave, or I'll have you beheaded," she said, lifting her snout.

"So let's go find the SeaWings," Clay said. "They're not on Burn's side, are they?"

Starflight heaved one of his long-suffering sighs. "No, Clay. They're allied with Blister, the middle sister, of whom the scrolls say —"

Glory, Tsunami, and Clay all tackled him at once. Sunny tried to come to his rescue, and the five of them ended up scuffling in the grass, laughing.

Clay caught a glimpse of the sky, blue and gold and empty of dragons, for now. He still didn't know how they would fulfill the prophecy and end the war. He didn't know how the other dragonets' families would react to them. He knew Burn was hunting them, and probably other dangerous dragons soon would be as well.

But he knew what he was here to do, and that was protect his friends, no matter what. He'd known it from hatching, even if he hadn't understood it. He didn't have to worry about finding his monster or being something he wasn't anymore. He would have to be enough for the prophecy just the way he was.

Big Heroic Destiny, he thought, *here I come.*

EPILOGUE

Wind howled around the small rocky island with the force of a thousand screaming dragons. It battered at the three on the cliff as if trying to tear off their wings.

One dragon was black as night, one red as flames, and one as pale as desert sand.

"Why did you bring me here?" Kestrel shouted, digging her claws into gaps in the rock. The wind seized her voice and threw it away.

Morrowseer ignored her. He stepped closer to the SandWing, their heads sheltered by their wings so they could hear each other.

"Trust me, you're the one," he said. "Burn and Blaze are the two who will die. We have chosen you to be the SandWing queen." Surf roared at the base of the cliff below them.

Blister regarded him with glittering black eyes. She was smaller than Burn, with a long, cunning face and a black diamond pattern running down her spine. She had an eerie stillness about her, like a venomous snake about to strike.

Unlike her sisters she had no scars. She was much too clever to do any of the fighting herself.

"And the dragonets will make this happen," she said. "The same dragonets who are now wandering loose around the countryside."

"We'll keep an eye on them," Morrowseer promised. "It's better this way. Once the word gets out, everyone will be watching for them . . . waiting for the prophecy to come true at last."

"What if they have their own ideas about who should be queen?" Blister asked.

"They won't. Besides" — Morrowseer spread his wings so the star scales caught the moonlight — "the NightWing dragonet has his orders now. He knows what he's supposed to do."

"What?" Kestrel yelled. "What are you saying?" She tried to crowd in closer, but the other two dragons spoke as if she wasn't there.

"I like that," Blister mused. "A traitor in their midst. Tear them apart from the inside. My kind of plan."

"We're good at those," Morrowseer said. A blast of wind buffeted the sea against the rocks and yanked at the dragons' tails. Thunder rumbled behind the thick clouds in the distance. "But we expect what we were promised."

"That won't be a problem," she said, running her forked tongue over her teeth. "Tell me, does your magic vision tell you where the dragonets will go next?"

Morrowseer looked at her sourly. "That's not how it works," he said.

Blister looked amused. "Well, let's hope it's to the SeaWings, then," she said. "And her? This is the trouble?" She tossed her head at Kestrel.

Kestrel caught the last question. "Yes," she roared. "Why am I here? Morrowseer, you said the dragonets were in danger."

"And you came running," he said. "Well, of course they're in danger. More than they know. But you're really here because you failed me."

Kestrel blinked her orange-yellow eyes and took a step back, glaring at him. "I failed *you*?" she growled. "I work for the Talons of Peace, not the NightWings. They can talk to me if they've got complaints. I kept those brats alive, like I was supposed to."

"But they don't need you anymore," Morrowseer said. "And neither do we."

Blister's claws ripped across Kestrel's throat before she could scream. Kestrel clutched at the blood pouring from her neck and staggered back, pummeled by the wind. Blister took another step and stabbed Kestrel in the heart with her poisonous tail.

The SkyWing collapsed to the rocks, thrashing in agony. Her mouth opened to scream curses or breathe fire at her murderers, but only dark red blood bubbled out.

Morrowseer glanced down at her, then reached out with one talon and nudged her body over the edge of the cliff. The wind caught her splayed wings and tossed her against the rocks until it got bored and dropped her in the ocean.

The sound of the splash didn't carry to the top of the cliff, where the other two dragons continued as if nothing had happened.

"There's one more," Morrowseer said. "A SeaWing named Webs. If he made it out of the mountain, he'll be looking for them, too. We need him dead before the rest of the plan will work."

"Not a problem," Blister said again. She stared out at the pounding sea below them. "What's one more dead dragon here or there on my way to the throne?"

Morrowseer smiled. "Then we understand each other."

"Give me the dragonets," she said, "and we'll both get everything we want."

The adventure continues in

WINGS OF FIRE

BOOK TWO:
THE LOST HEIR

The SeaWing started back in an eddy of ripples. He blinked at her in clear surprise. His eyes were a blue so dark they were almost black.

Tsunami pointed up at the surface. *Come on out of the water so we can talk,* she tried to signal. Hopefully he'd figure out what she meant.

To her surprise, he whipped around and fled. His tail smacked a wave of water in her face.

Well, that's *unfriendly,* she thought. She swam after him, swinging her tail to propel herself even faster. He glanced back over his shoulder, saw her chasing him, and put on a burst of speed.

Why was he running away? And how was he so *fast*?

"Stop!" she tried to yell through the water. "I just want to talk!"

Of course that didn't work. He didn't even slow down.

But then he twisted to look back at Tsunami, and so he didn't see the whale that suddenly loomed out of the deep in front of him.

Tsunami waved her talons and pointed. "Watch out!" she tried to yell in a cascade of bubbles.

The SeaWing smacked into the whale's side and careened backward. The whale was only slightly bigger than the dragon, with ridges all along its back and a flat, mild-mannered face. It made a weird squeaking groan and blinked at the SeaWing in confusion.

The dragon was still shaking his head, trying to reorient

himself, when Tsunami caught up, grabbed his tail, and pinned him to the sand.

Now what do I do? Tsunami thought. *I have to get him to the surface to talk to him, but if I let him go, he might try to escape again.*

She frowned down at the dragon. He wasn't struggling, at least. He lay on the sand under her talons, watching her almost curiously.

Tsunami pointed at the surface again.

The other dragon tipped his head to one side. Luminescent stripes lit up along his wings, flashing fast, then slow.

All right, Tsunami thought. *I can do that, too. Maybe he's testing me.*

She lit up her own stripes, illuminating the ones on her snout, then the ones along her tail, and finally her wings. *See? My stripes flash, too. I'm a SeaWing. Now let's go up and talk.*

Slowly she spread her wings and lifted up, prepared to grab him if he tried to bolt again. He scrambled upright but stayed with her. Encouraged, Tsunami swam a bit closer to the surface. He followed, but only for a bit before he stopped and looked around.

His stripes flashed again, this time along his neck and tail.

Impatiently, Tsunami lit up her stripes one more time, mirroring what he'd done.

The SeaWing's wings flared open with a whoosh that

scared fish into the reef. He lunged toward Tsunami, fast as a minnow. His front talons reached for her.

Tsunami roared, blasting him in the eyes with bubbles, and sliced her claws across his snout. She didn't know why he was attacking. Perhaps he thought she was an intruder, although he wasn't much of a guard if his first instinct was to run away, and his second was to attack with no reason.

He'll be sorry when he finds out who I am! she thought fiercely.

She kicked his underbelly hard with her back legs. He coughed up a stream of bubbles and fell back. Tsunami spread her wings and shot to the surface.

She burst into the air and kept beating her wings to rise into the sky. In the distance, she could see the cliffside cave and the worried faces of her friends poking out.

An enormous splash sounded behind her. The other SeaWing surged out of the ocean. His massive tail whacked the water twice as he lifted into the air, sending giant waves rushing in all directions.

He looked even bigger out here in the air. His hooked claws gleamed sharply in the sunlight. His dark blue eyes were fixed on her wings.

The first true citizen of her kingdom she'd ever met, and he was coming to kill her.